The Abnormalities of Stringent Strange

The Abnormalities of Stringent Strange

by

Rhys Hughes

Meteor House

The Abnormalities of Stringent Strange

Published by Meteor House

Meteor House

ISBN 978-0-9837461-3-3

First Trade Edition

This novel is dedicated to all the great science-fiction pulp writers of the 1920s, 30s and 40s who in cheap magazines created a fantastic literature of adventure, excess and wonder.

And also to the brave pilots who took to the skies in the early days of aviation not really knowing what might be up there.

"I am an apeman."

—The Kinks

Despite careful writing, proofreading and editing, a recent X-Ray scan has revealed the existence of an unspecified number of inconsistencies in the following novel. The publishers have decided to award a special prize to the reader who spots the most.

TABLE OF CONTENTS

THE PLANE TRUTH

Sunlight flashed on the wings of the single-engine Northrop Gamma as it banked around the small cumulus that was the only cloud in the sky. The monoplane performed a final barrel roll before coming in to land and the Pratt & Whitney R-1830 14-cylinder radial engine droned comfortably as the pilot adjusted the fuel/air mix. The overinflated wheels bounced once on the hot tarmac and the propeller clattered to a standstill. Then the pilot emerged and rubbed his gloved hands.

"She's a beauty, no doubt about it, doc. Handles like a French whore. I mean that the frills serve a purpose . . ."

"I comprehend the allusion," sighed Crinkle.

"Another winner, in my opinion."

The pilot removed his goggles and grinned. Stringent Strange was tall and muscular with a manly chin and the clear blue eyes of a hero. He was exactly the sort of fellow that girls should go wild over, but in fact he had to spend an unhealthy percentage of his test pilot's salary on prostitutes. It was his body that was the cause of this discrepancy. It was hirsute beyond belief, the torso of a gorilla balanced on the legs of a giant lemur; and the hairs were malodorous in the extreme.

"My worst fear has been confirmed," continued Professor Crinkle, as he rubbed his bleary eyes, "but there's nothing we can do about it. Jack is the winner and that's a plain fact."

"Knowing when to quit is a useful talent, doc!"

"Yes, I suppose so, dear boy."

Stringent began walking back to the control tower. He was in a good mood but he tried to hide his exuberance for the sake of his mentor, who trailed behind him with pouting lips. When a man's dreams are shattered in front of him, it's poor taste to whistle and skip. Tobias Crinkle, Ph.D., had devoted almost twenty-five years to the cutting edge of the aviation industry but dedication isn't enough on its own. Genius counts for more and his main rival had plenty of that.

His main rival had a name. Jack Northrop.

Although Stringent felt empathy for Crinkle, his recent flight brimmed him with an almost sexual joy and he strode ahead rapidly, not caring to be brought down by the glum expression and nihilistic mutterings of the disappointed professor; but at the entrance to the control tower he turned for a last glance of the gleaming Northrop Gamma, its aerodynamic spats giving the airplane a curiously anthropomorphic appearance, like a jazz musician performing a primal dance.

Stringent's psychology wasn't quite that of a normal man and he often saw resemblances that no one else could perceive, or would even want to, but on this occasion he could be forgiven his conceit, for the machine did actually have the semblance of a speakeasy reveler. Three steps at a time he climbed the spiral stairway to the control room and grinned at the man who sat on a leather chair in front of a transmitter. This man had been in constant radio contact during the flight.

"A beautiful plane, Mr. Northrop," Stringent said.

The seated man nodded once. "I'm glad you like it. I do feel bad about Tobias, but it's a cutthroat business."

"That's true. We appreciate the situation."

"Well, Jack," cried Professor Crinkle as he emerged into the room. "It only remains for me to throw in the towel and admit I'm beaten. Stringent here says your new Gamma is something really special and I know better than to ever distrust his word on anything connected with aviation. So I'm going to quit the business and sell up."

"That's a shame," said Jack. "You're a good designer."

The professor smiled wistfully. "Sure, but not a patch on you, and I'm not too proud to acknowledge the obvious. My own rival prototype, the Crinkle Crisp, just isn't up to scratch. Sure, it's faster than diarrhea in a Malay Peninsula missionary, but it doesn't have the maneuverability of your model. Look, I don't have a towel on me, just a pocket handkerchief, so I ought to throw that in instead."

He bunched up the square of filthy cloth and hurled it at Jack's head. It missed and struck the wall behind: a wholly symbolic gesture. The mucus acted like glue and it remained stuck on the wall. Stringent thought about wrenching it off, then decided not to.

Jack Northrop leaned back in his chair until the leather creaked and made a pyramid with his fingertips. "Listen, Tobias, my new Gamma is a superb small cargo plane and does everything it should to make it the best of its kind in that category, but that doesn't mean you should abandon all your ongoing projects. I'm extremely interested in some of your proposed innovations. The Flying Tail, for example. An aircraft without fuselage or wings, cutting drag to the minimum!"

Professor Crinkle shook his head. "I suspect you're just flattering me, Jack. Agreed, my Flying Tail is a pretty neat idea, but the tests I've run on miniature models prove that it's very unstable. And you've got your own low drag project, the Flying Wing."

Jack licked his lips and lowered his voice.

"Yes, that's a particular favorite of mine. But I'm going to come clean with the pair of you. There's something even more special in the works. A stratospheric cruiser with a highly experimental propulsion system that'll generate vast amounts of *free* power if it works properly. Forgive me if I don't say much more at this stage."

"You never cease to amaze me, Jack," said Crinkle.

The leather creaked again as the occupant of the chair stood up. "Time is passing rapidly and I have an engagement in Los Angeles this evening, so I should make my farewells now."

Stringent nodded. "Thanks for inviting us over, Mr. Northrop, and for letting me fly your Gamma." He turned to the professor. "I know you are sore disappointed, doc, but at least you've been saved pumping more cash into that ridiculous Crinkle Crisp."

"Yes, that *was* a rather large favor, dear boy."

"Think nothing of it," said Jack.

"Keep us updated about your triumphs, will you?" asked Crinkle. His reddening eyes blinked rapidly.

"Of course I will, Tobias. Maybe I'll see you again before 1932 is out, and if you decide to let Stringent go, there'll always be a job for him here. Have a safe journey back to . . . ?"

"Tallahassee. That's where we're based."

Jack's eyebrows shot up. "In Florida? But I always believed you had head-quarters somewhere in Nevada."

"We did. Then a freak sandstorm destroyed all our hangars. We had no choice but to relocate and now we're on the far side of the continent. Rent is lower and the climate isn't so harsh, plus I prefer the food and the local Seminole workers are reliable."

"And I enjoy swamp whores," added Stringent.

There was an awkward pause.

"Ahem . . . Yes, well, *many* factors contribute to the desirability of the Florida Panhandle as a suitable location for our operations, not that there will be any further products rolling off my production line. My intention is to cancel all Crinkle Industry programs. I've had it with aviation, Jack. I can't even face getting in a plane to return home. I think I'll take a train instead. Is that fine by you, Stringy?"

Stringent nodded dubiously. "I guess so."

Jack Northrop pulled on his coat and perched a hat on his head. "If I'd known you had to come so far, I wouldn't have invited you over just for a few hours and a solitary test flight. Damn it, Florida's two thousand miles distant and by locomotive it's a monstrous and vaporous journey. And I'm not referring to California when I honestly point out that you don't look in any fit state to go back right now."

"I *am* rather tired," admitted the professor.

Jack puffed out his cheeks. "In that case, why not spend the night here on the airfield? There's a cabin on the edge of the runway with a bunk bed and a kitchen and other facilities. I had it built so I could sometimes work late without having to go home."

Crinkle and Stringent exchanged glances.

"Why not?" they said in unison.

An Inflated Threat

They spent a quiet evening in the cabin and Stringent fried plantains and chilies with rice while Crinkle took out his pack of Tarot cards and dealt them on the little table provided. He always denied that he believed in the power of the occult but he carried his pack everywhere and consulted it at times of stress. He rapidly laid out three cards, pouted at them and recited them aloud, in a gloomy voice:

"The Hanged Man, The Devil and Death . . ."

"Sounds ominous to me, doc."

"Not necessarily, Stringy. I keep telling people that the Tarot is often used for harmless games and in fact is just a set of ordinary playing cards with an extra suit of trumps. The Vlachs, Slovaks and Magyars wouldn't see anything sinister in them! No more than they'd consider the black and white knights in a Staunton chess set to be two of the vile steeds ridden by the Horsemen of the Apocalypse."

"Aren't they, doc?" blurted Stringent.

"I most certainly hope not!"

"Well, if that's the way it is," shrugged the pilot.

Crinkle rubbed his chin. "Trust me, dear boy. By the way, maybe you should consider Jack's offer of employment. After I wind up my company you will be out of a job, and the country is in recession, and the Northrop Corporation's a pretty safe outfit."

"Don't know about that, doc. Seems a bit sudden."

Crinkle replaced the cards in their box. "Life is full of abruptness and dramatic changes are quite normal."

"What about you, doc? What'll you do next?"

The professor gritted his teeth, then said, "I've sold advertising space in this story to various companies."

"This story? What are you talking about?"

Crinkle sighed and smiled at his adopted son. "There are many things I never got round to telling you. I didn't want to frazzle your mind until you were old enough to cope with them. Things too odd to be feasible or even imaginable—and yet they are true."

Stringent swallowed hard. "What things exactly?"

"Dozens of them, dear boy!"

"Please tell me a few, won't you, doc?"

"Very well. When I found you in the jungle, there was a note pinned to your nappy. No one knows who its author was. It entrusted your care and education to whoever came across you first. That turned out to be me, of course, and so I raised you as my own. The note added that you possessed three abnormalities. Call them special powers, if you prefer. Nobody else has all three together, although a few individuals have one or two. These abnormalities might make you more powerful than normal human beings. At least that's what the note implied."

"Did it list what the abnormalities were, doc?"

Crinkle nodded. "Yes it did, but I kept them a secret because I didn't want you to grow up arrogant, pompous and pretentious, even though I'm not sure of the exact difference between those three faults. But I can smell smoke! The plantains are burning!"

Stringent Strange rushed back to the stove and lifted the saucepan off the gas ring. He inspected the charred contents and grimaced. "I guess if I add nutmeg we can get away with it."

"No, I detest that spice! Isn't there any cinnamon?"

With his free hand, Stringent rummaged through the spice rack. "Just some turmeric and paprika. Wait a moment! Right at the back there's an old jar of powdered cumin. Maybe . . ."

The moonlight that had been slanting through the little cabin window was suddenly cut off. Now the ring of blue flames on the stove provided the only illumination. "Clouds in El Segundo at this time of year?" cried the professor. "That's very weird."

Still holding the saucepan, Stringent went to the window and peered out. Then he emitted a loud gasp.

"It's a monkey-spanking airship, doc!"

"No need to curse, Stringy. Clearly we've got visitors. Maybe they are friends of Jack? I guess we ought to go out and welcome them properly. Can you see insignia on the tail?"

Stringent narrowed his eyes and nodded.

"A black hooked cross inside a white circle on a red square. Isn't that the symbol of the Manx Nation? You once told me there was an island where cats have no tails and that . . ."

Crinkle shook his head. "Just a bedtime story. I think this airship has come from Germany. The United States government is friendly with the Chancellor of that mighty realm."

"Well then, doc. Let's go and say hello!"

They stepped out of the cabin and blinked. The vast inflated body of the zeppelin was fifty feet above the runway. Half the wooden propellers in the nacelles span clockwise; the other half were in reverse, keeping the bulky sky whale in a stable position relative to the ground. There was no mooring post here, because Jack Northrop was a disdainer of lighter than air travel, but an anchor fell from the gondola on the end of a cable and smashed the tarmac where it landed.

Now they heard a drone and saw a second airship descending behind the first. This also dropped an iron anchor. Meanwhile a rope ladder was deftly unrolled from the first zeppelin and uniformed men began climbing down it, groaning as they swayed. There were at least twenty of them and they were all strapping figures with rippling muscles and therefore hearty appetites. Stringent was distraught.

"There's not enough food to go round, doc!"

Crinkle patted the pilot on his elbow. "Don't worry, dear boy, it's not your fault. Jack should have warned us they were coming." He rubbed his chin thoughtfully. "That's assuming he was expecting them. Perhaps they aren't really his friends? What if . . ."

The first figure had now reached the bottom rung. He turned to grin at the professor and his stepson. Then he reached for his holster and drew a peculiar gun, not an automatic pistol but something snub-nosed and shiny that bristled with aerials. He marched closer and grinned, his cliché of a monocle glinting in his left eye like a coin with a big cobalt blue iris for heads and an airfield at night for tails.

"Herr Northrop? How pleasant to meet you!"

"You've made a mistake," said Stringent reasonably. "This is Professor Tobias Crinkle and I don't think it's good manners to aim a weapon before you know anything definite about him."

"Mein Gott! An ape that can mimic speech!"

"How dare you!" rasped Crinkle. "You are referring to one of the best test pilots in the world. True, he was discovered in a part of Africa where gorillas tend to congregate, but so what? And yes, I admit it was also the location where missionaries have been known to enjoy unnatural sensual congress with the primates, but that evidence is purely circumstantial. At the very minimum he's half human!"

"Silence, Herr Northrop! We know you have been working on a secret type of propulsion system. We used electric ouija boards to learn this. We intend to kidnap you and take you back to Berlin where we will make you work for us under duress. With your aid, our futuristic flying fleet will lay waste to all Europe and America!"

"But Germany are our allies!" protested Crinkle.

"That's right, buddy. Just who the hell do you think you are?" snapped Stringent, shaking his most righteous fist. "Just wait until your Chancellor hears about this! He'll be furious!"

"Ha! That is the insipid delusion of a chump!"

"Now just hold your insults, Fritz! It's *chimp*, not *chump*, and like the professor said, I've got gorilla blood in me, not chimpanzee. Don't they teach taxonomy in your schools?"

The uniformed figure clicked its heels. "You have uttered an incorrect name in your pathetically pejorative attempt to address me. I have never been Fritz. I am Protogruppenführer Kaspar Stumpf, the nominated leader of the Pre-Emptive Nazis. I had a childhood friend named Fritz. I am not he! Do I look like I ought to be?"

"Well, that seems unlikely," conceded Stringent.

"Don't banter with the swine!" warned Crinkle. He turned to confront the invader. "What do you want?"

"I already told you—eight paragraphs ago."

"You can't expect us to listen to you if you won't listen to us," pointed out Crinkle. "I'm *not* Northrop."

"But you must be! For this is El Segundo aerodrome and that is the cabin where the renowned aircraft designer likes to snooze. And we saw you emerge from it with our inverted periscopes. Our reasoning is no less indisputable than a sausage! So you must come with us meekly or I shall be compelled to use compulsion!"

Crinkle snarled. "Don't you realize that by menacing innocent citizens of the United States you are opening hostilities with our government? It's an audacious act of war, no less!"

"Ja, but the Early Nazi catches der Wurm!"

"That's a species of dragon," Crinkle whispered to Stringent, "not one of those wrigglers in the ground."

"Thanks, doc," came the equally quiet reply.

The Protogruppenführer sighed. "Mein Gott! Why do you susurrate? You, Herr Northrop, are the pontificating procrastinator; and you, Herr Hairy, are a matted gibbering fool!"

"We're straying off the point," said Crinkle calmly. "This is nineteen thirty-two. We're not living in the Dark Ages and it's our duty to extend the hand of friendship to our fellow humans—so you should lower your gun and start being charming to us!"

The Pre-Emptive Nazi smiled coldly at this.

"Our electric ouija board has informed us that vicious war between our respective nations is inevitable within the next decade. Therefore we have decided to launch a pre-emptive strike by kidnapping your most capable aircraft designer, who will therefore be prevented from creating wondrous flying devices for the United States. Not only that, but we will pickle his brains and enjoy the benefits of his genius. My mistake, I meant *pick* his brains. Come along, Herr Northrop!"

Two of the other soldiers seized hold of Crinkle and dragged him off towards the rope ladder. Stringent sized up the situation. He would have to get physical soon, of course, but he decided to try talking his way out first. That was the mature thing to do. Melodramatically, he laughed in the face of the Protogruppenführer.

"You won't get far in those jumped-up balloons! What's the top speed of a zeppelin? Sixty miles per hour?"

"That means nothing to me. I think in der kilometers."

"It doesn't matter! You'll never get across the state line. The hydrogen you carry makes you a death trap. One tracer bullet and bang, sizzle, ugh! You'll never evade our air defenses!"

"Oh, I think we will, Herr Stinky. Do you wish to know how?" With a callous grin, the Protogruppenführer leaned closer and whispered a dozen words in Stringent's ear. The test pilot took a step back in astonishment and then glanced at the zeppelins, at the rows of lenses protruding from each gondola. He bunched his fists.

"Well, you'll have to fight me now, on the ground!"

"No, we won't." The Protogruppenführer discharged his weapon at the gaping jaw of Stringent Strange. Blue sparks leaped and danced about his teeth and he collapsed like a sack of doughnuts, the ones without cream in the middle, the toroid ones, you know.

"Stringy! You've murdered my adopted son!"

"Nein, Herr Northrop. Worry not your brow. The dunce is stunned. In a dozen hours he'll recover sense!"

The two soldiers pushed Crinkle towards the rope ladder. He stumbled and the Tarot cards in his pocket fell out and scattered across the runway. Perhaps one day an airplane would exist that had Tarot cards for wings, he thought. No, he was raving now.

Like some demented kind of doomed loon!

The Thief of Time

Stringent's entire skull throbbed like a whipped erection in one of those specialist brothels that he hardly ever visited, when he felt hands on his shoulders, shaking him back to consciousness. He squinted up into the concerned face of Jack Northrop.

"What the hell happened here, Mr. Strange?"

Gasping and drooling, he told Jack everything and then he staggered upright and gazed wildly around the airfield. The zeppelins had vanished and only the broken tarmac remained as evidence that anything dastardly had ever occurred during the night.

"They kidnapped the doc! I must get him back!"

Jack shook his head. "Hold your hormones there, Mr. Strange! Do you know in which direction they went?"

"Yes, I do. They're abducting him to Berlin."

Jack took off his hat and scratched his head. "So they must be heading west over the Pacific. I'll radio the coastguard and get some spotter planes sent up to fix on their positions."

"No, Mr. Northrop, I think they went east."

"Across the entire expanse of the continent? Without permission? But zeppelins wouldn't stand a chance of reaching the Atlantic seaboard. They would be shot down as a matter of plain protocol within an hour. Airship canopies are easy targets for ground guns and are terribly prone to getting fatal holes in them, remember?"

Stringent rubbed the bruise on his temple.

"They've planned for that, Mr. Northrop. The Protogruppenführer told

21

me how they use powerful projectors mounted on their gondolas to show pornographic films on the clouds; but if the skies are clear, the zeppelins project those films on each other, which is why both were sent together. The films feature Bavarian maids!"

Jack whistled through his teeth. "That's a very cunning stratagem, Mr. Strange. No pilot worth his orgones could ever bring himself to shoot big nude bosoms. These Pre-Emptive Nazis must be masters of psychological warfare and sensory manipulation."

"I've shot *over* big nude bosoms," blurted Stringent, and when he saw Jack's shocked face he added, "With my penis, I mean. When I was in an Algerian brothel. It wasn't perilous."

There was an awkward pause.

"Ahem . . . Yes, well," said Jack. "No need for details."

"I'm going after them anyway. I don't suppose you would be willing to lend me your Northrop Gamma?"

Jack Northrop pondered long and hard.

"Let me tell you something, Mr. Strange. Tobias Crinkle is someone I have liked for a long time. Although he's rather naïve—a less charitable authority might plausibly refer to him as a *cretin*——he does have certain visionary qualities. I do believe he's worth saving. But if I give you that plane, what use would it be? It's not armed, and even if it was, you could hardly open fire on the zeppelins, partly because of big naked breasts and also because you could never be sure which craft held the professor and which didn't. And even with extra fuel tanks you couldn't fly further than Bermuda, then you'd have to ditch in the sea. No offence, but it's the kind of mission only a monkey would try. I appreciate that apes and monkeys are different, truly I do, and yet . . ."

Stringent could contain himself no longer.

"I guess you're right, Mr. Northrop, but it does seem an awful shame. I hate the thought of what they'll do to him in Germany when they find out he isn't you. It might be even worse if they don't find that out and keep on working him until he ends up perfecting The Flying Tail. Then the world will be in deep implausible trouble!"

Jack held up his hands. "I'm not suggesting you don't go after him, but I don't think you should do it in the Gamma. I reckon you ought to use the stratospheric cruiser, the one with the new propulsion system—the plane that caused this mess in the first place!"

Stringent blinked. "But that's just a concept."

"Not quite," said Jack. "In fact the prototype has been constructed and is sitting in that other hangar right now; but it has never been flown and the engine hasn't ever been tested."

"What do you mean, not tested? But if . . ."

Jack smiled grimly. "I'm still waiting for permission. There was some concern at the highest level that this new type of engine might *transform* the nature of reality if started up. Frankly, I think that worry is a heap of bull-crap—at the most it'll only affect this planet—but I'm in no position to oppose the President. However, in the event of a national emergency I think it's only proper to disregard petty regulations; and such an occasion has arisen right now. Do you agree?"

"Lead me to her, Mr. Northrop!" chortled Stringent.

Jack turned smartly on the heel of his elegant shoe and walked off into the shadow of a large hangar. Unlike the other hangars in the aerodrome, this one was painted with a dazzling pattern of stripes calculated to make the eyes dance, a form of camouflage invented by the navy for battleships and scarcely ever utilized on land.

"In here. All ready to go. She's a beauty."

"Forgive my rudeness, Mr. Northrop, but I forgot to enquire how your engagement proceeded last night?"

"Not bad," responded Jack. "It was just a business dinner. I thought the pasta was fine, but not the yams."

"Were they baked or fried with a sauce?"

Jack reached the hangar doors, took a necklace from around his neck and held it up. A peculiar key dangled there. "Steamed," he said. "Let me tell you something about the engine of the stratospheric cruiser. It's a kind of pulsejet. The carrots were acceptable too. But it doesn't suck in air and expel heated gases and exhaust fumes. Didn't go with the wine, though. It sucks in *chronons* and disintegrates them so thoroughly that there's nearly no pollution. The olives were stale."

"What in the name of monkey-spanking are they?"

"Little black salty fruits mostly."

"No, I meant *chronons*, Mr. Northrop!"

"Oh those. The fundamental particles of absolute time. Tenseless time, in other words—the time that exists outside subjectivity. Tick tock time. My engine utilizes them for fuel."

"Isn't that risky, Mr. Northrop?" asked Stringent.

"Nah. Yeah. Perhaps. Dunno."

"In that case, I have full confidence in them!"

Jack turned the key in the lock and the hangar doors slid silently open, powered by some well-lubricated clockwork mechanism. The cylindrical craft that lurked in the shadows made the veins in Stringent's neck stand out. He blinked and his tongue lolled.

"This is a plane?" he spat. "The wings are tiny!"

Jack said chidingly, "That's so they aren't ripped off. The acceleration of this bird is unbelievable. Don't say you're scared of a little unbelievable acceleration, Mr. Strange? With a body as muscular and primal as yours, I bet you can handle lots of g-force."

"That's true, but this thing's more like a flying engine than any aircraft I ever saw. The nose is a jet intake and the tail's a combustion chamber. It looks like a torpedo, Mr. Northrop."

Jack slapped the pilot on his shoulder. "You've got it wrong. *Chronons* aren't combustible and there's nothing else inside to explode. I'll stake my reputation she's safe to fly. Safe for the pilot, that is. For the world and its teeming millions—who knows?"

Stringent wanted no further encouragement. He strode to the fuselage, peered up at the cockpit, reached out a long hairy arm to slide the canopy back and swung himself high and down into the pilot's seat. An ordinary man would have needed a stepladder to do this, but Stringent's hybridized genetics and jungle-born dexterity made the task easy for him. He secured his seatbelt and studied the console.

Jack called up, "The instruments are simple."

Stringent nodded. "Rudder, pedal and joystick. There's an altimeter and speed indicator. Hey, the fuel gauge reads empty! Aren't you going to fill the tank with *chronons* before I go?"

Jack laughed. "No need. The engine sucks them out of spacetime as it passes through reality; and they are everywhere, so don't worry about the range of this bird, she can fly forever, or at least until she corrodes away in mid air! The starter button's electric, just press it with your thumb and adjust the speed with the potentiometer on your extreme left. There's an emergency kit beneath the seat but no parachute. At the average speed of this baby you don't stand a hope of bailing out. If something breaks, you'd better glide her down—if you can!"

"Sounds tricky, Mr. Northrop. Wish me luck!"

"Sure. Remember that you carry no armaments. I don't advise trying to ram the zeppelins, even without projected bosoms, because of the bracing girders under the skins. You'll have to intimidate them into landing before they reach the Atlantic Ocean . . ."

Stringent grinned. "I've got a better plan. I intend to overtake them and continue all the way to Berlin. That's where I'll be hiding in wait for them when they arrive. I'll re-abduct the professor from under their very noses, then outrun their fastest pursuers."

"That's not really a better plan than mine."

Stringent nodded. "Yes it is!"

"No, it's not. Not *much* better. A bit better maybe."

"Good enough, Mr. Northrop."

Jack made a wry face. "There's no radio on board because I didn't have time to fit one, but I'll keep an eye out for published versions of this story, and if I find any, I'll skip ahead to learn how you fared. By the way, there were peas and beans mixed in the same dish and freshly baked bread. The hour was late when supper was finished but coffee was still offered at the end. Happy hunting, Mr. Strange!"

He stood clear and made ushering gestures.

So Stringent pressed the starter button and the cylindrical craft began vibrating along its whole length. A motor was turning a turbine inside the fuselage, directly under the cockpit, or so it seemed to the pilot, and wide hyperspatial vanes shaped like tesseracts were drawing in the particles of time itself, compressing them in a chamber until they disintegrated, then expelling the resultant stasis of nullity as a reactive exhaust. Some of this power was then fed back into the motor, a cycle of positive feedback that rapidly accelerated the turbine to maximum rotation. Stringent felt a deep ache in all his bones. He grimaced.

Jack was getting impatient. He had taken out a pocket watch and was carefully studying the passing seconds. Stringent released the handbrake, expecting the craft to roll slowly out of the hangar onto the runway, but it lurched like an electrocuted metaphor and shot skywards like a meteorite in reverse. Without his extensive experience at riding wild prostitutes, the pilot would have panicked, forced the joystick down and crashed into the ground instantly, but he kept his cool and swung the stratospheric cruiser around the control tower in a shuddering arc that flexed all the building's windows and made them sing unearthly music. Stringent tried to relax, to get a feel for the plane's character.

Jack Northrop had emerged from the camouflaged hangar and now he stood on the grassy verge and waved with dignity at the retreating cruiser before walking back to the control tower. Stringent was too busy fighting the controls to look down; he never again saw the man who was to do so much for the evolution of the aerospace industry but who was fated to be treated unfairly by his own government. But this is a work of fiction, not a rant, so let's not get too righteous.

The Passing of the Bosoms

With an excessive amount of physical effort, Stringent managed to make himself master of his machine. He felt vaguely uneasy that the plane had no name, but his overworked brain couldn't think of anything appropriate. It was also a strain that the cockpit window wasn't tinted and that he had to fly directly into the early sun, but he couldn't deviate from his course. Berlin was in this direction and he saw no reason to zigzag the whole way there, like a high frequency sine wave.

As the parched landscape rushed past under him, he started to feel an intense anxiety about the safety and health of Professor Crinkle. His filial love for the man who had raised him as his own son sometimes expressed itself in fits of intense blubbering, and now the oleaginous tears cascaded down his chiseled cheeks and something hissed on the floor between his legs, perhaps an exposed electrical wire. So he rapidly wiped dry his eyes and concentrated on the task in hand.

Despite the urgency of the task, neither of his hands were like those of the average man, and not merely because they were simian; no, it was the fact he possessed six fingers on both. He found himself wondering if this was one of the listed "abnormalities" mentioned by Tobias, and assumed it might be, and then he shrugged; but he couldn't suppress an acute pang of curiosity about the other two. What purpose did they serve? How did they mark him as different from his fellows?

His subconscious eructated a miasma of nostalgia and he sighed as he breathed it in deeply. Twenty years ago. Yes, that long already. It was in a remote valley somewhere in the Belgian Congo that Tobias Crinkle had chanced upon an abandoned baby, starving and hideous but not making an excessive infantile fuss, with steely eyes that seemed to augur the life of a hero if given the chance, in the center of a circle of mysterious ruins near the banks of the River Lomami.

Crinkle had travelled to the Congo to sell his revolutionary aircraft to the colonial administrators, devices with spinning rotors that could hover over the jungle and drop nets on escaping workers. The prototype worked perfectly well back home, so he later claimed; but in the tropical humidity it malfunctioned on its demonstration flight, crashing into the governor's palatial villa and beheading his wife. Needless to say, Crinkle's invention wasn't praised and nobody applauded.

Indeed, the professor was forced to flee blindly into the forest with an entire pack of dogs set loose on his heels. Poisonous snakes, spiders and the darts of hostile blowpipes slayed all the hounds one by one, but these dangers somehow missed him, and he stumbled into a swamp, where his blood was sucked by mosquitoes, leeches and ticks. After long despairing hours in this nightmare, he emerged onto solid ground amid the tumbled stones of an enigmatic temple complex.

And this is where he found the forsaken child who was to grow up into Stringent Strange. He took the baby in his arms and continued his lunatic plunge into dense jungle, and purely by luck he stumbled into a glade that contained a village. Thanks to drummed messages, the tribe that dwelled here already knew that a spindly pale man had struck a blow against their Belgian oppressors by slicing right through an important wife's neck with a divine sky sword. He was welcomed.

The chief of the tribe gave him his own hut and concubines and plenty of food and six months later guided him in person across a vague border into territory controlled by the Portuguese. From here he was able to sail back to the USA via Brazil. The Belgians did put a price on his head, but in time the matter just fizzled out and nobody ever took pot shots at him. Crinkle raised Stringent with the help of his sisters and aunts and the boy was fated to grow healthy and athletic.

Obviously, Stringent could recall none of this. He only knew what the professor had told him on those rare occasions when he had been induced to reminisce about the circumstances surrounding his failed projects. The pilot's earliest actual memories were all located in America and included such mundane experiences as peeling bananas with his feet on a suburban lawn, skateboarding on his hands, and flinging his dung at his neighbor's daughter. The standard childish pranks.

He remembered nothing of Africa and couldn't guess why he had been abandoned there in the first place. Had his real parents deemed him too ugly to deserve life? With this thought, self-pity consumed him and more tears dripped and sizzled on the wire . . .

Stringent shook his head to erase it of stupid sentiments. Such matters belonged to the past; it was essential he remain cool and focused until he could recover the professor. And now he shielded his partly blinded eyes with his left hand and allowed himself a short laugh. A pair of dots on the horizon proved that he had caught up with the zeppelins. He turned down the potentiometer and felt the engine splutter, but it didn't stall and with a gentle pull on the joystick he adjusted his angle to bring himself between them. That would surprise the rascals!

Then he noticed more dots rising over a mountain range.

"Dolphin-flogging interceptors!" he snarled.

A squadron of eight, no nine, biplanes was approaching the zeppelins from the north. Stringent recognized them immediately as Boeing P-12s, the modified 102 Model with 450 hp R-1340-7 engines. Primitive pursuit aircraft but effective enough, despite the fact they would soon be obsolete and broken up for spare parts in a Texas scrapyard. Certainly these planes would have no trouble blasting the airships out of the sky and that would mean the doom of the professor. He must warn them not to open fire! But he had no access to a radio transmitter.

He turned the potentiometer down another notch and the cruiser began bucking and wheezing. Stringent cursed and realized that it was incapable of slow precise flight. He had such difficulty fighting the joystick that the only option was to increase his speed again. He veered to starboard as the zeppelins grew large, overtaking them and swinging around in a wide arc. As he passed the airships he craned his neck to observe the occupants of each gondola, but through their murky portholes he was unable to discern which one Tobias Crinkle was aboard.

Nor did he catch sight of the Protogruppenführer, who obviously was deliberately keeping out of sight just to deceive Stringent. These Germans weren't fools—not by a long Bratwurst!

However, he *did* notice rotating parabolic aerials suspended below the gondolas and realized that an experimental form of RADAR had already been perfected by the Nazi scientists. Insulated wires ran from the aerials through holes in the gondola sides, and although Stringent couldn't see it, these were connected to electric ouija boards inside. Instead of worrying about this development, he kept his foot pressed hard on the rudder pedal and yawed his way sickeningly across the sky, wondering if the biplanes would attempt to shoot him down too, bearing in mind that Jack Northrop hadn't obtained flight clearance for him.

To be killed by friendly fire. A grotesque irony!

The turning circle of the stratospheric cruiser was considerable and by the time it had completed the maneuver, the biplanes were within firing range. But now the projectors on the zeppelins glowed into life and erotic images of naked girls appeared on the canopies. The girls were curvy and saucy and precluded any form of attack.

One Bavarian maid soaped down another and bubbles burst silently on her russet nipples. Then additional maids turned up and on some obscure impulse they all jumped into the same bathtub together. Yet more soaping and a little light massage of bosoms larger, rosier and milkier than clouds. Stringent found the plot extremely farfetched, but clearly the pilots of the interceptors had no such reservations . . .

Stringent watched as the biplanes started shuddering. He frowned. The clear air turbulence in the vicinity was mild, so why were these inherently stable aircraft behaving so erratically? It almost seemed as if each Boeing pilot had acquired an extra joystick that needed lots of rhythmic pumping before it fulfilled its function. Peculiar! One at a time, the biplanes veered away, a veteran pilot lighting a cigarette while his more callow comrades merely burned with smokeless shame.

The world was full of indecipherable happenings. No matter! Stringent swung the cruiser in another wide arc. If necessary he could keep circling the two zeppelins until he had learned as much as possible, then he would accelerate towards Berlin and spring his trap! He overtook the zeppelins a second time, thumbing his nose at them.

The crew of one airship had crowded the portholes and were gesturing at him. A hatch opened and a uniformed soldier fitted with magnetic pads inched his way along the outside of the gondola towards an exposed cage bolted to the nose. Barrels of what might be engine fuel had been stacked in this cage and a smooth chute protruded from it. The soldier reached the cage and lowered himself into it, one of the pads falling from his arm and tumbling towards the desert far below.

Stringent squinted. Was some sort of weird weapon being prepared for use against him? Before an answer to his question was forthcoming, more dots appeared over a different horizon. Five new planes were approaching from the south and they stood out vividly against the sky because of their coloring. They were all bright pink. Clearly the first squadron pilots had radioed the precise reason for their failure back to base and the authorities had taken rapid and relevant action.

They had decided to scramble the Sky Spartans!

This squadron was famed for its courage, its histrionic displays of wild aerobatics and the biting wit of its pilots. Stringent was fully aware that to qualify as a Sky Spartan, a candidate had to actively demonstrate before a panel of strict examiners that his erotic desires gravitated entirely towards other men and that his relationships with women were verifiably platonic. Most hopefuls failed this test; only the most determined entered the camp of proud, upstanding, elevated heroes.

Stringent grinned mirthlessly. The Bavarian maids couldn't save those Germans now, not even if they tripled the circumference of their bosoms and quadrupled the vigor of the soaping! But again, this meant the death of Crinkle, plummeting to the ground among a tangle of flame-enveloped fabric and red-hot girders and popping bodies. Ugh! The thought brought fresh drops to the apeman's tear ducts.

He regained control of his emotions. Was he some kind of softie? No, he had six fingers on each hand and was special and needed to act in full accord with his uniqueness! He peered closer. In the vanguard of the Sky Spartans was the sequin-decorated aircraft of Oscar Rosebud, the famous Pink Baron. One of the few pilots envied by Stringent for his flying skills, Rosebud was unconventional in his approach to flying. He had decorated his wings with tiny sparkling sequins.

Critics scoffed at his ostentation and vanity.

In fact these sequins were shaped like miniature annular airfoils and more than doubled the total surface area of the wings, contributing to lift and reducing the stalling speed of his biplane to a crawl. The Pink Baron was probably the most agile flyer in the world. Exploiting the gyroscopic pull of his powerful engine he was able to execute a 180° turn in a single length of his own fuselage. As Stringent struggled against his controls, he felt acute envy for Rosebud's freedom.

And now the five pink biplanes broke formation and buzzed like angry peeled bees around the zeppelins. Then the Pink Baron made a theatrical show of removing the safety catch on his Hotchkiss machinegun, blew a kiss at the nearest airship, and removed the gold lamé glove from his right hand, because he preferred to feel the trigger with his bare finger. Before he could unleash the first volley directly at the hydrogen-filled vessel, the pornographic films suddenly stopped.

New films started. They featured blond men in crotchless Lederhosen dancing and prancing around bowls of gherkins. Immediately the biplanes began vibrating. Rosebud lost all interest in his machinegun and appeared concerned only with manipulating the mysterious second joystick already noted by Stringent. The other Sky Spartans followed his example. One by one they veered off, just as the earlier interceptors had done, returning to the horizon over which they had come.

Stringent was alarmed. Nazi technicians inside the airships had clearly fitted new reels to the projectors, but that task should have taken several more minutes, especially the job of selecting such specialist material. But the films had changed smoothly and efficiently. Had these Germans been pre-warned that the Sky Spartans were on their way? How else could they have known? It was deeply worrying.

Stringent squinted as he made another pass. Next to the RADAR dish was a curious phallic object. He paled. It couldn't be! Were the Nazis so far ahead they even possessed a working GAYDAR? The Americans had been desperate to acquire such a device for years, but the technology had seemed a long way ahead in the future.

He shook his head. His government really ought to be informed about this! He watched in disbelief as the phallus tracked his movement across the sky, pointed directly at him and drooped. A moment later, the content of the films reverted to Bavarian bosoms. Now that the Sky Spartans had gone, the Nazis were taking no chances.

Stringent had forgotten about the soldier in the cage at the front of the gondola, but that villain didn't reciprocate his neglect. From the corner of his eye, the apeman saw a dark cylinder ascending rapidly towards him. A levitating barrel? Before he could turn his head to inspect it properly, the object detonated and he was thrown forward, striking his head against the hard cockpit console. His nose burst . . .

A Daft Mad Bonkers Blast

The cruiser jerked and twisted, but it didn't flip over. With blood pouring into his mouth, Stringent instinctively checked his altitude and speed. The explosion had knocked him almost one thousand feet higher. With a sigh of annoyance he berated himself for his lack of attention, and as he began still another orbit of the zeppelins, he kept his cobalt gaze firmly fixed on what was happening in the external cage.

The soldier stationed there was lifting up the fuel barrels and dropping them into the mouth of the smooth chute, propelling them far beyond the gondola. Instead of plummeting down and smashing open on the ground, they fell only a little way and then began rising in an arc, accelerating as they did so. Some sort of timer or altimeter on their surface then gave the signal for a charge to be set off that burst the barrels and ignited the fuel into an expanding shell of burning vapor.

Stringent was puzzled. He could understand how intelligent and highly motivated Nazis with generous state funding and the help of electric ouija boards could perfect hitherto unreliable circuits to create a valid RADAR system before the Americans; and even at a pinch how the fiendish brutes might turn what was supposed to be pure theory into practice and develop a practical GAYDAR; but Heighth Charges weren't even a *concept* in any research laboratory he'd visited. How did they fly? What made them rise? They span rapidly as they flew, he noted.

It was something else to warn his government about. But only after he had rescued the professor. Perhaps Crinkle already had answers to all the questions that were troubling Stringent? It's not unknown for captors and hostages to strike up friendships. If the Protogruppenführer still believed that Crinkle was Northrop, he may have revealed all his technical secrets to his prisoner. Stranger things often do happen, especially in spy novels, not that this is one of those. And yet . . .

"By all the gibbons of genuflection!" Stringent cried.

His mind had wandered again and a second barrel exploded near him, rocking the cruiser and causing the untoughened glass over the dials to shatter. He pressed the rudder pedal down hard and twisted the joystick, but to his horror the plane barely responded. The shockwaves had done serious damage to the hydraulics. One more blast and he was a deceased apeman, no question. He looked down and saw that the soldier was now hefting a third barrel towards the chute.

Stringent made a decision. He might not survive a third detonation and even if he did, it would lose him control over his rudder and ailerons, so it was definitely prudent to vacate the area as fast as possible. With painful slowness, the cruiser swung around in a wide circle. When it was pointing in the direction of Berlin again, he turned up the potentiometer. A second later came the third explosion. The dial fell off the potentiometer, and try as he might, he couldn't get it back on.

But at least he was speeding away from danger!

Or was he? It was a debatable point.

True, the zeppelins were far behind him, and the soldier who had flung barrels at him was faced with the prospect of inching along on the outside of his gondola without one of his magnetic pads—and Stringent did pray hard he would fall off—but the apeman's relief was cut short by a bolt of pure agony that shot through his spinal cord. Too much acceleration! The potentiometer was stuck on maximum.

So the g-force kept increasing, pushing him back in his seat, causing his eyeballs to ache and lights to flash in them. He winced as the beating of his heart became irregular and his blood turned sluggish in his arteries and veins. The pressure on his chest was stronger and more painful than during a massage he'd undergone in an Algerian brothel when a fat whore had danced barefoot on his sternum. He couldn't stand much more of this. He was about to lose consciousness . . .

There must be some way of slowing the cruiser down! He blinked at a knob that said WITHDRAW and pulled it impulsively but it only loosened some ratchet or catch under him and his chair slid back, so he was forced to cling tightly to the joystick to keep himself in a position where he still could reach the rudder pedal. Desperately he groped and pulled at another knob that he assumed might have the opposite effect. EMERGE it said. But no, his chair didn't lock back in place. Instead, a booster engine started up somewhere and worsened the situation.

With difficulty he peered closer at the second knob and saw that most of the letters had fallen off. What it actually said was EMERGENCY USE ONLY. This didn't bode well for his near future prospects, but perversely he started to feel better. Perhaps he was now acclimatizing to the rigors of sharply increasing velocity? After all, his gorilla body really was very sturdy. With a gasp, he greeted the appearance of the sea on the horizon directly in front of him. He had managed to traverse half the continental United States in only fifteen minutes!

He laughed in wonderment, despite his terror.

Then a light started flashing on the console. The numbers and symbols on one dial seemed to be indicating that every available *chronon* had been used up from the present. A second light began flashing. This showed that the cruiser had switched to using *chronons* from the future. It was all very confusing. If only Jack Northrop had given him a test flight before he had embarked on this ambitious mission!

But that was asking too much, of course. The opportunity hadn't been there and everything had happened the only way it could. It was better to simply focus on getting to Berlin in one piece, or failing that, in ditching somewhere safe, preferably not in the middle of the Atlantic Ocean. The booster engine wasn't throbbing in time with the main engine and curious creakings and poundings filled the cockpit. Tentatively he pressed down on the rudder pedal. Nothing happened.

The controls had jammed, probably more a result of the unimaginable velocity than the damaging effects of the Heighth Charges. But who knew for sure? He gritted his molars and wondered how he would ever land the cruiser, bearing in mind it could never run out of fuel. He would circle the world eternally: his skeleton slumped in the chair, while on the ground a terrible war raged between Germany and the USA, a synthetic apocalypse the Nazis were almost certain to win.

"Of all the rotten ends to my career!" he huffed.

He fell into a funk and watched the azure ocean undulate beneath, the crests of tiny waves sparkling in bright sunlight. Suddenly a vast shadow fell over the expanse of water. A circular shadow. And now another. And another.

They came together, overlapped, moved apart, like the umbrae of giant inhuman balloons. More Nazi vehicles? The cruiser shook violently, as if in the grip of several competing gravitational fields. He felt lighter in body, if not in mind. What did it mean?

Before he could crane his head up to view the origins of this incredible shadow play, he was distracted by a low solid line in the distance. He had reached Europe already! Was this the coast of France or Britain? He flew above fields, towns and rivers. The large circular shadows were here too, moving aside and allowing the sun to slip a beam through any gap, like a gold knife between ribs, or like a better and more original simile through the interstices of verbal logarithms. Yes.

A rapid patter turned the cruiser into a percussion instrument. Rain at this altitude? Impossible! No, not rain, something harder. Hailstones? But he was above the weather, cruising high in the ionosphere. Then he noted that the air was full of debris, particles of solid matter suspended no less magically than pebbles in water. They struck his wings and fuselage with the force of micro-meteorites, denting the metal, making a racket beyond endurance. At this velocity, even a single piece of gravel could puncture the hull and enter his body like a bullet.

A larger piece of shapeless rubble cracked the cockpit window, but the special glass held together. At least for the time being . . . Stringent felt the sweat pour from his brow and turn the dried blood on his nose and mouth back to runny liquid. The hammering grew louder and the engines whined like lost dogs made of cogs and vanes.

"Where the hell are you when I need you, doc?"

A rhetorical question. Stringent knew perfectly well that the professor was currently located on a zeppelin, an involuntary guest of the fiendish Protogruppenführer. Why bring up the matter again? Lazy editing on the part of this author, that's why. But in these circumstances the apeman can be forgiven his outburst, and I must be forgiven for leaving it in, because the strain we are under is truly immense.

"Blistering baboons!" he gasped. "What's this?"

It was a storm of cogs. A big clock had broken apart and all its innards had flown up into the sky. An hour hand whirled past like a scimitar and missed his left wing by inches, but some of the cogs were sucked into the intake of his main engine. A horrid screech went up from the turbine. The cruiser stuttered and began to decelerate.

Then the booster engine also shut down. The plane went into a shallow dive. Stringent licked his gooey lips. At least now he had a slim chance of making a crash landing he might survive! Not something to be sneezed at, unless he intended to spatter the cockpit with gory snots. But seriously, it *was* an improvement in his situation

More sea appeared and then vanished. Clearly he had just passed over Britain. Possibly the cogs had come from the inside of Big Ben! But how and why? Belgium rushed past in a dull flash, and yet he was slowing all the time. It was an ironic thought, but it seemed likely he'd make it safely to Germany after all. Probably not to Berlin, though; that would be much too contrived for comfort. He grimaced.

He was losing height almost as rapidly as speed. It took ten minutes to cross Luxembourg, despite its modest size. Now he was over the frontier and the forests of Germany rose up to meet him. He tried to steer between the mountains, and despite the stiffness of the rudder he managed the task and found himself in a narrow valley. Down he went, until he grazed the treetops. Wood snapped, metal squealed.

Then he was tumbling and the window fell out and pine needles were everywhere and the scent wasn't unpleasant. And finally he bumped to a hard but not fatal stop on a forest floor.

It was twilight down here, so thick were the trees all around. Checking for broken bones and not finding any, Stringent mumbled a quick prayer of thanks to no particular deity and began searching for the emergency kit that Northrop had mentioned. He eventually found it in a recess under the seat and opened it with his eager fingers.

There was a flare gun and a box labeled FLARES. Stringent tore open the box and was bewildered to discover a pair of trousers that widened for no reason near the ankles. He shook his head and checked the gun. It was loaded with a single cartridge. The only other item in the kit was a packet of vitamin bubblegum. The apeman stuffed this in his mouth and chewed in a frenzy of disappointment and hatred.

He had difficulty sliding open the canopy of the cockpit because of the branches outside that pressed against the cruiser and frustrated his efforts, but he persisted and finally managed to widen it enough to crawl out. The air that rushed into his lungs was remarkably pure; fresh but also scented with sweet pine and, bizarrely enough, thickened with an almost tangible primitivism. He felt perverse gratitude that he hadn't reached Berlin after all, for the factories of that metropolis undoubtedly would have offended his bruised nostrils with the smokes of ersatz chemical compounds, but he chastised himself for this selfishness. He shouldn't forget the professor! It was vital he get to Berlin without delay!

He stumbled through the forest until he found a wide clearing. Then he had his first chance to look at the sky. What he saw caused him to sink to his knees and whimper. So *these* were the source of the three overlapping spherical shadows! Three new moons . . . or were they planets? Far closer to the Earth than the old moon had ever been, they loomed and pulled at each other like squabbling cousins. Stringent felt the cross-currents of the gravity on the liquids controlling balance in his inner ear, on the hairs on his head, even on his mind's thoughts!

"Corking cantaloupes! It's like something out of one of those science fiction magazines on the newsstands!"

And so it was. Stringent occasionally read those publications and was a particular fan of S.P. Meek, Ray Cummings, Neil R. Jones, Charles R. Tanner, Raymond Z. Gallun, Henry Hasse and maybe half a dozen other half-forgotten pulp masters you've never heard of. Well, you might have heard of Cummings, I suppose. He wrote lots of tales about men getting themselves shrunk in order to have bizarre adventures on the surfaces of atoms. He's still quite obscure, though.

And yet, even for science fiction magazines of that era, three planets at the same time seems a bit overdone . . .

Still dazed by the sight and also by his ordeal, Stringent aimed his gun upwards and pulled the trigger. The flare streaked high and a parachute opened, but instead of a burning lump of magnesium, a banner unfurled itself and rippled on the mild breeze.

WHY NOT TRY GLOOPMITE! A BYPRODUCT OF THE BEER INDUSTRY THAT MAKES A YEAST DRINK ENJOYED BY GIRLFRIENDS WITH SLIGHTLY ODD TASTES. GO ON, YOU NEVER KNOW! ALSO LEGAL AS A SANDWICH SPREAD!

Stringent laughed bitterly and dropped the gun.

So that's what Crinkle meant when he referred to selling advertising space in this story! It wasn't just a question of product placement, mused the apeman, as he spat out his VitaPop Bubblegum, but a case of utterly overt and intrusive commercial propaganda. Bah! He watched the banner under the parachute. Instead of drifting back to earth, it hung in one spot for a few minutes and then started rising. The gravity of the other planets was stronger even at that low elevation.

What had happened to the world since the morning?

There was no point standing here trying to work it out for himself. He needed to speak to some locals, get answers from them, so it was crucial to leave the valley and maybe find a village. It didn't matter too much in which direction he headed, but he decided to go east, towards Berlin. The forest here wasn't like the jungles of the Congo. It was dense and hard to penetrate, yes, but there were no poisonous snakes, predators or thorns as long and sharp as stilettos, and even Stringent didn't know if he meant the knives or the heels. You can choose.

Not much more than an hour later he broke out of the undergrowth and found himself on a road. He set off with a light step, partly because of his relief, partly because of the pull of the rogue planets, but he managed less than a mile before he met a vehicle coming the other way. It was a jalopy of some kind, steam powered obviously, for thick fumes poured out of its windows.

The occupants saw him immediately and pulled over. Stringent knew only a few very basic German phrases. As the driver leaned out of a window, the apeman pointed at his blood-covered nose and said, "Das ist keine Wurst! Wo sind die ganzen Nutten?" But the response of the driver was most un-expected. He answered:

"Hey dude, why are you jawing the ancient lingo?"

"You speak English?" cried Stringent.

"English!" The driver scratched his head. "What's that?"

His companion in the passenger seat said, "English is the old name for American. Yeah, read that in a book."

The driver squinted at Stringent. "That's not my freak. I never learned any of the dead languages. Too bad!"

"You're speaking English now!" the apeman protested.

The driver laughed. "This is German, man. Are you on some powerful mushrooms? I heard there's a mind blowing variety growing in the woods around here. Think I ought to come back with a sack and stock up. Well, are you going to climb inside, dude?"

"By all means. Thank you," said Stringent.

"We'll take you back to the community and get some herbal remedies inside you, just to be on the safe side. You might have internal bleeding, you see. And I reckon that bashed nose could benefit from some healing crystal energy. Maybe a massage too."

"I'm glad you came along," remarked Stringent.

"We saw your distress advert, man."

"I won't trouble you for long. I'm going to Berlin to meet a friend and I can't risk missing him. We must return to the USA and if I'm not ready to greet him, he won't get another chance."

"The USA? Ha ha! This joker is a comedian!"

The driver and his passenger chuckled and slapped their own thighs in gestures of mirth. Stringent, who was crammed into the narrow back seat, leaned forward to exhibit his look of dismay. "What's funny about that? I fail to discern any wit in my statement."

"The USA doesn't exist. It was annihilated nearly a century ago when the Yellowstone Supervolcano erupted."

"Who told you such lies?" bellowed Stringent.

"Take it easy, man! The history books tell the story. The only zone of North America that's still inhabitable is Canada and you really don't want to go *there*, not unless you think it's cool to end up as a human sacrifice. I reckon you may be suffering from concussion. We'll check your aura for specks when we reach the community."

Something awful now occurred to Stringent. He said bleakly, "Do you mind if I enquire what decade this is?"

The driver and the passenger exchanged amused glances. "Why, we're in the teens, of course! Between the noughties and the twenties. Some say it's the brashest phase in every cycle."

Stringent gulped. "Are we in the 21st Century?"

"Tee hee! What a jester! This is the 22nd, buddy, no more, no less. The beautiful year of 2112 in fact. Yeah!"

PITHY PULP WITH PIPS

Stringent Strange wasn't like other men. Not only did he have six digits on each hand, the body of a gorilla, an unprecedented vigor with whores, as well as two more presently unknown, possibly momentous abnormalities, he was also capable of recovering from severe mental shocks in less than ninety-five percent of the time required by the average human male. This enabled him to sit in the back of the jalopy without trying to jump out and hide forever under a roadside hedge.

Something extremely serious had gone wrong, and he began to suspect he knew what. Hadn't Northrop informed him that the cruiser gobbled the very particles of time? His flight from El Segundo to this valley had taken away so many *chronons* from spacetime that whole years, even centuries, had been consumed by his engine. Time had been forced to speed up and he was already in the future! Everything that had belonged to his life back home was dust or unheard echoes . . .

It wasn't that he had been propelled forward through time like the pilot of a time machine. No, it was more a case that Time itself, and with it the backdrop to his existence, the real world, had shifted all around him. In a sense, he had stayed in place while everything else had slipped backwards, falling into a temporal chasm created by the accelerated loss of *chronons*. An avalanche of time had passed over him; and he had emerged, blinking and frightened, in a changed landscape.

The future can be reached in two ways. Either by moving forward in a static universe or by remaining static while the universe moves backward. The little-used second option had been his fate. He had run on a treadmill made of pure time—and won the race!

His mind struggled to cope with the implications. The future had been born prematurely, without having a chance to mature properly at the rate of one second per second. Thus there couldn't be any intervening events between the start of the cruiser's flight and its finish because there simply hadn't been enough *time*. So anything that may have 'happened' in history between those dates wasn't real. Or rather, momentous events such as the volcanic annihilation of the USA had been generated retroactively by the necessity of explaining their outcome!

Stringent bit his bottom lip and wept. During the entire period between 1932 and 2112, the effects of every event had preceded its causes. And it was his fault! No, wait a moment, it was Northrop's! No, it was Professor Crinkle's! No, it was the Protogruppenführer's! Yes, that was better. This final judgment enabled him to regain control over his emotions. He made an effort to smile, but tears still shone on his face and dripped like greasy gems of deliquescing sissy lubricant.

But the driver and the passenger in the front seats didn't seem troubled at all by his sobbing. Did this mean they were comfortable with the truth of a man expressing emotions in public? How weird! And yet this *was* the future. One hundred and eighty years had passed since his own age. Even social attitudes can evolve, or devolve, in such a span. He smiled without effort now. The future is another country, he told himself; they do things differently there. But he wasn't sure who "they" were and this was perhaps the most fretful aspect of his position.

As the jalopy bounced down the road, the driver and passenger finally introduced themselves. The driver was called Moonwash and his friend was known as Quorn Joy. They found it hard to pronounce or understand Stringent's own name when he offered it, but the mirth occasioned by the effort reduced them to happy chuckles.

Quorn Joy reached into a pocket of his brightly colored coat, found a packet of cigarettes and offered one to the apeman. Stringent frowned. He never smoked, although he knew from the propaganda of his own age that tobacco is good for the health; and yet the picture on the packet displayed not a tobacco leaf but a stylized marijuana plant. So he hesitated. Only the most bohemian appreciators of jazz in the hardest to find speakeasies ever cared to inhale the fumes of that exotic weed, as far as he was aware. Did these people mistake him for a jazzer?

"Go on, puff on an Arbeit," urged Quorn Joy.

"That's just the brand name, man," explained Moonwash.

"But what does it do?" asked Stringent.

Quorn Joy inserted a cigarette in his own mouth, ignited it and inhaled deeply, releasing the pungent vapors from his nostrils in curling ribbons that filled the interior of the vehicle.

"Do? Why, Arbeit macht, like, frei, man!"

His voice was hoarse and languid. Stringent declined again and Quorn Joy returned the packet to his pocket. Now the apeman realized the jalopy wasn't steam powered after all: the smokes he had observed issuing from it belonged to these burning tubes of delirium leaf! He ought to ask about the power source for the wheels. He did so. Moonwash gestured through his window at the overhead planets.

"All our energy is renewable, sustainable and biodegradable. There's a sort of spherical flywheel under the bonnet that is continuously pulled off balance by the changing patterns of gravity created by the three planets as they move closer together or break apart. The gravitational fields of those worlds are never in equilibrium! The motion of the sphere turns gears that operate a dynamo and recharges a battery that is used to power an electric motor that propels us where we choose."

Stringent whistled appreciatively. "Ingenious!"

"Yeah," nodded Quorn Joy, "but the output of the dynamo is small and it takes a long time to recharge the battery, so after every journey a jalopy must be allowed to recuperate for a week. Luckily, our community is only a few kilometers from here. We rarely use machines to get around, but we feared you might be too injured to walk."

"That was very thoughtful of you," said Stringent.

"Think nothing of it, dude!"

"Excuse me, are you pacifists?" asked the apeman. "I mean, from the way you speak and act I wondered . . ."

Both Moonwash and Quorn Joy turned their heads and gaped at him in disbelief. Then they chuckled and returned their attention to the road. The sunlight slanted through a break in the overhead planets and illuminated a collection of tepees and tree houses just ahead. The jalopy slowed, pulled up next to a geodesic wicker dome.

"Of course we are, man! Did you think we were Rushans? Everyone in Germany is a pacifist. We're all HIPZIS here! How come you're so out of touch with events and facts? You're not from outer space, are you? There isn't a *fourth* rogue planet up there?"

Stringent clutched his brow in despair. "Too many references to things I've never heard of! Slow down!"

Quorn Joy grinned. "Sure thing, that's the pace we like!"

"Mild and easy!" agreed Moonwash.

Stringent licked his lips. "Let's take it one item at a time. I first want to solve the language issue. My native tongue is English, and that's what I'm speaking now, but you seem adamant it's German. I am therefore worried that you might be incurable lunatics; and I require you to prove, with use of convincing words and gestures, that you are, in fact, perfectly sane and trustworthy. I have issues to raise!"

Moonwash said, "Fine, we'll answer any questions you ask, but I think we should do it in more positive surroundings than the inside of a jalopy. Come inside my yurt for a bowl of yogurt. Then we can jabber about the heavy stuff to your heart's content."

He opened the door and jumped out. Quorn Joy followed his example. The apeman eased himself out of the cramped seat and stretched his legs on the ground. He was surrounded by tree houses, domes and huts. There were people everywhere, gentle, graceful figures. Animals too. Children in brightly colored clothes played with lambs or toy sitars, and women with dreadlocks made pottery, meditated or did yoga between the tepees. Nose rings were common. The men sat and smoked marijuana, blew into ocarinas or played games with lentils.

"This is our humble community," announced Quorn Joy. "As you can see, it's a vegetarian eco-village based on the main HIPZI principles. We love peace and nature and innocence."

"Welcome to Goodvibe!" said Moonwash.

GOOD VIBRATIONS AND EXCITATIONS

The yurt wasn't made from animal skins. None of the tents were. Animal products were frowned upon in Goodvibe with the exception of milk and yogurt. Stringent found the interior spacious, especially as there was so little furniture, and comfortable enough for his taste. A woman with blue cheeks served him herbal tea in a quaintly wonky clay mug; she appeared to be Moonwash's girlfriend. Another girl entered and sat on Quorn Joy's lap, her breasts bare and daubed with red and green stripes. It seemed that body painting was a normal custom here.

The apeman sipped the tea. "Very refreshing!"

"Mint and nettle," said Moonwash. "The best combination for serious concussion and possible broken ribs."

"I think all my bones are intact," replied Stringent.

"You do have an immensely strong body," concurred Quorn Joy, "and rather a hairy one too, believe it or not."

Stringent smiled thinly. "I already noticed that."

"You're not some sort of nature god, by any chance?" Moonwash was suddenly excited; he leaned forward.

"I'm afraid not. Just an abominable mutant . . ."

"Ah well! Have some food with us."

The woman with blue cheeks went to fetch bowls; Moonwash jumped up to help her. They returned with a healthy feast. Having an enormous appetite and enthusiasm for fruit and vegetables, Stringent barely touched the yogurt, but he devoured the pears, apples, plums, tomatoes, grapes, lettuce, chives and celeriac. When he had finished, he sat back, sighed in gratitude and beamed at his candlelit hosts. "Thanks. And now I just need to take a crash course in modern history!"

"You know nothing at all about Germany? You weren't kidnapped by a Pectoral and taken to Bronson Alpha?"

"Once again, I don't understand those references . . ."

Quorn Joy stroked his chin carefully. "The words you spoke when we first encountered you were Antique German, the same kind uttered by our ancestors back in the 20th Century. Since then, the language has evolved and changed, as every language does over time, and by pure coincidence it now exactly resembles American." He paused and then added, "Which is the language once called English."

The apeman guffawed. The chances of such a fortunate transformation were incredibly slim and yet that was no argument against the process. A caterpillar doesn't have to turn into a butterfly of its own species; it might change into the caterpillar of a moth.

Why not? Apart from the fact it's a biological impossibility. But that's just splitting hairs. Hairy caterpillars.

Or gorilla hairs. Smelly and thick. But warm.

"Tell me about the HIPZIS . . ."

Moonwash opened a fresh packet of Arbeit joints. "Hippie Nazis, my friend, that's what it stands for."

Quorn Joy added, "A long time ago, the Nazis were a warlike people ruled by a dictator named Hitler who waged war on Europe and the USA and defeated them. His prime advantage was a secret weapon, a radical type of aircraft called the Tarotplane."

Stringent gasped at the mention of this device. If Moonwash or Quorn Joy or the females noticed his discomfort, they were tactful enough not to say anything. The lecture continued:

"So the Nazis ruled the world and many bad things occurred. It was a real downer of a time, but Hitler died and after the passing of years, the regime mellowed. Hitler's successors were each a little less fanatical than he. Eventually they were pure hippies."

Quorn Joy looked at Moonwash for approval. Moonwash nodded and added his own summation of events:

"And that's the origin of the HIPZIS, man! That's us, man! We're the end result. You want to know something? I read a novel last month about a parallel Earth where Hitler lost the war. It was terrible, man! By losing when he was at the zenith of his malevolence, the Nazis became forever preserved in the world memory as evil killers, and therefore would serve as symbols—as touchstones, man!—for future troublemakers. By losing, they never had a chance to mellow out and become associated with peace and harmony. What a freaky idea, huh? Mind blowing! That novel was a satire, man, and a twisted comedy!"

"Did Ray Cummings write it?" blurted Stringent.

"Never heard of him. Nah, it was by some dude called . . . I can't seem to recall. Sort of Spanish name . . ."

"Felipe ¿Que Dick?" suggested Quorn Joy.

"That's him!" cried Moonwash.

The women, who were called Nutloaf and Tantra, now decided to take part in the conversation. Until this moment, Stringent had assumed, like most men of his era, that their function was mainly decorative. So he was amazed to discover they were highly intelligent beings despite their lips, thighs and bosoms, all very alluring. They asked him what else he wished to learn and when he asked about the three rogue planets they gave him a detailed account of their discovery.

"A scientist by the name of Jiggery P. Bronson was the first to observe them, just before they entered the solar system. He was an American, for this happened before the supervolcano erupted, as will be obvious when you hear the rest. Actually he only observed one of the planets, the first one, Bronson Alpha, and he calculated that it was on collision course with Earth. As it happened, he was slightly out, but it skimmed near enough to cause an immense amount of damage."

Moonwash took up the tale, waving his arms and exhaling smoke like some sort of more original simile than a dragon. "The gravitational pull uprooted the tallest buildings in every land, pulled them apart in mid-air. All the debris is still up there, in dense clouds that are blown thither and hither by the winds of the jet stream. That's why all airplanes have been banned from flying higher than 100 meters. Sometimes, when the planets are aligned in such a way their combined pull is less, the components of those clouds come down as hard rain."

Tantra displayed a large cog. "This fell through the yurt only a month ago. Sliced a cucumber on a platter clean in two! It's only a matter of time before someone in Goodvibe is killed!"

Stringent nodded with understanding and sympathy. "It was that junk that brought my own aircraft down . . ."

Tantra touched his arm and he thrilled to feel the heat of her flesh on his hairy bicep; he needed a woman!

She said, "The pull of Bronson Alpha didn't just uproot buildings but also encouraged simmering chambers of magma just under the surface of the earth to break through the crust."

"Hence the Yellowstone Supervolcano," said Nutloaf.

"Incredible!" moaned Stringent.

"The lava spread and covered most of the USA, although Alaska and Hawaii were spared, because of their geographical separation. Jiggery P. Bronson lost his life with every other American scientist. The lava cooled and entombed the entire country. Bronson Alpha went into a weird orbit with Earth and no one's quite sure if it's entirely stable or not, so there's still a danger it might collide properly with us. Poor Jiggery never got to witness the advent of a second rogue world also headed for Earth, but it was named after him in his honor."

"Bronson Beta?" asked Stringent.

Quorn Joy shook his head. "Greek letters weren't used in this instance. The International Radiotelephony Spelling Alphabet was used instead, so the second world is Bronson Bravo."

"And the third is Bronson Charlie," said Tantra.

"That's the really weird one, man!" cried Moonwash. "It sounds like a harmonica as it grazes our magnetosphere. Like a lonesome mouth organ on the platform of some godforsaken train station out in the desert. That's just my own interpretation, though!"

"The music of the spheres," grinned Stringent.

"Yeah, disappointing, ain't it?"

The apeman was bemused by this negative reaction. "Why? What kind of music do you like?" He fixed a sardonic stare at the marijuana cigarette and added nonchalantly, "Jazz, I bet!"

"Some. But we generally prefer groovy psychedelic sitars, funky drum patterns and rhythmic electric bass."

"Fair enough, this is the future," conceded Stringent.

"For the time being," said Tantra.

The apeman pulled a piece of apple peel from between his front teeth, examined it dispassionately and said, "I'd love to stay and hear more, but my friend will be arriving in Berlin soon. In fact, if this is the year 2112, I'm extremely late already! I must go."

"Don't be crazy, man!" objected Quorn Joy.

Moonwash nodded. "You're in no fit condition. You should stay here and rest for tonight, at the least. Tell you what, why don't we take you to Berlin tomorrow? We haven't had an outing for weeks. All five of us should go. It's a totally cool city, my friend!"

"But the jalopy needs recharging and it's too small," Stringent pointed out. He didn't want to appear rude, so he grinned and blinked and did his best to look sheepish. Tantra laughed.

"No one travels such distances by jalopy. We'll take the cable car. That will get us to Berlin in a few hours."

"And it's good fun!" added Nutloaf.

Stringent nodded and his smile was genuine and warm as he regarded his new friends. "In that case, I accept."

"Great!" Quorn Joy stood up. "I'll fetch you a hammock."

"You can sleep right here, man, in this yurt; and if there's anything you want or need, just say," said Moonwash.

Stringent cleared his throat and muttered, "Well, there is one thing. I'm ashamed to ask, to be honest. It's just that I haven't spent the night with a woman for a long time and I'm feeling quite constricted, you know, down there. In the man area. I don't suppose . . ."

"Sure thing, dude! That's a totally normal request!"

"Plenty of willing girls in Goodvibe. The HIPZIS are into free love as an article of faith. Oh yeah!" cried Moonwash. "Shall I ask around to see who might be interested in a tumble?"

"I'll go and call Hogbreath," offered Quorn Joy.

"She's down by the compost toilet," said Moonwash. "I'll fetch her on my way to the spare hammock store."

"No need," chorused Tantra and Nutloaf. "This specific task is one we can fulfill. Both of us at the same time. Provided our guest regards it as an acceptable arrangement, of course . . ."

Stringent managed to croak, "Yes, I do!"

A TUMBLE IN THE HEY!

Stringent was surrounded by warmth and when he moved all the warmth moved too, and the warmth was poetic because it emanated from the nude bodies of two lovely girls. They all lay entwined in the largest hammock provided by the community, a threesome special woven from extra strong hemp and knotted tightly enough to survive constant vibration. Enveloped in bliss, the apeman grinned and sighed.

Nutloaf and Tantra had stripped him naked and bathed him in a trough full of dandelion, daisy and buttercup petals, then they had slowly rubbed their own bodies with oil squeezed from vanilla pods. He had offered to help with this operation and they hadn't dissuaded him. Now they smelled like ice cream and he was delighted. There was nothing for it but to start licking them all over, from top to bottoms.

Nutloaf had long sleek black hair and brown eyes; she was athletic but curvy nonetheless. Tantra had wavy red hair and green eyes; she was also athletic and curvy. With taut stomachs, generous but firm breasts, russet nipples and smooth thighs, both girls were experienced in the arts of love. Or maybe it's a science. They moaned and writhed as he attended to them, but somehow they also managed to reverse their positions, so that now he was under them and they were in control.

"Lie still and we will make love to *you*," they whispered, but Stringent felt a twinge of irritation at these words. He hated how the word 'love' is so often used as a timid euphemism for "sex." Call the act what it is! Both girls were experienced in the arts of sex. Yes, that's better! He didn't raise any objections as they covered him in kisses, pausing only to pick gorilla hairs from between their fine pearly teeth.

He closed his eyes and surrendered to the sensations, trying to deduce by touch alone which nibble belonged to Tantra and which to Nutloaf. He felt all his energy concentrating in one region of his body, flowing along his electrified nerves and pulsing with his blood down arteries. Alerted by some feminine intuition to what was happening to his physiology, Tantra and Nutloaf both focused on that particular zone with their swift fingers and hot moist tongues in panting mouths.

Then one of the girls mounted him and slid herself down until the part of him that seemed the center of the universe connected with the center of another universe, her universe, and this second universe tried to envelop the first. But it seemed the first universe didn't want to be absorbed just yet. The second girl took over and also slid down him until she reached a point where her own universe could feast on his. But still there was some indefinable resistance, some reluctance . . .

Stringent could bear it no longer. He had to act!

With an immense effort, he sat up in the hammock, pushing Tantra to one side, Nutloaf to the other, like a porpoise gently rising between two oddly conjoined waves, which is a simile no more precise than the act it's supposed to clarify. His face was twisted in a leer of lust but he managed to utter coherent words, despite the drool of anticipation that flecked his pulsing lips like the crests of those waves.

"I want you both, I need you both, but there's something you must do for me. It's a kink I have, a perversion . . ."

Tantra and Nutloaf shrugged. "Fine. Tell us what it is and we'll do our best. Whatever your freak, we won't judge."

Stringent was too excited to feel shame. "I can't actually perform if it's for free. I mean that it would turn me on even more if you pretended to be prostitutes. Can you do that for me please?"

"Of course! But we don't know what prostitutes are!"

Stringent panted, "Girls who have sex for money. They get paid to let men exploit them. They pretend to enjoy it, and maybe some do, but cash is the primary reason for the institution."

Tantra and Nutloaf exchanged troubled glances.

"We can't think of anything sexier than role playing games, and we'd love to oblige you in this instance, but . . ."

"What?" blared Stringent, his eyes bulging.

"There's no money in Goodvibe. No money anywhere in Germany. It's against our principles, you see. Against the HIPZI code. There have been no coins or paper notes in circulation here for the past hundred years. But you can pay us in some other item, if you insist on acting out this fantasy. How about fetching that bag over there and using its contents as a form of improvised currency? On the shelf."

Stringent squinted at the bag in question. "Lentils!"

Instantly his manhood went limp . . .

Through the Treetops to Berlin

The five daytrippers finished drinking their cups of herbal tea and stepped out into the mild morning. The three planets had moved away; the largest of the trio, Bronson Alpha, was at apogee, its furthest point from Earth on its highly eccentric orbit. The sunlight had plenty of room to radiate and cheer up the plants and animals that roamed the forests and glades of the narrow valley. Well, the plants didn't roam, that's just a figure of speech, unless you count growing as roaming.

Stringent Strange felt unmanned by his activities of the night. He kept his eyes downcast and shuddered at regular intervals; but neither Nutloaf nor Tantra seemed especially concerned by his failure to perform. As for Moonwash and Quorn Joy, they were totally absorbed by the freshness of the air and the sweetness of the birdsong.

The two HIPZI males led the way to the cable car gantry. The apeman blinked and sniggered when he saw it. He had expected a modern system with an enclosed metal cabin, electric motors and pulleys; but this was an unpowered device, or rather it was powered solely by gravity. The cabin was a wicker affair like the basket of a hot-air balloon, very rickety, and it dangled from a rope that resembled a vine. This rope was suspended from the trees and vanished into the distance.

"This is a joke, surely?" he blurted.

"No, it goes all the way to Berlin," said Tantra.

Moonwash gestured at a frail bamboo ladder that led up to the gantry. Stringent climbed it gingerly, wincing as it creaked and swayed and each rung bent under his weight. It was a long way up, over a hundred feet, for the trees in this valley were giants.

As if reading his mind, Quorn Joy called up, "The gravity of the plants has made all planets grow higher."

"It's the other way around, man!" laughed Moonwash.

"Oh yeah!" Quorn Joy lit a joint.

Stringent reached the gantry safely and needed just a little more urging to step into the wicker cable car. Nutloaf was next up the ladder, followed by Quorn Joy, Tantra and Moonwash.

"It's all downhill from here," laughed Tantra.

"That's fine for my purposes," Stringent mused, "but how will you get back to Goodvibe after we arrive in Berlin? This is a one-way line, by the look of it. Won't you be stuck there?"

Nutloaf explained the system. "There are two separate networks. The capital is the hub of both. To an observer in Berlin, all the incoming lines slant upwards away from the city and the outgoing lines slant downwards. The further a village is from Berlin, the higher will be the ingoing line at the point where it passes through, and the lower the outgoing line. Here in Goodvibe the difference between the two isn't great. The height disparity can be seen at its most extreme on the borders of Germany, but we're not going outwards; and in fact, to travel by cable between some settlements, you must go to Berlin and change there."

"An awfully complex layout for such a simple system! Don't the lines ever get tangled?" wondered Stringent.

Moonwash laughed. "There's a vast pole in the center of Berlin where all the lines meet. It's like a weird three-dimensional cobweb. Real freaky sight! But perfectly organized and free to run! Anyway, hold on tight, I'm about to release the handbrake, man!"

"Groovy, funky, cool!" commented Quorn Joy.

Stringent grinned, but he suddenly paled as the wicker cabin squealed and lurched down the line. Moonwash decided to oil the pulley wheel; he climbed out of the window and pulled himself onto the roof without any kind of safety harness. The apeman caught himself wondering if HIPZIS were brave or just too constantly stoned to worry about danger. Now the motion became smoother and Moonwash returned the same way. On the walls of the cabin were wicker benches.

"I used olive oil, man! The pulley likes that best!"

As the cabin accelerated, Stringent said, "Surely if Berlin is hundreds of miles distant, the angle of the line will be very shallow, too shallow to account for our current high velocity?"

Nutloaf replied, "If it wasn't for the rogue worlds, what you say might be true, but they exert an upwards pull on our cabin and so keep the angle between it and our destination steep."

She offered him fresh fruit and he accepted.

Stringent sat and gazed out of the window. Trees and greenery and a few birds went past. In the distance he saw another line dangling among the branches of a tall pine. He frowned. Maybe this wasn't such a wrong place after all? It was peaceful and kind; the lack of money might be the biggest passion killer in his experience, but looking at it from a broader perspective, it was a minor sort of Eden.

"A world of peace and beauty!" he breathed.

"What was that, my friend?"

"I was just thinking to myself that Earth has become a utopia. Clean air, good food, free love (although I prefer the expensive kind), gentle people, harmonious communities . . ."

Moonwash and Quorn Joy spluttered; Tantra and Nutloaf gasped. It was at this point that Stringent realized he'd said something wrong. What was the problem? How had he offended?

"Have I insulted you in some way?" he stammered.

"No, no, man! Of course not! It's just the naivety of what you said. A world of peace! That's childlike talk!"

"You're forgetting the Rushans," explained Tantra.

"Are they evil?" asked Stringent.

"In our opinion, yes. In their own, probably not. They kill and destroy and care only for splashings of gore."

Quorn Joy wiped his eyes. "Makes me sob like a squonk to even think about the sorts of things they get up to!"

"Real nasty people, the Rushans," said Moonwash.

"Let's avoid Russia!" said Stringent.

"Be serious, dude! There are no Rushans in Russia. There are Rushans only in Canada. Russia's full of Zombie Scholars. There was a plague and it escaped from a secret research laboratory near Moscow and it infected the entire population of that nation, dissolving their souls but giving them an insatiable urge to read textbooks."

"And revise for non-existent exams!" added Nutloaf.

Tantra and Moonwash nodded.

"The Rushans wouldn't dare go anywhere near Russia. It's not that the

Zombie Scholars are more powerful than they are, but the plague's highly contagious. The Rushans are Canadians and stay in Canada. That's where their prophets told them to stay. But they're making plans to get rid of all rival populations in all other lands."

"Including us," trembled Quorn Joy. He puffed desperately on his joint and then slowly relaxed with a smile.

"I'm rather confused," mumbled Stringent.

"Who isn't?" snorted Moonwash.

"So Canada is inhabited by terrible people who do awful things? What kinds of things? Do they cut off hands and thread them on necklaces? The friend I'm going to meet once told me that the Belgians planned to do that to him! But they didn't catch him . . ."

"Can we change the subject please?" pleaded Quorn Joy.

"That stuff's a bad vibe!" said Moonwash.

But Stringent was in his element now. He counted off various kinds of hideous tortures on his hairy fingers. "Do the Rushans like to boil victims in molasses? Do they force them to dance on hot embers? Do they impale them on sharpened telegraph poles and dance frenzied and drooling round them long into the bloodcurdling night?"

Tantra and Nutloaf shuddered.

"This cat is chilling the scene!" growled Moonwash.

The apeman blinked. "Pardon?"

"You're causing a downer," explained Quorn Joy.

"I'm sorry!" croaked Stringent. "I got carried away. I won't ask another question about the Rushans, honest!"

The four HIPZIS seemed relieved by that promise. The apeman licked his lips and found himself making a reappraisal of his previous judgment about the miracle of the convergence of language. He'd been too hasty in his assessment that German had mutated *exactly* into English. There were many words used by these people that weren't known to him at all: and he had won a literacy contest in Salt Lake City in 1929, coming away with a year's supply of free pulp magazines as his prize! His new friends tended to pepper their banter with curious words such as "funky" and "groovy" that were only comprehensible in context.

Fortunately, Stringent was a master of contexts . . .

He continued to stare out of the window. A large bird with purple and gold wings flew close through the vegetation, kept pace with the cabin for a minute, then swooped away. The apeman felt a pang of envy. Would he ever get his hands on a plane again?

Flying was his life, the only thing he was good at.

At least until he discovered what his so-called abnormalities were and how they functioned. Then he might be good at other things too. It was an uplifting thought, not quite as uplifting as thermals under a pair of elegant wings but adequate for the time being. He made a wry face. Then he saw a billboard flash past. It said: ESPERANTO CHOCOLATE. FOR THAT DARK CREAMY CROSS-CULTURAL FLAVOR! More product placement! With a sigh, Stringent muttered to himself:

"Crinkle is responsible for this!"

"What was that, man?" asked Moonwash, in the act of lighting a joint. Quorn Joy and the girls turned to look.

"Nothing," said Stringent. "I was merely thinking out loud. I remarked that the professor—he's the personage I'm going to meet—was at fault for selling advertising space in this tale. That's why there are billboards in the treetops, where they don't belong."

"Yeah, dude, but what was the name you uttered?"

"Crinkle. Tobias Crinkle. What's wrong? Why do you look amazed by that? You can't possibly know him!"

"Maybe not," said Quorn Joy, "but he has the exact same name as our Führer, which is quite a coincidence."

"Yeah, my friend, nobody else has that name."

"It's such a weird name, man!"

Stringent frowned. Then it occurred to him that perhaps the professor had thrived under the command of the Protogruppenführer, had settled in Germany, married a female and fathered children; one of his great-great-great-great-great-great-great-grandsons might have been given the name of the renowned inventor, the man who had helped Hitler win the war with his Tarotplane. As a sort of tribute.

Yes, that seemed entirely feasible. The apeman stroked his chin and he did this because it's one of the traditional gestures in a paragraph without any dialogue; when you're already frowning you can't frown again. Either you arch your eyebrows, pout your lips, squint, blink or ruffle your hair. I prefer chin action; so the chin it is.

"This Führer of yours isn't a bad man, is he?"

Moonwash clutched his sides in pantomime mirth. "By no means! He's the leader of the HIPZIS and one of the most attuned souls in the cosmos. He loves rabbits, man! He plays the dulcimer, man! He can roll a gigantic spliff with both hands tied behind his back and smoke it right down to the roach in just one long massive drag!"

"But he's no pothead, dude," added Quorn Joy.

"That's right," said Moonwash. "He's a mighty brainbox and is able to solve cryptic crosswords and integral calculus and other tough shit. What else can I say about him? He's cool!"

"Also, he's a clockwork robot," added Tantra.

Stringent resumed his chin rubbing. "Sorry, did I hear you correctly? I thought you said 'clockwork robot' . . ."

Nutloaf nodded. "That's right. Please don't do the overacting routine. I can forgive impotence but not contrived and unjustified surprise. Yes, the Führer is a clockwork robot. Is that odder than zombie scholars, debonair werewolves or macrobiotic vampires? No, it's not. And all of those things exist on our world. Plus, according to what you've told us, you're a hybrid of gorilla and man from the past. So how dare you feign incredulity at the news that our Führer is spring loaded?"

"I can also forgive impotence," declared Tantra.

Moonwash and Quorn Joy did their best not to smirk. Stringent turned his head to conceal his ripe blushes. He was directly facing the window. The trees rushed past, a blur of green and brown, with birds and squirrels and pine martens sitting among the fruit and nuts. Once he caught sight of a group of owls; they seemed to be playing backgammon. Surely that was an optical illusion? The rocking of the cabin was regular and compelling. Other lines came into view between the leaves, and wicker cabins hurried under them. He yawned and closed his eyes.

He must have fallen into a sleep that lasted hours, for when he awoke, there were many lines outside the window, a thick web of them, and they were made furious by whooshing cable cars full of commuters dressed in brightly colored cotton clothes. Nutloaf said, "If you lean out, you'll get your first view of Berlin. Don't worry, it's safe. All the outgoing lines are at different elevations to the incoming."

Stringent rose from his bench and followed her suggestion. He felt the rush of cool air on his face and it was very welcome. He saw how forests converged at a circular city of shining marble, like a vision from Ancient Greek mythology, and at the center of this magnificent metropolis was an awesome tower strung with cables, the transport hub of the gentle HIPZI empire; and the complex interplay of thin shadows over the wide streets, public squares and pools made a shifting grid of obscure function. With a cry of joy, he turned to his companions.

"It's the same way I always imagined Atlantis to be!"

Nutloaf grimaced. "But Atlantis was raised up from the seabed by the gravity of Bronson Alpha and it doesn't look anything like Berlin! There are no statues in Atlantis, for one thing!"

"I don't care! This is simply marvelous," enthused the apeman, "and I can't wait to greet the professor's probable descendant. Do you think your Führer will be happy to accommodate me?"

Moonwash scratched his head. "I don't know about that, man, but he's bound to let you visit him. Oh I see, my friend! For one moment I thought you were talking about his buttocks . . ."

Stringent blanched. The language barrier again!

Meeting with Der Führer

The wicker cable car would have smashed straight into the pillar with loss of all life if Moonwash hadn't applied the handbrake in time. Squealing to a stop just a few inches from disaster, the HIPZIS jumped out of the cabin onto the ground. Stringent followed and looked up. They were at the base of this thrusting hub; a spiral staircase wound around the pillar to the very summit, where the outgoing lines began.

The pillar was a flurry of activity, with the newly-arrived commuters stepping out of cabins at ground level, and others climbing up the steps to the dizzying gantries to reach cable cars that were preparing to depart for outlying regions; it was both crude and impressive. The apeman felt sorry for the porters who had to unhook the wicker cabins from the lower lines and carry them up the stairs to the upper.

Dressed in cumbersome furry uniforms, these porters worked tirelessly and not once did Stringent hear a curse escape their rather thin lips. After watching them for a few minutes, he realized that they weren't human but bipedal felines. He pointed at one and nudged Quorn Joy, who fumbled in his pocket for a joint and sparked it up.

"Oh yeah, the stevedore cats. Berlin's full of them."

"But there hasn't been enough time for evolution to change a domestic four-footed creature no bigger than a melon into such strong anthropoidal monsters! So how could this happen?"

"They're mutants. The first time Bronson Alpha passed close to Earth it damaged our magnetic field and allowed hard radiation to penetrate the atmosphere. The cats got a big dose."

"I thought they were men wearing fur coats!"

"No way! Only vegetable fibers are used in our textile industry. These porters do all the manual labor for us."

Stringent was shocked. "That's a form of slavery!"

"Why do you say that, dude?"

"Because it's a well known fact that cats are lazy!"

Quorn Joy laughed. "Yeah, maybe where you come from, but not here. In fact they insist on working for us."

Stringent shrugged. Clearly the radiation had transformed not only the physiology of the felines but also their psychology. It was as plausible as anything else. He said, "Will you give me directions to the Führer's home now? I assume he lives in a palace."

"He does indeed, but he has a frugal lifestyle nonetheless." Tantra took him by the arm. "We'll go with you."

"Really? Don't you have business of your own?"

"Nothing urgent." Tantra conferred with the others and after a moment she turned back to him and said, "We came here on a whim but there's no reason why we should abandon you."

"Yeah, man, let's stick together for the duration."

Stringent was pleased. "Great!"

They set off down a long avenue and the apeman felt happy and full of energy. He liked Berlin already. Apart from the whirring of wicker cable cars, a sound one got accustomed to quickly, the city was relatively quiet, much less frenetic than Tallahassee or El Segundo. There were no power tools or other noisy machines at work in the streets. Many trees rustled in the soft winds and people sat on benches or on rugs in parks, laughing or singing or befriending young deer.

There were many statues on plinths dotted seemingly at random, but a more eclectic jumble of artistic subjects would be hard to conceive. Stone and crystal men and women and bipedal felines were joined by sculptures of rabbits, frogs, butterflies, bread rolls, guitars, owls, mushrooms, nature gods, teapots, robots, octahedrons and even statues of sculptors in the act of making new statues. The ambience was relaxed but not lethargic, quite unlike the draining aura of California.

Half a dozen windmills turned picturesque papyrus sails and generated electricity for modest domestic usage.

Berlin was a white chess city, shaped into cubes, three sided pyramids and other polyhedra, but charming at the same time. The human element was a constant factor in the equation . . .

A little further along they passed a makeshift stage. "Wow! Groovy! A music festival!" warbled Quorn Joy.

"They have them often in Berlin," said Nutloaf.

"Who's playing?" enquired Stringent.

Moonwash went to ask a technician; he came back with news that was meaningless to the apeman. "Plenty of fab bands, man! First up is Jacque-in-le-Box, with Ruby dubDub on drums; followed by Everyone's Cup of Tea, who play really extreme shit! Then the legendary Havkvind with the Orgone Accumulators; then the sentiment proggers Knip Dyolf; rounded off with The Self-Raising Flower!"

"She's truly mind blowing, man!" gasped Quorn Joy.

"Sounds painful," said Stringent.

Moonwash continued, "That's the first half. After an interval for drugs and wine, the Sages of Atlantis are due to perform, not just on their own but with The Undivided Amoebae! This extravaganza will be topped by The Thing that is Scarcely a Thing playing backing organ for the hotshot Vindaloo Bottoms; next up, the HIPZI KINGS with local boy made good Djingo Rhineland; and the whole shebang will be given a grand finale by the maximalist Admirable Restraint."

"My ears hurt already," remarked Stringent.

Quorn Joy's eyes narrowed. "This cat is chilling the scene!"

"Forgive me," spluttered the apeman. "I didn't mean to offend you by casting aspersions on your tastes . . ."

Quorn Joy chuckled. "I wasn't referring to you, man! I was referring to the cold effects cat, the cat over there."

Stringent followed his pointing finger and beheld a bipedal feline with a machine that blew dry ice over the stage. The creature was testing it for faults. There were none. Other cats were busy installing stroboscopes and adjusting microphones and speakers.

"It'll be a fabulous festival, man, I just know it!"

"We must attend," insisted Tantra.

Stringent pondered. "Perhaps. It depends what my friend wants. I was hoping to take him back to the USA, but now that country's just a cooled lava flow, maybe he won't want to go."

"One way to find out, dude—ask him in person!"

"I will indeed," concurred Stringent.

"The palace is over there! See the creamy building?"

Every building in Berlin was whitish, but the apeman had no difficulty working out which particular edifice Moonwash was referring to. Unlike its pseudo-quasi-neoclassical neighbors, the façade of the palace wasn't propped up by columns or adorned with carved nymphs, dryads, satyrs or sitars. It was an outburst of bulging domes and nowhere could a straight line be discerned. It also seemed to be the hub of another transport system with extremely busy outgoing lines.

"Huge!" gasped Stringent. "The biggest palace ever!"

Tantra squeezed the apeman's elbow. "That's just a trick of perspective and if you look close you'll see that the cables are very thin and the cabins that run under them are miniatures."

Nutloaf nodded. "It's not a second transport network at all, but a cheap communications service. The Führer's able to send scrolls or messages in other formats to any part of Germany."

"But there are no incoming lines!" Stringent said.

"None. He has alternative methods of keeping himself informed about events in his dominions. Let's go and see if he's free to receive you. If he's too busy, we'll still get a fulsome welcome from his ministers and gifts of wine and weed. It's the custom here."

They approached the front of the palace and ascended wide stone steps to the entrance. Security was incredibly lax and the unarmed guard at the gaping portal merely blinked good-naturedly at them and asked for a light for his joint. Moonwash obliged. They stepped over the threshold into the lobby. It was dark inside; the skylights had been covered for some reason and all lamps extinguished. The aroma of smoky wicks was pungent. The apeman felt a prickle of unease at this.

He groped his way forward and heard a strange rustling just ahead. As his eyes began to adjust to the dimness, he realized the lobby was full of shambling figures that didn't have the outlines of human beings. Was the place packed with cats? His unease turned to fear. Then the curtains over the skylights were torn down. Sunlight slanted, filled the immense lobby. Stringent found himself confronted by . . .

Gorillas! Two hundred or more of the beasts!

Suddenly they started dancing, a weird and primeval routine involving enormous bananas, a sort of sedate and yet powerful pavane that only the supreme primate god, Zumboo, might have choreographed convincingly. But Stringent didn't believe in Zumboo, nor in the other ape and monkey deities, Thomp, Spanko and Basha. He retreated a step, but these gorillas didn't charge him. They continued to dance, completing their moves with a crisp efficiency that was as metaphorically *unhairy* as their bodies were thickly matted. Could they be fakes?

Much to Stringent's amazement, his HIPZI comrades weren't alarmed in any degree by this performance. Although they clearly hadn't expected the spectacle, it didn't faze them. They tapped their own feet and gyrated their hips to the complicated rhythms.

"Funky hirsute footwork, brother!"

"One banana, two bananas, three bananas, four . . . But how many make a bunch, dude? It's a fruitful paradox!"

"I wonder if this is part of the festival, man?"

Stringent frowned. "It seems somehow too much of a coincidence not to have been arranged for my benefit."

"An egocentric supposition," Tantra cautioned him.

But a voice grated through the pulsations of the dance. "No, my dear, he's quite correct. It *was* put on entirely for him. It's a themed welcoming party. I had to express my almost unbearable delight at meeting him with an exaggerated display of atavism."

"Who said that?" demanded Stringent.

A pair of metallic hands came together and produced a clap like two colliding similes concerned with thunder. As if they were interconnected levers in one of those newfangled calculating machines that Stringent had been reliably informed were used by the United States Census Board, an agency that no longer existed, the gorillas came to an instant stop. In his ears the silence roared like laughter. Very quiet laughter, obviously. The sort that people do behind your back.

Around the immobile ranks of the gorillas trundled an object. It was a trapezoid box mounted on three castors. Prehensile arms protruded from the sides; Stringent counted at least eight of them. Mounted on top of the box was a smaller box festooned with artificial expressions and on top of that was a clear glass bowl and inside the bowl throbbed a naked brain in pale purple water that gurgled often.

"What in the name of all unholy tinkering is that?"

Moonwash and Quorn Joy lowered their voices respectfully. "It's the Führer! We told you he was a robot."

Nutloaf added, "Actually he's a cyborg, part man, part machine, but he runs on clockwork, that bit was true!"

Stringent noticed the wind-up key on the side of the box and nodded at her words. He waited for the thing to speak again, but the brain pulsed for many moments before the inorganic voice made its next statement. "I have been expecting you all day, Stringy."

The apeman spluttered, "What did you call me? Only one person ever called me that! How did you know . . . ?"

"Stringy, dear boy, don't you recognize me? Just because I'm a brain in a bottle fused to a robotic body doesn't mean I'm not the same poor fellow who adopted you as his own son. Are you so shallow that your powers of recognition are only muscle deep?"

"Tobias Crinkle?" cried Stringent. "Is it you, doc?"

"Most certainly it is, dear boy!"

"But how? How? Tell me!"

"All in good time. Come and hug me first!"

Stringent flung his arms around the trapezoid; three, maybe four, arms wrapped around him in return. Reticulated tantalum tentacles is what they really were, he realized. So what? A hug is a hug is a hug. Stringent broke the embrace with tears in his eyes.

"And you put this show on especially for me?"

"I did. First themed event I ever arranged for you, huh? But there'll be plenty more where this came from!"

The gorillas were frozen in awkward postures like ritual paintings. The Führer faced them. "At ease, boys!"

And with gasps of relief, the figures reached up to remove their gorilla masks and reveal faces dripping with sweat. They had been phoneys after all; they were just plain men in suits! Well, that shouldn't come as much of a surprise. Ultra-disciplined gorillas aren't that easy to come by and the notion of keeping animals captive and then making them work seemed at odds with the HIPZI ethos, despite the fact that cats did all manual labor in the city; but they were an exception.

"How did you know I was coming here, doc?"

The Führer laughed. "With my electric ouija board! The biggest of its kind is located right here. All the technological achievements of Germany are at my disposal. True, there has been little radical innovation since the Nazis turned into HIPZIS, but many astounding inventions existed before that time, so I don't worry much about the stagnation of science! Some of those inventions were designed by me!"

"You mean the Tarotplane?" asked Stringent.

"Ah, I suppose one of your travelling companions told you about that? No matter. Now you're here, you must come into my private quarters and make yourself at home. These 'gorillas' are my personal bodyguard but they don't see much action, despite the numerous threats of assassination from Rushan agents or Debonair Werewolves, so they were happy to perform a little dance for you, but now I should let them take a break. Please follow me, sonny, and make yourself at home."

The apeman gazed at his friends, at Moonwash, Quorn Joy, Tantra and Nutloaf. He felt an absurd affection for them and protested, "Hey, can't I bring all my buddies along too, doc?"

The Führer clicked impatiently but nodded.

"Wait a moment, man!" said Moonwash. "To be perfectly candid, we'd rather go to the music festival outside."

The three other HIPZIS nodded in agreement.

"Fair enough," replied Stringent.

Quorn Joy cried, "Farewell for now, dude, but you know where we are if you ever need us for anything."

"Take care, brother!" added Moonwash.

The apeman raised a hand in a wave, then he turned to pursue Crinkle, who was already accelerating away.

Stringent caught him up and kept pace with him. The Führer was in a hurry to return to his private quarters. His clockwork motor hummed like lips. As he trundled across the lobby's smooth floor to a broad staircase, one of his extendable arms shot out and lit the wicks of lanterns hanging in chains from the domed ceiling. "It's far too dark in this palace. I intend to have more skylights created and arrange a system of mirrors to bounce the sunlight into the darkest corners."

"That would certainly be less wasteful, doc."

The Führer shrugged his metal shoulders. "Until then, the lamps must suffice. They use olive juice for fuel."

"Oil, you mean! Not juice!" cried Stringent.

Crinkle chuckled. "Perhaps, my dear boy. I'm good with aerodynamics and certain coefficients but useless with plain domestic matters. Although I know I'm a genius, I sometimes wonder if other people don't think I'm a regular or possibly irregular fuckwit."

"That's what Mr. Northrop said, doc."

Crinkle's brain convulsed. "Jack called me a fuckwit?!"

Stringent blushed and waved his arms dismissively, as if he was trying to fend off wasps or baseballs. "No, doc, that wasn't the word he used. I'm sorry for misleading you. *Cretin*, he said."

If the clockwork robot had possessed lips, he might have pursed them with an accompanying clank. Instead he merely grated, "I see. But there's no point feeling resentment about things long dead. The world of 1932 is dust blowing in the wind, Stringy."

The apeman nodded wisely. "What if the air's still, doc?"

The Führer's tentacles waved. "Eh?"

"I mean," elaborated Stringent, "that inside old rooms with shut doors and windows, there's no wind to blow dust around, so maybe 1932 still exists in an intact condition there?"

"It's some sort of hypothesis, I suppose, dear boy."

They reached the base of the staircase. Before Stringent could wonder how a robot with wheels might climb stone steps, the Führer extended no less than six tentacles and employed them as legs. He resembled a bizarre but gigantic hunched crab or deformed ant as he scuttled up. The apeman ran after him. At the summit of the staircase were a marble landing and a statue of Jack Northrop in an alcove.

The professor turned to the left and hastened along another corridor to a circular door that opened like an iris or the aperture of an old fashioned camera when he pulled on a rope that dangled from the ceiling. Without a backwards glance he glided through. Stringent went after and the door shut behind him. He found himself in an office or stateroom filled with objects from many different historical eras and cultures. Not all the artifacts were human or from Earth. Three golden globes stood nearby, representing the three Bronson worlds in outer space.

The apeman blinked. Professor Crinkle was already standing behind a desk studying papers with an interchangeable eye. He looked up, frowned with tungsten wrinkles and bellowed:

"Who are you? How did you get in here? Guards!"

AN IMPLAUSIBLY LONG SALUTE

Stringent took a step backwards, lifting his arms to protect his face from attack; but the professor began laughing. "Just a little joke of mine, dear boy. Please don't take it too seriously!"

The apeman exhaled slowly. "You had me worried for a moment, doc. I thought you'd became a psychopath."

Robotic palms rubbed together. "Not yet! Not yet!

Stringent gazed around the room. A map covered one wall and rather usefully it depicted the current global political situation. The continents were all still in their regular places, for not enough time had elapsed for significant tectonic drift, and even the former boundaries of nation states were mostly unchanged. But they were labeled differently. The apeman studied the names in fascinated horror.

He saw that the HIPZI FEDERATION comprised Germany, Austria, Switzerland, Liechtenstein and Chaud-Mellé. This grouping of peaceful communes was bordered to the west by the Debonair Werewolf Domain in what had once been France; to the north by the Macrobiotic Vampire Empire, which covered all of Scandinavia and most of the Baltic States; to the east by the enormous Union of Zombie Scholar Republics; and to the south by Big and Little Italy. It seemed that Big Italy was an ally of the HIPZIS and also ruled by a robot.

"Muscle Leany is his name, and he's steam powered. I don't approve of burning up fossil fuels and yet . . ."

"I understand, doc. You have to be diplomatic."

"Precisely, dear boy! Take a seat, by the way. We can't have you on your feet all afternoon. Fancy a drink?"

The apeman perched on an elegant rocking chair. "No thanks, I have been nibbling juicy fruit all morning."

The Führer resumed talking, but Stringent's eyes kept wandering back to the map. He saw that Africa comprised a complex swirl of overlapping circles, like a Venn diagram, and realized that these must be variations of the old tribal territories. As for America, the site of the former USA was a blank, devoid of towns, roads, even rivers, but Canada had been renamed the Rushan Ascendancy and was bristling with urban centers and ports, a superpower in the making or on the make.

Crinkle was preparing to disclose why he was a brain in a bottle. "So after the zeppelins reached Berlin, the Protogruppenführer took me down into his secret lair and began torturing me for information. They refused to accept I wasn't Northrop; and in the end I gave up denying it. They set me to work on radical aircraft designs. I attempted to perfect my Flying Tail, but it never worked. So I designed something new for them, a plane with enormous Tarot Cards for wings."

"Oh yes?" Stringent's feigned interest became real.

The Führer managed a cobalt smile.

"The Tarotplane won the war because its predictive capabilities were even more powerful than those of an electric ouija board. Depending on what situations and predicaments might be imminent, the wing designs would change to alert the pilot and flight crew, so enemy fighters in the air, anti-aircraft batteries on the ground and bad weather might be easily avoided. We flew rings around everyone!"

"Gadzooks, doc, that's totally consistent geometry!"

Crinkle cleared his osmium throat with an iridium cough. "Some of those rings were Mobius Strips, dear boy, but there's no point going into detail. The point is this: my invention was so highly regarded that Hitler himself decided I was too important to be allowed to die. He instructed his best scientists to find a way of making me immortal. And so cyborgs were created and my brain was transplanted into this machine. It was an absolute triumph and plans were made to transplant the brains of every man, woman and child in the Reich."

"But I haven't met any other robots yet, doc!"

The Führer nodded clankingly. "Because there aren't any, Stringy. I don't count the Protogruppenführer in that statement, because a different kind of immortality experiment was conducted on *him*, and it wasn't as successful, though he's still alive; but before the general populace could be converted into machines, Bronson Alpha turned up and disrupted the fabric of civilization—rending it apart like a bear with a dagger! Ripping centuries of achievement into ribbons!"

"The technique of transplanting brains was lost?"

"Indeed so, my boy. I am unique."

"What about that Muscle Leany you mentioned?"

Crinkle waved a dismissive tentacle. "He was never a human being in the first place. He's a real robot, not a cyborg. The Protogruppenführer is also a kind of cyborg. But anyway . . ."

"What about Mr. Northrop, doc? Is he one too?"

"Alas no, Stringy. Jack's dead."

"Bronson Alpha has a lot to answer for, doc!"

"All the Bronsons do, dear boy. But let's not talk of such gloomy stuff. The world as you see it is fairly stable. Civilization has taken a backwards step, but one hopes the reason is for it to choose the right path on the fork in the road; clearly we took the wrong path last time. The only thing that's threatening a renaissance of human achievement is the appalling religious practices of the fiendish Rushans . . ."

"My HIPZI friends refused to speak about them."

"Yes, that doesn't surprise me."

"Why are they so scared of them, doc?"

The Führer entwined a few tentacles together thoughtfully, sighed and rubbed the bottom part of his jar, where his chin should be. Then he took a long hard look at the apeman, came to a sudden decision and propelled himself out from behind his desk.

"I'm going to tell you everything you ought to know about those foul beings, dear boy, and that's because I need to enlist your aid against them. They are a threat not only to the world, but also to the entire cosmos; and we are perhaps the only ones who might be able to stop them. You are the best pilot I've ever known, Stringy."

"Do you have some flying job for me, doc?"

Crinkle nodded, but then he trundled towards a pair of windows. "The time has come for my daily salute. Why not join me on the balcony? This is a hallowed custom of my status."

Stringent shrugged and followed the cyborg as it opened the windows, swung them both wide and glided out onto a spacious balcony with low railings. A few people were gathered in a plaza below. They blew smoke rings and cheered when they saw the professor's chassis. He leaned over the wicker railings to smile at them.

"Some days, quite a crowd gathers for the occasion. I fully realize that today most of Berlin will be heading towards the festival instead. In fact I think I can hear the final sound check. I never got accustomed to the kind of music these people like. I still prefer the atonalities of Bartok, Varese, Schoenberg. Guess I'm old school."

"That classical stuff's a bit above me, doc."

"Then you'll appreciate living here, my boy. The famous composers of the past have all been forsaken. The Zombie Scholars study the scores, of course, but they never play them."

"Sound like a bunch of mindless academics to me."

"Spot on, dear boy! But shall I tell you what the real problem with the educated living dead is? It's the fact they only think *outside the box*. And when I say box, I mean coffin . . ."

"I get it, doc. But what happens next?"

"Why, I salute my citizens, Stringy! Might as well do it now and get it over with for another day. Ready?"

The apeman nodded and then he was astonished to see a metal tentacle on the Führer's right side suddenly shoot up at a sharp angle into the sky. It was a replica of the Nazi salute that Stringent had noticed in newsreels of German political rallies back in the early 1930s, but it extended much further than Hitler had ever managed, for Crinkle's vanadium arm seemed infinitely stretchable; and as it went up and up, the gripping apparatus on the very end changed into a mesh.

"What happened to your hand, doc?"

"I've turned it into a net. All part of the ritual."

The apeman continued to gaze at the ascent of the tentacle through the air. It vanished into a cloud of debris, one of many that darkened the sky at various points above Berlin. For five full minutes, Crinkle held it there, and then he retracted it. The net was full of junk: nuts and bolts and other components of clock towers. He turned and went back inside the palace. The small crowd applauded and dispersed. Gliding smoothly, the Führer approached a disposal chute and emptied the debris from the net; then he converted the net back into a hand.

"Every little bit helps, but it's mostly a symbolic gesture," he sighed. "I started this ceremony not long after Bronson Alpha arrived. There are still millions of tons of junk up there."

Stringent nodded. "What about my flying job, doc?"

"Indeed. Well, it concerns . . ."

A blurry psychedelic chord vibrated the windowpanes. The first band had started playing. Spaced out drumming underpinned weird banjo notes and amplitude-modulated cracklings that resembled the reception of valve radios tuned to unknown foreign stations. Stringent winced and looked at the Führer's desk, hoping to find some loose items to stuff in his ears, but nothing suitable stood there.

Crinkle noticed his distress. "Use the letters, boy!"

The apeman realized that the professor was referring to the detachable letters on the large electric ouija board. He removed the "q" and "x" in the belief that their loss wouldn't impair the working of the device too much, and inserted them in his lugholes.

"That's better!" he breathed at once.

Crinkle modified his voice so that it would vibrate against Stringent's jawbones, allowing the apeman to hear him through bone induction rather than air induction. This operation, impossible for a man to perform, was a doddle for a cyborg equipped as marvelously as the professor was. Now the Führer came to an abrupt decision.

"Stringy, I truly think you're the right man for the task I have in mind. The world is in grave danger. The Rushans have opened a portal to a rival dimension and made it possible for *other beings* to come through. There's evidence that what is about to enter our dimension, if it isn't here already, is indestructible. So everyone is doomed. I need you to face this intruder and do the impossible—annihilate him!"

The apeman digested this news for a moment. "I hate to point this out to you, doc, but that's not a flying job."

Crinkle smirked. "You won't operate alone, dear boy. I'll be with you every step of the way, even though I don't take steps but trundle along on castors. And there *is* a weapon that can destroy an indestructible being. I know that's a violation of logic, but what's that compared to the violation of a universe full of sentient beings? There's a mythical gun in existence that can kill anything, anything at all. I'm hoping against hope this means it can even kill our unwelcome visitor."

"You want me to fire this gun in self-defense, doc?"

"Maybe, Stringy. But that won't be your main role. To get that gun we have to go on a long journey, a journey to a very remote location; and the only way of reaching that location is by a special plane, a plane that can't be flown by any human, feline or robotic pilot who has ever tried. It's too unstable. I believe that *you* can fly it."

The apeman flushed with pride. He had an urge to beat his chest with his fists, but he repressed it. "I'll try!"

"Well, dear boy, this is the way it is. After the Tarotplane won the war and Hitler died and the regime became mellower, I rose up in the party to the point where I could command funding for my own personal projects. Eventually I was elected as Führer, of course, but even before that I was a big shit—I mean shot—in HIPZI politics. So I took my abandoned Flying Tail out of mothballs and tinkered with it. Finally got it working! But it's a temperamental monster, Stringy . . ."

"You seriously want me to pilot your dream machine?"

"Are you happy to, dear boy?"

"You bet, doc! Happier than an eel that doesn't once get mistaken for a whore's garter during its slimy life!"

There was an awkward pause.

"Ahem . . . Yes, well, we needn't worry about eels at this stage, and the suspension methods of a sex worker's stockings are also irrelevant, but at the rear of the palace is a hangar, and inside that hangar is the Flying Tail and she's loaded with fuel and supplies for a long voyage. I suggest we go there right now and get her started."

"I'm with you all the way, doc! You can rely on me!"

He turned and began walking towards the circular door but the Führer called him back. "One moment, Stringy! It's time for a commercial break. I did warn you about the need for advertisements during this story, didn't I? You haven't forgotten about them?"

The apeman blinked. "No, doc, but . . ."

"This next advert is for a cosmetics company, Stringy. See this tube of lipstick here? This is what's being promoted. I'll get the ball rolling. Just make sure you're facing out of the page—towards the reader. And it helps if you can make your eyes diverge."

"Out of the page? I don't understand any of this!"

"In *that* direction, Stringy!"

"There's nobody there, doc. Just a wall."

"It's a special kind of wall, Stringy, a fourth wall: it doesn't truly exist. It's an optical and literary illusion."

"You're messing with my mind, doc!"

The Führer pointed directly at you, yes you, sitting there, holding this book in your hands, and said, "The reader is out there. It takes practice to know which way to face, but you'll get it in the end. Watch me and try to emulate my motions and smarminess."

He held up the lipstick in one tentacle. "Tired of looking like a frump with those lips of yours? Don't weep! A few strokes of Lohengrin's Labial Lushgrin will soon defrumpize you."

He beckoned to Stringent below page level.

The apeman reacted sluggishly to his cue. He stepped forward, tried to make his eyes point in different directions and stood awkwardly with his hairy arms at his sides. "Fab," he said.

Crinkle sighed deeply beyond the left margin, out of the line of sight of the reader, thus seeming to maintain his unruffled pose. "Available in crimson, pale pink and papaya. Remember: no added rainbow clippings. It's suitable for boys as well as girls."

"And cats," added Stringent in a monotone.

The Führer and the apeman froze in position and grinned for maybe five seconds, and then relaxed. The commercial break was over. "You were rather unconvincing, Stringy!"

"Sorry, doc, acting is just not my bag."

"Please don't improvise next time. Cats indeed!"

"My eyes are smarting, doc!"

"Hazard of the profession. You'll get used to it."

The Führer led the way to the door and pulled the rope that opened it like an iris. But in the corridor he drew back and allowed the apeman to overtake him. Stringent was halfway down the staircase before he turned to see where the professor was. Crinkle was only a few steps behind him but the statue of Northrop in the alcove had undergone a change. It now sported a vast clown's smile outlined in thickly applied lipstick. Without uttering a word of explanation, the cyborg vaulted past the apeman on his multiple arm-legs and scuttled down a side passage that led to the hangar at the palace's rear. Stringent followed.

They emerged inside the hangar. And there she was. The Flying Tail! Stringent laughed with unalloyed joy.

ALL ABOARD THE FLYING TAIL

Just as the apeman was about to climb into the cockpit with the professor, he was hailed by four voices. He turned to behold Moonwash, Quorn Joy, Tantra and Nutloaf coming slowly towards him. He took the letters out of his ears in order to hear clearly what they were saying. Then he noticed a fifth figure behind them who was tagging along somewhat uncertainly. It was a bipedal feline dressed in a caftan.

"How did you get into the hangar?" squealed Crinkle.

"Through an unlocked hatch, man!"

"But the location of those isn't generally known to the populace. Only spies and saboteurs are aware of them!"

Moonwash shrugged and drew on his joint. "No sweat, dude. Here we are anyway. We want to talk to Mr. Strange. We'd like to introduce a new friend to him. Is that cool with you?"

The Führer was nonplussed. "I suppose so."

Moonwash indicated the feline by blowing smoke in the cat's direction and declared, "This is Purrfect Day."

"Good afternoon," said Stringent politely.

The cat grinned and crooned:

"I was drinking sangria in the park, baby, when these cool dudes came up and we got chatting. They mentioned you and I thought how far out it would be to meet you, man, so I asked for an introduction, baby, and they were groovy enough to say yeah!"

"I see," responded Stringent.

"You don't mind, do you?" asked Moonwash.

"Not at all," said the apeman.

"To be honest, the first band weren't good," added Tantra, "so we took the opportunity to seek you out."

Purrfect Day seemed to notice Crinkle for the first time and his slitted eyes narrowed. "Well, hellooooooooooo. How groovy to meet our glorious leader in such an informal situation!"

The Führer creaked in dismay. "But there are no formalities among the HIPZIS. You ought to know that . . ."

"Did I say 'informal'? I meant *unguarded*."

And he abruptly widened his jaws, but what issued from his throat was a baritone howl. Stringent was bemused by this incongruity, but the effect on the professor and his friends was far more extreme. They stiffened and the color drained from their faces, though in Crinkle's case it was a nude brain behind ultraglass that paled.

The Führer hissed, "Assassin! It's a coup d'cat!"

"He's not a cat!" cried Nutloaf.

"Indeed I'm not, baby," said Purrfect Day.

And indeed he wasn't. With a lightning paw he groped under his sleek chest fur for a hidden row of buttons and popped them in rapid sequence, a glissando of disrobement. Off his shoulders slipped his body suit until it was merely a fabric puddle on the floor of the hangar. And now he stood in his true glory, a purple dressing gown covering fur coarser than any cat would dare to wear, a cigarette holder in one languid paw, his pointy ears and slavering fangs carefully posed.

Stringent whistled as the enormity of the danger sank in. "Some sort of wolfman in mutated cat's clothing!"

"We call them Debonair Werewolves!" cried Crinkle.

The creature performed an elegant bow. "For our part, we prefer to be known as *louche loup-garou*. But that's not important right now. Prepare to be expunged, you foolish tin can!"

And he fitted a cigarette to his holder. But it wasn't a cigarette: it was a cartridge containing a flechette; and the holder was a miniature recoilless blow-pipe; and once the holder was between the slobbering black lips, the weapon was armed and dangerous.

"Throw yourself between me and the projectile, Stringy!" shrieked the professor in a powerful paroxysm of paralytic panic. As if that alliteration wasn't enough, he perilously pulsated.

"Man, this is really heavy!" gasped Moonwash.

Stringent stepped forward to obey the Führer's command, but was too slow. The werewolf had already exhaled the stinking breath in his occult lungs and the armor-piercing flechette had been released from its metal jacket and was spinning out of the cigarette holder's ebony barrel directly at Crinkle's important brain. It penetrated the ultraglass, causing a dozen teardrops of pale purple preserving liquid to leak out, and buried itself in the mass of throbbing grey matter.

"I've been hit, Stringy! It's a lobotomy!"

"What should I do, doc?"

"Kill the assassin, then give me a hug!"

Stringent noticed that the hole in the jar had already healed itself, and he supposed that ultraglass wasn't exactly like the old kind. This thought wasn't uppermost in his mind as he turned on the werewolf, but it was an interesting observation nonetheless.

Moonwash, Quorn Joy, Tantra and Nutloaf were paralyzed with horror and revulsion. Every fiber of their souls reacted negatively to any display of violence, and the apeman guessed they would even disapprove of what he was about to do to Purrfect Day.

But the Debonair Werewolf was resigned to his fate and determined to face it in the most stylish manner, so he struck a rehearsed bored pose, his right paw covering a phoney yawn.

"Any last words, Fido?" growled Stringent.

The werewolf took no offence at the name. "I've nothing to declare but my genus, which is *homo lupus chic.*"

"Can't you do better than that?" cried the apeman.

"Very well. You do realize this isn't an average assassination of a brain of state? No, it's a carefully planned takeover of the entire HIPZI political set-up! Our agents have been insinuating themselves into German society for many years and we've established quite a devastating fifth column. It's the day of reckoning for peaceniks!"

Stringent snorted. "I expected something more sentimental than that. If I had to deliver a bunch of last words, I'd talk about how my life has been a marvelous journey, and about how every journey on any itinerary has a destination, and death is a destination, and once a destination is reached it is time to send a postcard home . . ."

"Oh really, my dear fellow, get it over with."

"You lycanthropic interloper!"

"Indeed." The werewolf grinned sardonically and waited for the blow that would put him out of the world forever. The apeman delivered it with a monkey wrench he found on the floor. Purrfect Day died with the grin fixed on his lips; Stringent was reluctantly forced to admire the inhuman courage of the paranormal beast.

The monkey wrench clattered to the ground. The HIPZIS looked as if they were about to be sick and even the professor undulated his tentacles in revulsion. Stringent steadied himself by leaning against the fuselage of the Flying Tail, then he recalled that it didn't have a fuselage and jumped quickly upright to avoid falling over.

He gazed down at the cadaver of the assassin and felt a certain amount of pity for the clobbered monster, now a tangle of bloody fur and tattered dressing gown. It was only following its supernatural nature, after all. Let those among us without fangs cast the first spanner. He turned as his ears caught the sounds of fresh conflict.

"Can you hear that? Distant screaming outside!"

"Better than nearby screaming inside, man," observed Moonwash with a terrified stutter. "But uncool anyway!"

It grew louder. Fists pounded on the hangar wall. The Führer clutched his brain bottle with one tentacle and rasped, "I have a bad feeling about this. Get us out of here, Stringy!"

"But, doc, we have to take you to a hospital."

Crinkle scowled, so Stringent appealed to the HIPZIS as the screaming and knocking increased in volume.

"Yeah, dude," said Quorn Joy, "he urgently needs some chamomile and raspberry tea. It's the only remedy for severe brain lesions! But why don't we find a hospital outside Berlin?"

The screech of an unlocked hatch made him jump.

"I'm fine!" insisted the Führer.

The apeman didn't believe him, but saw it was completely pointless to argue. Intruders were running towards him: half a dozen werewolves, one still in his cat suit because the buttons had jammed. Stringent doubted he could kill all six with the spanner; he turned to usher his companions into the aircraft, but they had already anticipated his intention and were now crammed into the rear seat of the cockpit, squirming and waiting for him to take the controls. He vaulted inside.

The Debonair Werewolves reached the door just as it closed and raked it ineffectively with their sharp claws.

Flechettes pinged against the reinforced windshield.

"A revolution, doc!" gasped Stringent.

The Führer nodded, but the action seemed to cause him pain. "No time to open the hangar doors, but there's a weak point in the wall. The hangar was breached by a piece of falling sky junk a year ago, but I didn't bother to rebuild the damaged section properly. It's made of papier-mâché. I kept that fact a secret, of course. There!"

He jabbed a directional tentacle at the spot.

Stringent studied the control panel. He pressed a button marked START and an engine hummed into life, but the power output was low. Clearly it was an electric motor. A concealed propeller turned somewhere and with a casual flick, the Flying Tail trundled forward, building up speed with an excruciating lassitude and crashing through the weak segment of the wall at the undizzying velocity of two miles per hour. The werewolves howled in rancor and loosened their cravats.

The apeman grappled with the controls down the runway and found he couldn't lift the craft off the ground at all. He soon ran out of runway and had to twist the joystick savagely to avoid hitting a tree. They rolled over a grass verge and bumped along one of the boulevards that led back to the center of Berlin. All around was chaos.

The music festival had been abandoned in disarray. Musicians scurried everywhere, tripping over electric cables and hitting themselves senseless on the corners of monitors and amplifiers; groups of doomed HIPZIS tried to defend themselves with plucked flowers; but the Debonair Werewolves showed no mercy to anyone. Abandoned cat suits littered the parks. There had never been any bipedal felines in the first place: the phenomenon had been a diabolical trick from the outset.

"The underhanded pawed rascals!" cursed Stringent.

"Man, we can't leave our brothers and sisters like this! We should help them escape the carnage!" wept Moonwash.

"That's just not possible," said the Führer in an unemotional voice. "It is better to escape now but return in the future to wreak an awful revenge against these unlikeable lycanthropes."

"Revenge? But, dude, that would be, like, unethical, man!" Clutching his face in his hands, Moonwash trembled. He was comforted by Quorn Joy, who in turn had to be comforted by Tantra and Nutloaf. Despite the horror etched on their faces, the girls seemed to be coping better than the men in the dreadful situation. Stringent noticed this and his typical 1930s prejudices were challenged in a way that makes this tale more acceptable to a modern female readership, I hope.

He shook his head clear of such metafictional concerns and devoted all his concentration to the task of flying.

Vibrating at constantly shifting frequencies, dilating and contracting in an unnerving manner, the Flying Tail lurched up into the air, accidentally buzzing a group of werewolves who were harassing the lead singer of the Sages of Atlantis by knocking off his pointy hat. The bullying beasts had to throw themselves flat to avoid being hit, a serious blow to the image of unruffledness they liked to cultivate.

Further along was a scene of futile heroism, as the Führer's bodyguard bravely attempted a counter-attack; but they were outnumbered and soon fell with flechettes embedded in their necks. The apeman couldn't detach his gaze from this tragic spectacle, but Moonwash had a different peril on his mind and shook the pilot's shoulder.

"Watch out for the cables, man!"

Stringent veered just in time to avoid one of the lines that radiated out from the central transport pillar. A wicker cabin glided past full of fleeing HIPZIS; a second cabin containing werewolves pursued it. Somehow the monsters had fitted two cable cars onto the same line. Now it was obvious why they had so willingly worked as stevedores: to gain wide experience at a variety of operations that would be useful when the uprising began. It was doggedly malevolent and cynical.

Crinkle began groaning, but when Stringent expressed concern for his health, the professor seemed to recover and merely stated how pleased he was that the Flying Tail was a viable aircraft. "I don't know about that, to be candid, doc!" returned the apeman.

And in fact he had terrible trouble holding the weird airplane aloft. It kept stalling and losing height abruptly; then it would pick up speed again and soar effortlessly for a moment before jerking to the side. It frequently appeared to want to go in every direction at once, and on these occasions the frame flexed disconcertingly. As for the motor, it stopped and started at will. Stringent gritted his molars.

"You know something, doc? I always expected your Flying Tail to be like a normal plane but without wings or fuselage; in other words just like a standard tailpiece, with rudder and fins. I never guessed it would be the perfect reproduction of a fox's brush!"

"Didn't you? Are you disappointed, my boy?"

"No, doc. Just astonished . . ."

And with a mighty effort he yanked the joystick to the right so that the aircraft narrowly missed a second outgoing cable. "But I don't understand how the bishop-bashing thing works. It's very underpowered and the least aerodynamic thing I've ever flown!"

The professor said, "Head south, Stringy!"

The apeman nodded and smiled. He was starting to get the hang of the bizarre airplane already, proof that he was indeed the finest living pilot, even better than Oscar Rosebud, the long deposed Pink Baron. He turned the unpredictable craft and headed back over the massacre that had once been the harmless capital of a gentle population. Teams of invaders were toppling the marble columns, breaking the statues, raiding private houses for food and magazines, posturing.

"The festival was the signal for this takeover," lamented the Führer, "I should never have given my permission for it." Then he added, "Keep her pointed to the south, my dear boy."

"Where are we going, doc? Will you tell me?"

Professor Crinkle grimaced, but whether from physical pain, or some curious ethical consideration, or simply because he's required to do so in this paragraph, will never be known.

"Yes I will. We must pick up the gun I mentioned, the one that can kill anything. Our first duty is to save the universe; only later should we seek retribution against the Debonair Werewolves." His brain reddened as he peered out of the window. "Look at that one in the garden; he's devouring an entire box of chocolate liqueurs!"

"Looters and land pirates, doc. No better."

"Yes, Stringy, and we'll make them pay one day. But to return to what I was saying, there's a long flight ahead of us, most of it over territory that is hostile or just plain surrealistic."

"Do you feel up to such a voyage, doc?"

The Führer touched his jar. "Despite the fact the evil projectile entered my brain, I'm actually feeling better. It destroyed cells in there but I don't yet know which ones. They're dying even as I speak; and when they're all fully dead, I'll have a better idea."

"Don't you mean a *worse* idea, doc?"

"In total, yes. My overall brainpower will certainly be diminished to a degree; but what I meant was that I'd have a better idea of which aspects of my cerebral processes have been degraded or obliterated. For instance, it might be my motor functions or my short-term memory that suffers; or perhaps my libido or ability to empathize with others; or maybe even my mostly latent psychic endowments."

"I hope you don't become dangerous, doc!"

"Ha ha! Me too, Stringy. I'm a cyborg after all, with the power of more than thirty bears. But we'll worry about that when it happens. Just do your best to keep this bird in the sky . . ."

"I still don't know how it works, doc!"

"Well then, I shall inform you. It's not a true airplane, but a powered glider, with only a modest electric motor to take it to a certain altitude. At that point, the engine automatically cuts out and the craft begins to swoop back to Earth. But the gravitational fields of the Bronson worlds also pull upon it. By skilful manipulation of the complex controls, it's theoretically feasible to catch every gravity-thermal and stay in the sky permanently. A difficult task, though, bearing in mind that the Bronson planets are always changing their relative positions."

"Well, that's one way of flying, I suppose, doc!"

"Indeed. There are many others."

Stringent frowned and said, "There's something I want to ask you. One of the zeppelins that kidnapped you flung a few Heighth Charges at Jack's stratospheric cruiser while I was in it. They were spinning barrels without wings. How did *they* stay aloft, doc?"

"Spinning, you say? In that case, what you witnessed was undoubtedly an application of the Magnus Effect."

And the professor went on to explain that any object moving sideways while rotating along its horizontal plane has a tendency to rise, depending on the direction of that lateral movement. It was a phenomenon suited to the aviation industry but rarely used.

During this lengthy exchange, the HIPZIS had been too traumatized to utter a word. Finally Quorn Joy removed a packet of Arbeit joints from a pocket and pushed a reefer between his quivering lips. "Anyone mind if I light up?" he asked in a tiny voice.

Stringent was a man of his own time. "Why should I mind? Doctors in all the journals agree it's healthy to periodically fill the lungs with smoke. I guess that the advice for tobacco also applies to marijuana, and even if it doesn't, it's best to assume it does."

The Führer groaned inwardly at this and a feeling of hopelessness rose up inside his soul like canal water in a leaking old cellar. The apeman had leap-frogged eighteen decades of history and was as much a castaway here as was a microscopic sailor stranded on the surface of a floating coconut. Could he really be relied upon to complete the difficult quest that Crinkle had asked him to take on? Or would the anachronism of his presence be a gross handicap to the successful discharge of his task? Time alone would tell. Time always tells. The snitch!

As for that microscopic sailor: how dare he enter this story without an invitation! Isn't it rude when a metaphor takes liberties? Something needs to be done to discourage the others . . .

"Man, I got the munchies bad!" rumbled Quorn Joy. "Any food on this plane? I could eat a soybean horse!"

"Did someone mention whores?" asked Stringent.

"It's the language barrier, man!"

Moonwash rummaged in an overhead locker and discovered a sack of emergency supplies; but there was only one edible item inside. He held it up and rapped it with his knuckles.

A coconut? But Quorn Joy wasn't displeased.

"That'll do just fine, dude!"

A Little Trouble in Big Italy

The crypto-cubist cyborg that also happened to be Führer of a devastated
federation of hippie Nazis had started to run down to the point where his
speech was slurred. So he wound himself back up, one tentacle grasping and
turning his own key until the big and powerful spring inside him was again at
maximum tension. They had been flying for many hours and had finally
crossed into the biggest Italy.

The only friend of the HIPZI FEDERATION, Big Italy comprised the
entire peninsula apart from its heel, sole and toe, all of which belonged to Little Italy, a political entity that consisted mostly of islands, two of them as large
as small countries, namely Sicily and Sardinia. Neither Italy had a decent air
force but Muscle Leany had recently installed some batteries of steam-powered
vertical iron cannon.

Stringent would need to watch out for those and avoid any shells that
were puffed his way, at least until they could find a way of notifying the Big
Italy government that the HIPZI Führer was on board. Muscle Leany was
quartered in a villa on the shores of Lake Balbo, an expanse of water named
after the man who had established a colony in what had once been called
Libya, a realm that no one had heard anything from since Bronson Bravo had
spiraled into Earth orbit.

Although an ally of Germany, the tastes of the citizens of Big Italy in
music and art were significantly different from those of the HIPZIS. The
main thing here was jazz and violently rhythmic poetry; the clothes were less
colorful. The Big Italians enjoyed cellar clubs and abstract painting, and
Muscle Leany and his Beatnikshirts had a harder edge than the meek Teutonic

dreamers, but both sides preferred to stress their shared distrust of traditional government structures.

As the apeman steered the Flying Tail over the tall mountains that fell away in overlong prose descriptions, he caught sight of a sheen of water below and said, "The sight of all that liquid is encouraging my bladder to complain, doc. I think I need to go!"

"Me too, man, I'm bursting," concurred Moonwash.

"Don't be foolish!" grated the professor. "There are no toilets on board this aircraft. You'll have to hold it in."

"Sorry, doc, I'm not sure I can. I haven't been since before the start of the novel and it's affecting my flying skills. I can't cross my legs because that might interfere with the pedals."

There was a general discussion among the back seat passengers and it was decided to request a stop at the next landing place. Crinkle grumbled and beeped, but finally agreed to the proposal. "Very well. Take her down towards the lake, Stringy. See that grey building? That is Muscle Leany's abode. May as well pay him a visit."

"So that's Lake Balbo, is it? Cool, man!"

The HIPZIS seemed excited and relieved at the idea of standing again on firm ground, but Stringent had a hard job getting the Flying Tail into a survivable landing approach. The crosswinds were tricky and the runway turned out to be a laughably short stretch of beach on the shore of the lake beneath the villa. But he managed it successfully and killed the motor. As he opened the cockpit doors, he saw that a delegation was striding down a steep path to meet them. He squinted.

"Are you sure they'll be friendly, doc?" he asked.

"Yes, yes. I know these people!"

The delegation was formed of men in polo-necked sweaters and horn-rimmed sunglasses who wore the insignia of a golden saxophone on their belt buckles. These were the Beatnikshirts and they never smiled but that doesn't mean they were unhip, dig? Quite the opposite. They scrutinized the new arrivals with inscrutable expressions. They seemed as black and strong as freshly brewed espresso.

"But can we communicate with them, doc?" Stringent asked. "I don't think I know any Italian phrases."

Nutloaf whispered in his ear, "Most Big Italians speak a lingo called Scat and no other, but Muscle Leany also speaks good German, so you'll be understood no sweat by him."

This was ironic bearing in mind how much heat that coal-fired robot gave off—everyone who stood in his presence expelled moisture through their gaping pores, even other robots.

In fact it turned out that these Beatnikshirts spoke fluent German. One of them gazed through his tinted lenses at the professor and said, "I don't like your shape. Are you a square?"

"Take me to your Douche!" cried the Führer.

"Hey, I thought you wanted to meet Muscle Leany, doc!" protested the apeman with a frown of mild surprise.

"That's his official title. Leave the diplomacy to me."

"Sure thing, doc. I won't interfere."

The Beatnikshirts conferred amongst each other. "Skibby da bap, dah be bap bah da bam! Dibbah de do!"

"Do bap bap, de bap bap bom, sabbady bah!"

The first official who had spoken said, "We have now agreed that you really are the Führer of the HIPZIS and not an impostor, so you and your friends may proceed to the villa."

"Is Muscle Leany at home?" asked Crinkle.

"He is indeed, daddy-o."

The Führer accelerated up the steep path and Stringent and the HIPZIS followed him; the Beatnikshirts brought up the rear. They were wheezing and gasping by the time they finally reached the house and similar sounds greeted their arrival, for they were met on the sooty veranda by the rusty Douche himself, and he was leaking steam. The coals inside him glowed and spat and made his belly blush.

Stringent took a closer look at this robot. The steam gushed out of the cracks between his metal plates and the holes of his missing rivets at such high pressure that the apeman frowned at the wastage. Couldn't someone fit this dictatorial contraption to a turbine? He remembered that he ought to say nothing that might cause an international incident; he had promised the professor to button his labials.

But it would be a strain to remain silent!

The first thing Muscle Leany said when he saw his guests was, "Look at that hairy old smelly brute. I bet he can juggle bananas! Can he? Well, can he? What a funny throwback!"

The professor explained tactfully, "He's not my pet but my pilot. How are you, Signor Leany? It has been a long time. Bad news, I'm afraid. My country has just been taken over . . ."

"Really? Come inside and tell me about it."

They stepped over the threshold. Stringent peered all about and noted that the walls, floors and ceiling weren't actually painted grey; they had originally been white but layers of discharge from the badly maintained resident dictator had accumulated over a period of years. Everything was coated with soot, ash and smoldering embers that had spilled out of the robot. It was like walking through an indoor battlefield. No wonder the Beatnikshirts only wore black garb!

"May I use the toilet, doc? Will you ask him?"

Muscle Leany overheard this request. "Of course you can, you comical hybrid. What's it like being so organic? Don't tell me, let me guess! No, I give up, it's too difficult. Ha ha!"

The apeman gritted his teeth. "Where is it?"

"The bathroom's down that corridor." Muscle Leany jerked a thumb as sharp as a spike and exhaled steam.

"Can we go as well?" asked the four HIPZIS.

"Ha ha!" laughed Muscle Leany, turning to the professor. "Makes you grateful to be mechanical, doesn't it?"

Stringent grumbled as he hurried down the specified corridor. "What a perfectly obnoxious clanker! I'm sorry I ever asked to land the plane now. I should have wet my pants instead."

As he relieved himself in the porcelain urinal he decided he would ask the professor if they could depart as soon as possible. All his life he had been subjected to insults but he had always been free to respond with his fists; he simply had no experience at restraining his emotions. How much abuse could he take from the Douche?

After he had finished, Moonwash took his place, then Tantra, Nutloaf and Quorn Joy. Stringent was intrigued to know how the girls managed to utilize such a high urinal, but he didn't stay to look, and he was too timid to ask later. They would have told him if he had. And then I would know as well. But he didn't, and so I don't.

The apeman dragged his knuckles in minor irritation as he looked for the professor down various passages and in random rooms. The HIPZIS joined him in the search; Moonwash heard muffled voices and followed the sounds to a circular chamber where the Führer and the Douche were deep in conversation across a table. The Beatnikshirts stood to attention along the far wall, like jazz sentinels.

Crinkle was saying, "That's bad, very bad!"

Muscle Leany answered, "Yes, the situation is growing worse. I had to expel the Rushan Ambassador last week. His extreme occult belligerence had become intolerable. Evil is afoot."

"Luckily I run on castors," joked the professor.

The Douche was unable to resist temptation. "Well spoken! And if evil is afoot, by logic it must be armless!"

He glanced up, saw Stringent and the HIPZIS, and beckoned them into the chamber with imperious gestures.

"Evil isn't really harmless," he explained.

"I know!" snapped Stringent. "It's my body that's the ape, not my head, I'm not stupid!" Then he noticed the professor's expression and regained control of himself. "Thanks anyway!"

"Ha ha! Don't mention it. I appreciate a human being who knows how to monkey around convincingly . . ."

Stringent grinned a wide grin he didn't feel.

"Take a chair, dear boy," said the professor. "I'm not seated myself, of course, because I don't have buttocks, but don't let that put you off." The apeman sat gratefully next to him, and Moonwash, Quorn Joy, Tantra and Nutloaf also sank down onto seats.

Muscle Leany said, "I'm just keeping your master—who also happens to be your stepdad—up to date with the latest geopolitical news. A horrid situation has just got much worse."

Crinkle nodded and his brain wobbled.

Stringent tugged at one of his depleted uranium elbows. "Shouldn't we be getting back on our way, doc?"

The Führer swiveled one of his prehensile electric eyes at the apeman, its pupil contracted to a point, like a schoolboy subjected to hypothetical reducing rays. "Grief, no! The Douche has invited us to stay for supper. It would be very impolite to refuse!"

Stringent opened his mouth to object but nothing intelligible came out, so he fumed in impatient silence, doing his best to avoid catching Muscle Leany's eye. The sight of the dubious dictatorial device, spilling heaps of anthracite dust onto the ground with the mildest motion of its body, filled him with a livid loathing that was decidedly Luddite in its lurking lunacy. Something along those lines anyway.

The HIPZIS didn't seem concerned by the concept of the delay, though it was clear they weren't wholly at ease in their surroundings. The Douche ignored them and continued to debate affairs of state with the Führer, and Stringent found himself listening very attentively to the points raised until he finally felt compelled to interject, "All this talk about the Rushans isn't worth an unsalted peanut to me, doc!"

The professor sighed and apologized to Muscle Leany. "He's from the past. I'd better explain it all to him . . ."

"Go ahead. I'll order the food," grinned the Douche.

He bent forward and opened a little iron door in the knee of his left leg and rummaged around until he found an iron bell, which he lifted out and rang thrice between finger and thumb.

The notes it produced might have been doleful and gothic had the bell been large, but they sounded merely dull and drab; yet their desired effect was achieved almost instantly. The Beatnikshirts turned smartly on their expensive heels, marched off to the kitchens and presently returned with trays loaded with victuals, serving the diners with supercilious efficiency while humming intricate be-bop tunes.

One of these tunes was actually a coded advert for ZOOT SPARKLE'S FANGPASTE, GUARANTEED TO PUT A SMILE ON THE LEAST DEBONAIR WEREWOLF'S FACE. Nobody else in the room was aware of this message and I don't recommend the product.

The apeman found himself staring at a plate of color-coded spaghetti and he jabbed this pasta matrix unhappily with his fork. Professor Crinkle neglected his own dish of cogs and springs while he lectured Stringent on Canadian history. "Everything went wrong everywhere with the first visit of Bronson Alpha. After Yellowstone erupted, the Canadians were free at last to become the dominant power of North America. They saw what the HIPZIS were doing and wanted the same thing for themselves. But hippie culture can go two ways. There's a dark side to all that stuff; and that's the path the Canadians tumbled down."

"Are you referring to Black Magic, doc?"

The Führer nodded and continued, "Three prophets rose among them, preaching the law of sorcery and occultism; and it's whispered that those prophets turned themselves into weird demigods as a result of the arcane and perverse rituals they performed."

Stringent absorbed this information with a growing sense of unease in his appendix that had nothing to do with his inedible pasta. He felt afraid of something, some energy in the professor's words. "Did those prophets have human names, doc?" he moaned.

The Führer sighed deeply, and in case you're wondering how and why a cyborg could and would do such a thing, it's because he can. No other reason. He said, "Yes, dear boy, they do. They are called Geddie, Lifesun and Pert. They preach the Rule of an entity they call Rush, and that's why their devotees are named the Rushans."

"But sorcery doesn't actually work does it, doc?"

"Unfortunately it does, at least in our universe. Maybe in some parallel dimension where Hitler lost the war—perhaps in the cosmos imagined by the writer Felipe ¡Que Dick!—it's hokum, but not here, alas. No, Stringy, weird occult shit has authentic power."

"You swore, doc!" tittered the apeman joyously.

The Führer frowned. "Didn't you note a previous occasion where a bad word accidentally slipped off my technetium tongue? You missed a prime opportunity for bountiful chortlement there, dear boy! That's a word I just coined, by the way. But to return to what I was saying: until very recently those prophets (who might be demigods, don't forget) have been happy to remain in Canada; and in fact they have forbidden their followers to dwell abroad, with the exception of a few spies and ambassadors. Every soul in Canada was needed for a ceremony—a magic ceremony based on warped psychology and diabolic philosophy."

Muscle Leany interrupted at this point. "Did you mention Felipe ¿Que Dick? He's one of my favorite authors but I like Philip José Farmer even more. Ah, those diabolical Rushans!"

Then he returned to his repast of raw embers.

The professor extended a tentacle to touch the apeman's shoulder in an affectionate but heterosexual manner.

"Listen closely, Stringy. From what the Douche has just told me, Rush *in person* is about to enter our cosmos from an adjacent universe. It seems that Geddie, Lifesun and Pert have succeeded in their nefarious design! If this is true, there's even less time left for the Earth than I feared! We need to get hold of that special mythical gun as quickly as possible; and it's a pity we can't insult our host by jumping up from this table right now and getting back aboard the Flying Tail."

Stringent asked. "But how does the Douche know that Rush is ready to infiltrate our spacetime continuum?"

"The Rushan ambassador dropped a few obvious hints and said he was going to be recalled next week, to be in attendance when Rush arrives, so Muscle Leany wiped the glib smirk off his Canadian visage by expelling him. The ambassador stormed off, but before he left he poured a bottle of poison into the lake, killing the fish."

"The chimp-pumping rogue!" fumed Stringent.

The Douche wiped his pig iron lips with an asbestos napkin. "Some of the eels in there were my friends," he said obscurely. Then he finished his last ember and belched sulfur dioxide. Instead of apologizing he seemed proud of this industrial eructation.

The supper came to an end. The sun was setting and its crimson beams slanted sideways through the window and seemed to ignite the dead coals that lay in profusion everywhere, an optical illusion that proved unsettling to the human guests at the table. Muscle Leany suggested a game of cards but the Führer refused, much to the apeman's relief. "We're exhausted and need a good night's sleep," he said.

"I'll order your rooms prepared!" roared the Douche.

He took a second bell from the compartment in his right knee and rang it and the Beatnikshirts ran off to make the beds in the spare rooms. Now the sun had vanished over the horizon and it was twilight: the body of the robotic ruler glowed, reminding Stringent of a red light district. Clearing his throat with a cough he ventured, "I don't suppose you could furnish me with something to aid my sleep?"

"Certainly I can!" boomed Muscle Leany.

"What do you require, Stringy?" asked the Führer. "Extra sheets, two pillows instead of one? A teddy ape?"

"Actually, doc, what I really need is a prostitute . . ."

There was an awkward pause.

"Ahem . . . Yes, well, I doubt our host is able to procure one of *those* at such short notice, my dear boy."

Muscle Leany raised a good-natured hand.

"Sure I can! This villa is equipped with a resident whore. Don't worry, I use her myself from time to time."

The apeman beamed. "Why, thank you, Signor Leany!" He thrust his hands into his pockets and was delighted to discover a few coins in both. This currency had come with him from 1932 and because of inflation its value should have increased. He was confident he could afford a session with a prostitute that would last until morning. Then he'd be in the right frame of mind for *any* adventure!

"I'll send her to you at midnight," said the Douche.

"Gee, that's perfect for me!"

One of the Beatnikshirts returned to declare that the beds were made, and at Muscle Leany's urging the company abandoned the remains of the feast and tramped out of the chamber and down long passages to a suite of rooms. The HIPZIS elected to sleep all together in the biggest bed in the biggest room. This suited both the professor and the apeman. At the entrance to their respective rooms they bid each other goodnight and the apeman expressed the forlorn hope that Crinkle's brain would feel better by the morning. The Führer sighed.

"Some groups of nerves have definitely died in there, dear boy, and I think it might be my Psi-Suppressor Cluster that has gone, which is bad news—but it could be a lot worse."

"What does that particular cluster do, doc?"

"It limits sensitivity to psychic phenomena, Stringy. Without it, I'll be able to transmit and receive telepathically, receive disjointed visions of future times and bend long spoons."

"I can bend spoons, doc! I bent a spanner once."

"Not with my bare hands, dear boy, but with the energy of my mind. I'll also be able to discern specters."

"Aren't those talents useful?" frowned the apeman.

Crinkle shrugged. "Maybe, maybe not. It could be that I'll be freaked out every second of every hour of every day. Already I'm feeling uneasy. I'm picking up an unhappy vibe."

Stringent pouted but had nothing more to say, so they bid each other goodnight again and departed to their separate rooms. The apeman lay in his bed with wide eyes, impatiently counting away the minutes. Finally, after what seemed an age, midnight arrived. He heard the chiming of an antique clock somewhere. Then he sat up rigidly. The handle of his door was turning. She was coming to him!

The door swung open. A shape entered the room. This was going to be the first woman Stringent had enjoyed for 180 years. She seemed to be carrying a lamp near her abdomen, but the light it gave out was dull. She moved closer, but he didn't find her motion as graceful as he'd hoped. On the contrary, she rumbled and clanked . . .

When she reached the bed, he was able to get a good look at her. The red glow came not from a lamp but from a stove in her belly. She was a coal-powered robot! A fossil fuelled floozy! Was Stringent about to learn the true meaning of a steamy session?

BIGGER TROUBLE IN LITTLE ITALY

Stringent woke abruptly. Somebody was doing something to him. It was still dark but some animal instinct inside him told him that the room was full of intruders. Had the Debonair Werewolves tracked him all the way from Germany? That couldn't be. His mind struggled to understand this situation. A handkerchief was being pressed down hard over his mouth and nose and it stank of chloroform.

He lashed out but his fist struck only the dozing iron framework of the undressed robot that lay at his side. He had serviced her well but without fixing her, if you take my meaning. She was utterly satiated and wouldn't awake even if a supernova went off.

But the intruders weren't very interested in her. Stringent realized that he was about to lose consciousness and there was nothing he could do to avoid his fate. Then it all went black.

He struggled back to awareness hours later.

He was in the rear of a car, stretched out on the seat. It wasn't the sort of car he'd been used to driving back in Nevada or even in Florida. It was a limousine and it was longer than he'd ever imagined a car could be. The interior seemed to stretch forever towards the front seats, where the driver sat like a flea on a cobra's head. There were at least five-dozen other rows of seats in between, you do the math.

At different points along the entire length of the car sat men. Most of them cradled submachine guns; some of them munched pizza, the purist marinara variety, which features a thin topping of tomato, garlic, olives, basil and oregano, but no cheese.

"I recognize you! The Beatnikshirts!" gasped Stringent.

The man in the row of seats directly ahead turned with a grin. Then he removed a toothpick from his mouth. "Nah, buddy, that was just a ruse to give us access to the Douche's villa. We infiltrated a month ago and been waiting our chance ever since then."

"A revolution of some kind?" spluttered the apeman.

"Nah, buddy, we don't care about the internal politics of Big Italy. We care only about its foreign policy, namely Muscle Leany's attitude to his southern neighbor, Little Italy. He has been leaning hard on us and that's why we need to teach him a lesson."

"You mean to say that you are Little Italians?"

"Yep, buddy, we're a bunch of fifth columnists. We were trained to do impressions of the Beatnikshirts, with our turtleneck sweaters, Vandyck beards, berets and the be-bop jive talk. It wasn't easy learning Scat, I tell you! De bam de bop bah bam dah!"

"Scooby de bam, deebe de dah, dabbah!" came the reply from another man four rows ahead. Then giggles.

"But what do you want with us?" demanded Stringent.

"You're our hostages," explained the first man. "It's very simple really. We figured that as you were guests of the Douche you must be important to him. So we're going to use you to bargain for less harassment from the big iron bully. You are our insurance."

Stringent scratched his head and for the first time realized that no one had tied him up or secured him to the seat in any way. "I never realized that Muscle Leany was that kind of ruler. I thought his jazz republic was as peaceful and soft as Germany . . ."

"That just ain't so. You see, he follows the *hard* bop groove."

The apeman licked his lips. "Right."

"Don't listen to them, Stringy!" came a familiar voice. It was Crinkle himself, maybe eighteen rows ahead. The ultraglass bell jar with the nude brain peered over the top of the distant leatherette seat. "They're liars, my dear boy! These guys are gangsters!"

And he lashed out with one of his tentacles and tore off the clothes of the fake Beatnikshirt closest to him. Beneath was a sharp Armani suit and a silk shirt with platinum cufflinks.

"Shut up, canister!" growled the gangster. And with a few accomplices he overpowered the professor and held him immobile. "Yeah, the game's up. We're the Cosa Nostra Damus!"

"You won't hold him for long," said Stringent. "He has the strength of many bears. Sock it to them, doc!"

The gangsters roared with laughter at this.

"You underestimate us. We have seized hold of his clockwork key and are twisting it the wrong way; we won't finish until his mainspring loses most of its tension. He's very weak already and won't be allowed to wind himself up until the journey's over."

Stringent growled, "Picking on a poor attenuated cyborg! What cheap kind of Mafia-style outfit are you?"

The first thug removed his horn-rimmed sunglasses and said, "Less of your lip, monkey boy. You're all coming with us back to Sicily, where we plan to put you in a smelly dungeon."

"Man, that's the pits," came the voice of Moonwash.

It appeared the HIPZIS were also inside the limousine, occupying one row each at various points along the entire length. "My name's Fredo and let me warn you against escaping!" said the first thug. The thug who had been divested of his raiment by the Führer added, "Yeah, and my name's Caldo. All the Little Italians in this vehicle are related to each other. Don't mess with the Cosa Nostra Damus!"

"Tell me about yourselves," suggested Stringent.

Fredo pondered this request. "Sure, why not? The Cosa Nostra Damus plans all its crimes in the future, thus escaping punishment in the present. We tend to issue ambiguous threats that can equally apply to anyone; and if you're not careful I'll be forced to make you an offer you can't interpret or clarify. That's what we do, pal."

Stringent was none the wiser but decided not to push the point. So he changed the subject. "Although you've warned me against making a break for it, I really am very strong. I have the arms of a gorilla and I'm certain I could overpower you, climb all the way to the front seat—smashing your brothers' skulls as I go—finally wringing the neck of the driver, taking his place and then applying the brake."

Caldo shook his head emphatically. "That's sixty rows of seats, buddy, some of them with collapsible backs or other traps, not to mention all the concentrated submachine gun fire."

"You're right. I was just probing for weak points. Plus I wanted you to do the math for me. Many thanks."

"Do any of you heavy dudes mind if I smoke?" came the forlorn voice of

Quorn Joy. Fredo muttered something about it being a filthy habit, but he gave his permission all the same.

"Look there!" came the voice of Nutloaf.

From her tone it was obvious she was referring to something out of the window. Stringent peered and saw a steam-powered vertical iron cannon. It was surrounded by men who were shaking their fists at the limousine as it sped past. Caldo laughed loudly.

"That's why we didn't bundle you on an airplane for the long journey to Little Italy. We would have been blasted out of the sky! But those iron barrels are fixed and can't be moved. We can zoom past far beneath them and be safe from any discharge."

"You fiendishly clever scoundrels!" cried Crinkle.

Stringent wasn't so sure about this. He said, "I reckon the Cosa Nostra Damus has overlooked one thing, doc. This car is so long it'll never make the first bend without jamming. While the highway is dead straight, it's a viable method of transportation, but when the road starts to curve, dip and twist, the driver will have to stop!"

Fredo and Caldo bellowed with mirth.

"You idiot!" they choroused. "This highway is straight all the way. It's the famous Etna Road (known in old German as the Etnabahn) and runs without a single degree of deviation to Sicily. If we chose, we could use a car ten times as long as this one . . ."

"Oh dear!" said Stringent beneath his breath.

The Führer sighed and said, "They speak the truth, dear boy. Bronson Alpha is to blame. When it passed over, it caused not just Yellowstone to erupt but all the Italian volcanoes too. Etna's lava was dragged behind the planet as it travelled through the sky, and when Bronson Alpha went over the horizon, cutting off its gravitational pull, the ribbon of now solid lava fell back to earth, creating a highway that stretched from Etna all the way to the Swiss border in the north."

Now the driver felt compelled to speak, despite his remoteness. With only one hand on the steering wheel, he turned in his seat and called back in a faint voice, "You think this car's long? You should have seen the one owned by the Chicago gangster Upside Downy, Jr. before the apocalypse. That was a Duesenberg and was so long that it never needed to be driven anywhere, because the moment it was pointed towards its destination, it was already at that destination and in some cases had even passed it. Then it was just a case of Upside Downy getting in the back door and jumping over all the seats until he reached the row next to his destination. I often fantasize about driving *that* car!"

Stringent had nothing to say in response to this. In fact he had nothing more to say about anything much. He made himself comfortable on his seat and gazed out of the window. They glided past several more vertical cannon. The hours rolled away. He listened to the idle chatter of Nutloaf and Tantra and he slowly grew bored. Then something occurred to him. He sat up straight and called out:

"Hey, doc! Any chance you might let me know precisely what my two other abnormalities are? Maybe they can get us out of this situation? For instance, if one of them involves making myself impervious to bullets, it would be a useful talent to deploy."

The professor merely groaned in reply. "My brain's hurting bad. Feels like a tidal bore of psychic influence is rushing between my synapses. It's definitely my Psi-Suppressor Cluster that's dying. It has almost gone; and the visions are flooding my mind . . ."

"Sounds mind blowing, man!" approved Moonwash.

But Stringent felt only concern for the injured cyborg. "Doc! Keep a grip on yourself. Don't give yourself away to them! Don't listen to them! Visions are a bunch of losers, doc!"

"That's not always the case, dear boy. Sometimes they are significant and transcendent. I'm seeing something now, a picture from the past. I'm back in the jungle, the forests of the Congo. There's a theater troupe lost among the dense vegetation! An English theater troupe doing a tour of the African colonies. But they've wandered off the path. I think one of them is your mother, Stringy! Your biological mother! Ah, the vision fades to grey and disappears. Sorry about that."

Stringent bounced up and down in his seat. "Don't apologize, doc! I'm delighted to learn my mother was a human actress! And English too! I've never adhered to the view that all Limeys are a pack of pantywaists; only the vast majority are. But if my mother was a woman, then it's my father who was the gorilla. I wonder how they met? Maybe he raped her or used her as a prostitute in his treetop nest?"

There was an awkward pause.

"Ahem . . . Yes, well, I don't think that male gorillas ever pay for it, my boy," said the professor, "but anyway, I don't want to be a fully-fledged psychic. It's far too upsetting. I need to find a technician who can build a mechanical Psi-Suppressor Cluster and graft it in place. Otherwise I'll be forever cursed to know secrets that men aren't supposed to know, such as the fact none of the wives of our kidnappers are faithful to them. In fact, they are currently planning orgies."

Fredo had heard enough. "Shut up, will ya?"

Caldo reached in the pocket of his Armani suit and drew out a plastic disc on a length of chain. He dangled this object threateningly in front of the Führer. "Yeah, or I'll plug ya!"

The dawn came and the sun rose; then it travelled across the sky and was eclipsed by the three Bronson planets at various points on its voyage. Because of this constant alteration of light and shade, the air heated up to different temperatures within relatively small areas, altering pressure and causing micro-winds to constantly blow. This detail plays absolutely no part in the plot. I wanted to leave it out but my editor insisted it remained in place; or maybe it was vice versa.

In the late afternoon, with the sun nearly touching the western horizon, they finally crossed the frontier into Little Italy. They didn't stop to have their passports scrutinized; the driver pushed his foot down hard on the accelerator and the limousine bashed through the lowered wooden barrier just like in the films. Exciting, huh?

The remainder of the journey lasted a further eight hours. By the time the limousine had reached Palermo, capital of Sicily, it was already much too late for bed. The men of the Cosa Nostra Damus bundled the hostages out into the night and forced them to march, at gunpoint, up a tall flight of stone steps and along a dank corridor. They were inside a prison and the claustrophobia quotient was high. The prison was a square tower that had been built hundreds of years ago.

An oak door with an iron grille was unlocked and the captives pushed inside. This was the dungeon that was supposed to remain their home for the next few weeks, or for however long it took Muscle Leany to come to terms with the kidnappers. The dungeon was devoid of furniture but pasta on the floor had been scattered to serve as a carpet. It crunched or mushed as the apeman paced back and forth, depending on its state of preparation. While the Führer laboriously wound himself back up to maximum power, Stringent rubbed his heroic chin.

"Maybe I can break down that door with my hairy shoulder, doc?" he suggested, but the professor shook his head and reminded the apeman that the strength of the biggest gorilla wasn't sufficient to splinter such tough wood. Even if Stringent was joined by the HIPZIS, they would rebound with bruises and the door wouldn't be dented. Crinkle was full of respect for Sicilian oak doors and regarded this one in particular as an example of superb craftsmanship. He added:

"I tell you: it would take twenty-nine bears to force it open!"

"Then we're stuffed, doc!" said Stringent.

"Heavy, man!" cried Moonwash.

"Wait a moment. I have an idea!" replied Crinkle.

He tiptoed on his tentacles to the metal grille and peered through it. A guard stood in the corridor outside. A bunch of keys were fixed to his belt and in the wall behind him was another barred window. Then the Führer crossed the dungeon to the far wall. There was a barred window here too. He frowned, nodded and whispered:

"I can't stretch a tentacle through the grille in the oak door to snatch the keys from the guard because he's facing our way and would instantly see what I was doing. But if I extend one of my arms through this other window, it can circle the entire world and reach through the window in the corridor and take the keys from behind him. Then I'll retract my arm and bring the keys back here to us!"

"Can you really do that, doc? It's a long way!"

Professor Crinkle smirked. "25,000 miles, dear boy. It has never been done before, but this seems like a good point in the novel to try. If I fail, this passage can be deleted before the book gets published and no reader will ever be aware of my humiliation."

"Heck, doc, I wish I could read the book right now to see if it contains this passage or not; and then I'd know!"

"I think it does, man! I'm standing right in it!"

"No, Moonwash, I just think you've wet yourself. How can I be sure? How can I know without doubts, doc?"

Professor Crinkle chuckled.

"Don't worry, Stringy, we'll find out the old fashioned way! Firstly I'll press myself as close to the wall as possible. Every little inch helps. Now I'll reach out my most flexible tentacle. There it goes. I just need to force it outwards and keep lengthening it. The mental processes involved in this operation are curious in themselves: a state not dissimilar to meditation is created in the forepart of the midbrain."

He grimaced and strained. Every metallic fiber of his being vibrated to the melody of his suppressed grunts.

Out in the world went the arm, further and further.

Or farther and farther. I've never been sure of the correct spelling, and neither is Crinkle. But he doesn't have time for such nitpickings; he's too busy extending that tantalum tentacle. The effort involved was intense; he flexed his metal plates and made a noise like a broken celesta, which is a seldom-played type of keyboard instrument, and I know this even though I've never seen or heard one. Drops of lubrication oil bloomed out of his microscopic pores: the perspiration of a clockwork cyborg. He shook and grunted like a randy boiler on heat.

"How far have you stretched it, doc?" cried Stringent.

"Just crossed Spain and Portugal . . . Felt the leaves of olive trees brush past my elbow . . . Women are hanging laundry on my arm but they won't get it back . . . Now I'm over the Atlantic Ocean . . . Seagulls flapping round my hand, perching on my thumb . . . Albatross has done its business on my knuckles . . . What's this? The rigging of a tall ship . . . A crossbow bolt has been discharged at my wrist and has bounced off . . . Lashings of rain and flying fish . . . Soon be in America . . ."

"Give Washington D.C. a wave from me, doc!"

"No can do, Stringy . . . That city no longer exists . . . The lava covered every square inch of the USA . . . I think I'm over land now . . . Just need to concentrate and stretch, stretch, stretch . . . Lots of seabirds perching along the entire length of my arm, but nothing has come to peck my hand . . . It's all dead here, I'm afraid, with no lizard, groundhog, cheerleader . . . I think I've crossed the entire continent. . . Now I'm over the Pacific Ocean . . . The velocity of my tentacle is immense!"

"You seem to be heating up, doc! Are you alright?"

The professor fumed and puffed and gears deep inside his lower frame started to whine. "Yes . . . I think so . . . Just passed Hawaii . . . Felt the rising vapor of a volcano . . . Now I'm in Japan, China, Turkestan . . . This is just a summary, you understand? My arm couldn't really go this fast without it melting, but I'm running out of wordage . . . I'm back over the sea: it must be the Mediterranean! Soon be here again . . . Take a peep at the guard and check that he's still facing forward."

The apeman moved to the door, peered through the grille and saw that the guard hadn't budged. But behind him, through the window, something was approaching over the picturesque landscape. It was the cyborg's hand on the end of his arm! Against all expectations, the Führer had succeeded in circumnavigating the globe with it; now it reached the window, slipped between the iron bars and hovered near the guard's belt. Stringent hissed instructions: "Left a bit! Down a bit! Up a bit! Right a bit! Bingo!" Thus the delicate operation was a triumph. Crinkle held the bunch of keys and slowly began retracting his tentacle.

Once his arm was back outside, and the keys were clutched even more tightly in his fist, he was free to retract it at maximum speed. It snapped back like a whip made from a complete line of latitude unpicked from the Earth's surface with a gigantic hook and snipped into a lash with a pair of super massive scissors. But less of that.

It retreated over the same lands and oceans it had already crossed. The seabirds were returned to their original locations, but not the laundry: that had all been pecked to gusty ribbons.

The tentacle was now only a mile or so long, but it had lost most of its elasticity, and the professor had to reel the rest of it in manually. When he finally managed to draw it back into the dungeon, he opened his fist with a fair amount of apprehension; but no one had stolen the bunch of keys in transit. He passed them to Stringent.

"Your arm is covered in albatross crap, doc!"

"Yes, dear boy, but a more polite name for the substance is *guano*. It's used for fertilizer or as an ingredient in explosives." He sighed. "It seems my arm is fated to hang limp and useless forever, but at least we have the means to escape our grim confines."

Stringent scratched his left buttock, found a flea there, examined it for a moment and then cast it aside. "Say, doc, if your arm is so flexible, why didn't you just loop it around the prison, which is shaped like a tower, and save yourself the trouble of reaching all the way around the entire world? The difference in mileage is vast!"

There was an awkward pause. The professor looked at the apeman and the apeman looked at the professor.

Finally Crinkle spoke. He said, "Um!"

Thin Crust and Thick Roof

It was a simple matter to unlock the dungeon door from the inside with a single turn of the appropriate key and then overpower the guard, who was paralyzed by the plot twist. They hurried along the corridor and down the steps, out of the prison, into the city. Dawn's blush was redecorating the eastern sky. With no coherent plan of action, they simply ran in a random direction, hoping for inspiration.

As they ran, Stringent said, "Tell me please, doc, what's the best way to address you? You seem to have lots of names and titles. Should I refer to you as Tobias, or as Crinkle, or as the professor, or as the Führer, or as the clockwork cyborg? Why do you have so many names? It's confusing for an apelike test pilot like me . . ."

"That's the fault of the author of this text, Stringy. He's clearly hoping his novel will be translated into Portuguese and so he's preparing for that eventuality. Unlike in English, repetitions sound awful in Portuguese, so it's better if he can refer to a character in many different ways. That's the only truly plausible explanation."

"Are we likely to be translated then, doc?"

"Well, Portugal's about the only country where his work is successful, so I guess there's a mild chance."

"What's the author like, doc? Is he a good guy?"

"I've never met him, my boy, and I have no desire to. I loathe him and everything he stands for, in fact."

"What did he do to you, doc?"

"Well, he turned me into a cyborg for one thing!"

109

"Yeah? For what thing, doc?"

"What do you mean, my dear boy?"

"For what one thing did he turn you into a cyborg?"

"No, Stringy, I didn't mean . . ."

As this conversation doesn't serve to move the action along, it shall be abandoned and I'll take the opportunity to report that the little brave band of escapees ran down alleys and up cobbled streets and across plazas and only finally stopped to catch their breath outside an all-night pizzeria. The apeman now realized that he was hungry. He mentioned this; and Nutloaf, Moonwash and Tantra all agreed that they were famished too. Quorn Joy only reported that he felt peckish.

"That's not the same as ravenous, man, but I could still masticate one of those margherita pizzas, dude!"

Stringent hesitated. When stranded in enemy territory, it's not normal to just stroll into a restaurant. Could they risk entering this place without being recaptured? What if the chef grew suspicious and reported them to his masters? What if he tried to hit them with a pizza shovel? Everything depended on how they behaved. Maybe pure sang-froid would carry them through: the sheer cheek of the act. The apeman checked his pockets and discovered he had only a single cent left; thanks to inflation this would be more than adequate to pay the bill.

"But what's your opinion, doc?" he asked.

"Yeah, man, you have psychic abilities now. Use them to learn if we'll get trouble inside," said Moonwash.

The professor sighed. "I'd rather not, because they make the rest of my brain ache. I think we should just take a chance and do it. Probably at this time in the morning the chef is too tired to notice anything unusual about us. Come on, we might as well go in."

And he was the first to open the door and enter.

Stringent and the HIPZIS followed and they selected a table in a quiet corner. There was only one other customer in the establishment: a fat man who had fallen asleep among the crusts of his pizzas. A waiter came up to them and asked, "What do you want?"

"I'll have a margherita," said Quorn Joy.

Tantra, Nutloaf and Moonwash didn't want cheese toppings. "Marinara for each of us, please," they ordered.

"I'll also have a marinara," said the professor, "but can I have nuts and bolts instead of oregano on mine?"

The waiter frowned, smoothed a thin eyebrow with one hand, flicked a napkin with the other, and finally came to a decision. "I suppose so, but it will cost you extra. Rusty or fresh?"

"The bolts rusty. The nuts unsalted," said Crinkle.

Now it was Stringent's turn. So far everything had proceeded smoothly enough. He beamed and said, "A margherita for me, but instead of olives can I have sweetcorn and pineapple?"

The waiter froze. The color rose in his cheeks.

"Intruders! Spies! Saboteurs! Alert the enforcers! Summon the hitmen! There are heretics among us! Help!"

The Führer rapped the apeman on the head with a tentacle curled into a spiral. "You fool, Stringy! We're in Sicily now, not Chicago! Nobody in Sicily puts pineapple on his pizza!"

"Sorry, doc, I wasn't to know! I'm half gorilla!"

"Well, I can't be too hard on you, I guess. But now we're going to have to flee more rapidly than before . . ."

They all jumped up from the table and hurtled into the street. The sky was getting lighter and brighter all the time: if one of the Bronson worlds didn't appear soon to cast concealing and confusing shadows, they would be easily spotted and arrested by the Cosa Nostra Damus. Still not having a plan, they ran randomly; and now gangsters were filling the streets and frowning deeply as they ran past.

Someone shouted: "Stop them! Sweetcorn!"

It was the chef. A burst of submachine gun fire followed his voice and a full magazine of hollow-nosed .45 bullets flattened themselves into lead amoebas on the walls of old buildings. More voices joined the fray. Fredo and Caldo could be heard bawling.

Stringent led them on a route so exceedingly twisted and devious that it should have thrown even a professional maze designer off the scent, but still the gangsters chased them. Then the apeman realized why. "It's your slack tentacle, doc! It's trailing behind you for a full mile and giving our position away. Tear it off quickly!"

The professor did so, laying the offending arm in the gutter of a steep alley. Water was pouring into this gutter from a broken pipe and the arm rapidly floated away like a sea serpent to the end of the alley and beyond. This would serve to fool their pursuers and send them the wrong way; but the reprieve would be brief, for if the escapees just kept running with no clear idea of where they were going, they would simply blunder back into trouble soon enough. What to do?

The Führer held his bell jar in two tentacles as he ran and concentrated his nascent clairvoyant powers to find a way out of the predicament. This desperate action of last resort paid dividends almost immediately. "Here's an abandoned garage to hide in!"

The apeman looked around. "Where, doc?"

"End of the next paragraph . . ."

They scurried around five more corners, found themselves confronting a cul-de-sac full of junk. They climbed over the junk and located a rotting wooden door that yielded easily to a gorilla's savage booted kick. Behind the door was some sort of garage.

They tumbled inside and coughed as they inhaled dust. In the center of the garage was a big object covered with a tarpaulin. Stringent extracted a splinter from his ankle and said:

"We're safe for the time being, but we can't stay here forever. What do you reckon we should do now?"

"That's a difficult question, my boy."

"If only we had some herbal tea!" lamented Moonwash. "Then we'd be able to, like, open our minds to positive vibes, man. Marigold, borage and cranberry is good for that, I hear!"

Quorn Joy nodded in confirmation. "Yeah!"

"Why don't we see what's under the tarpaulin?" suggested Nutloaf, and before Stringent could mock her for this absurdity, she had tugged off the green covering with a deft flick of her wrist. Beneath stood an object that neither the apeman nor the professor had seen since 1932. It was such an unexpected sight for them that they both were speechless for no less than three sentences. This one. And this one. And also this one. Then together they cried out: "The Crinkle Crisp!"

Tantra shrugged. "Another kind of airplane. So what? It looks really ancient and probably doesn't work."

Stringent shook his head disapprovingly. "You don't understand. The professor designed this one himself."

"What's it doing here, man?" Quorn Joy asked.

The Führer stifled a titanium laugh. "I now recall that I sold one to the Italian air force just before we went to visit Jack Northrop in El Segundo. This must be it! And so it has been languishing here ever since. What an amazingly contrived coincidence!"

He used his tentacles as grappling irons to hoist himself up and then he clambered along the fuselage towards the cockpit. He tried to peer inside but the windows were too dusty, so he called for Stringent to join him. A cyborg rarely has enough organic matter on him to use as a cloth; and if he had attempted to rub the glass with one of his metallic parts he would probably have scratched it. As it was, while he waited for the apeman, he scratched his own metallic parts . . .

Stringent's powerful and hairy arms enabled him to swing himself into a position right next to the professor. He wiped the glass. "The fuel gauge reads full, doc! She's ready to fly."

Tantra raised an objection. "But we'll have to move all the junk in the cul -de-sac to get the contraption out of the garage; and even if we manage that, there's no way to take off in such narrow streets. Whoever got it in here must have used a shoehorn!"

The Führer exuberantly clapped two tentacles. "But that's not the case at all, my dear! It can ascend just like a helicopter. I designed the Crinkle Crisp to have VTOL capability."

"That stands for Vertical Take Off and Landing," Stringent explained patronizingly to the beautiful girls.

Tantra still wasn't convinced. "It doesn't resemble any helicopter. The propeller is mounted at the front."

The professor folded six tentacles across his tungsten chest. "I see I'll have to explain the *channel wing* concept to you, my dear. When a wing moves in air, a pressure difference is created between its upper and lower surface. Higher pressure on the lower side lifts up the wing. It's a method that depends entirely on forward motion. But my alternative technique is to keep the wing in a fixed place and to draw in the air with a turbine, in other words to channel air over and under a static wing, creating the same lift, but applying it all vertically."

"With no lateral movement at all?" asked Tantra.

"Very little. Once the craft that utilizes this new lifting method is aloft, the angle of the turbine can be adjusted so that it now pulls the aircraft in the orthodox manner and the subsequent lift is created the old-fashioned way. But the upshot of all this theory is that we can escape the garage by going *straight up* through the roof."

"I'm not sure about that," said Nutloaf, pointing upwards. "I think those are wrought-iron girders. Their weight will kill the lift of your wings and we'll plummet back down. We'll have to remove each girder by hand first, but they're much too high to reach."

"The professor can reach them from here!" cried Stringent. He turned to the cyborg. "Extend those arms and do it, doc! You told me you have the strength of . . . How many bears?"

Crinkle answered curtly, "Thirty exactly."

Moonwash began to dance. "Dude, that's a lot of bears! Soon get that roof off with all those groovy bears!"

Stringent frowned. "Wait a moment! How many bears were needed to break open the dungeon door, doc?"

Crinkle said nothing; and his brain gave nothing away.

"How many?" repeated Stringent.

The answer came in a small voice, "Twenty-nine."

The apeman blinked. "So you mean all that around-the-world business was for nothing? Sometimes I really don't understand you, doc. But that's life, I guess. Just lift up the roof!"

"I can't, dear boy. Even at the maximum of my bear power those rusty girders are heavier than I can bear."

"Tee hee! Two uses of the word 'bear' in one sentence, doc! Is that bad writing or does the fact that the meanings are different absolve our author from blame? What do you think?"

But the professor had no opinion on the issue. "I'm picking up psychic emanations of a threatening nature! It appears our pursuers have located us. They're standing outside the garage right now. We need to act fast! If I still had my limp tentacle we could have used the *guano* on it to build a bomb and blown the roof off that way, but as it turns out this is an utterly futile paragraph; we're in trouble."

A voice could be heard in the cul-de-sac. "We know you are hiding in there." It was Fredo and he sounded both tired and angry. "Come out with your hands up or we'll do our worst."

"Can't you do better than that?" taunted Stringent.

"Ah!" cried Caldo. "So you really are in there. We weren't sure before but now we know! Prepare to die!"

"You are a fool, Stringy!" sighed Crinkle.

Quorn Joy was more confident. "Listen, man! They intend to do their worst. I had feared they were going to do their best and succeed in killing us, but they plan to deliberately fail!"

The professor shook his head in exasperation.

Something was hurled through the door: a spherical black object with a length of string dangling from it.

The string sparked and hissed and grew shorter.

It was a melodramatic bomb!

"Throw it back, doc! Before it explodes!"

The professor regarded it sadly. "Sorry, dear boy, I can't do that. Time for another commercial break, I'm afraid. There's no way I can reschedule it. Just help me out as best you can."

"Doc! What the heck's this one promoting?"

"Let me just check. Ah yes! CLEAN-O-PATRA'S WASHABLE PAPYRUS CLOTHES FOR MEN AND MUMMYS' BOYS. CHEAP, CHEERFUL, CLASSIC. ARE *YOU* TOO SPHINXY FOR YOUR SHIRT? ALL STOCK SOURCED FROM CERTIFIED PHARAOAH-TRADERS."

"No pyramid selling involved!" added Stringent.

The voices of Fredo and Caldo wafted in from outside: "Available in the best Cheops—we mean shops!"

"Stare out of the page!" hissed Crinkle.

"And don't forget to diverge your eyes," said Stringent.

"But it's painful!" they protested.

It was Nutloaf who saved the day. She picked up the bomb and waited until the fuse had burned down to a precise point. This timing was a very delicate operation. Then she hurled it with all her strength. As it left her grip, she flicked both her wrists, imparting spin to it. And so the Magnus Effect took over and it levitated easily.

Moonwash, Quorn Joy and Tantra instantly ducked down behind the Crinkle Crisp. The bomb exploded . . .

The blast cut short the advert, knocking the apeman to the ground and leaving a dent in the Führer's trapezoid. The HIPZIS cried out: "Come on, dudes, the roof has been blown off!"

And so it had. Like an improvised Heighth Charge, the bomb's energy was focused mainly upwards, ripping the iron girders out of the decaying brickwork and scattering them over the city of Palermo: one of them fell on the ultra-stretched limousine and bisected it neatly in two. But none of the HIPZIS were aware of this fact.

And neither was Stringent. He staggered to his feet, turned and jumped up the side of the Crinkle Crisp, sliding back the canopy and slotting into the pilot's seat. He squinted at the controls, worked levers and ignited the engine. It croaked into reluctant life.

"Hurry, doc! Lift the others, then pull yourself up!"

Crinkle responded with appropriate efficiency. He lifted Nutloaf first, then Tantra, then the two men. The aircraft had sustained some damage in the explosion but nothing serious.

Fredo and Caldo appeared in the doorway. They raised and pointed the submachine guns cradled in their arms. "Whatta mistake to make!" they screamed as they beheld the scenario.

And they opened fire. Zang tumb tumb! Peow!

Unfortunately I don't know how to spell *phchhyowngg*, which was the actual sound made by those bullets . . .

But that doesn't much matter, because the Führer waved his tantalum arms with astounding speed and dexterity and deflected every single one. Now the magazines were exhausted.

"Go, Stringy, go!" he bellowed, as he climbed into the cockpit. With a primal laugh, the apeman squeezed the throttle hard and the dormant old turbine screeched and wheezed, sucking in dust-laden air and diverting it through channels cunningly arranged to fool the wings into thinking they were moving forward and creating their own airflow. Not that wings are sentient, but you know what I mean.

Up shuddered the Crinkle Crisp. The professor frowned and said, "The engine sounds different from the way I recall. I don't think this is the 450-hp Pratt & Whitney Wasp C 9-cylinder radial engine I originally fitted. I guess the Italian air force changed it."

Stringent nodded. "Yeah, doc, it's got a harder hum. I reckon it's a Fiat AS.6 24-cylinder vee-type with an output somewhere between 2800 and 3000-hp; same as the Macchi MC.72, designed by Mario Castoldi for the Schneider Trophy way back in 1931."

"Stop showing off your author's knowledge!" chided Tantra.

"It's too boring!" confirmed Nutloaf.

Stringent glanced over his shoulder. "He doesn't really know this stuff off the top of his head; he looks it up and lets the reader assume he's more erudite than he is. It's the oldest trick in the book. And when I say 'book' I don't mean this book, but *the* book."

"The book of tricks," clarified the professor.

They were high above the ruined garage, so Stringent pulled the lever that changed the angle of the turbine.

They began to accelerate away from Palermo. "Where are we heading, doc? I've forgotten the plot again!"

"South, my dear boy. Always south."

Telepathic Winking Dinosaurs

The corrupt government of Little Italy had no vertical cannon to endanger the progress of the Crinkle Crisp, and Stringent managed to fly across the length of Sicily from north to south in perfect safety. Soon they were over the sea again, the smooth but filthy Mediterranean, and the apeman made sure his altitude never exceeded three hundred feet, because of the clouds of atmospheric junk that clustered very densely in this region. Halfway to Malta, Tantra asked him for a favor.

"Will you please teach me to fly, Mr. Strange?"

The cockpit contained three rows of seats. Tantra sat next to the pilot in the front; Moonwash, Quorn Joy and Nutloaf occupied the middle row; the professor had the rear row all to himself. Now he leaned forward and said with a sigh, "Really, my dear, this is hardly a good time for a novice to learn how to handle my invention."

Stringent shook his head. "I disagree, doc."

"But what if she stalls it into a dive and kills us all? The Rushans will stomp across the world unopposed!"

"Yeah, that's one consideration, doc, but look at it another way: at the moment you rely entirely on me to do the flying, so it makes sense to pass my skills to at least one other. Since the earliest days of aviation, females have flown, in fact there's a name for them: *aviatrix*. I have no problem at all with showing this gal the ropes."

"Wow, man!" gushed Quorn Joy. "You mean this thing is powered by cordage like our wicker cable cars?"

"Just a figure of speech," chuckled Stringent.

"Thanks, Mr. Strange," said Tantra.

The professor muttered unhappily to himself, but the apeman wouldn't be dissuaded from his decision to allow the HIPZI girl to take the controls and perform basic maneuvers under his careful direction. First he put the machine on autopilot, then he unbuckled his seatbelt and exchanged seats with Tantra. This was the tricky part.

She had to climb over him, wriggling her buttocks on his pelvic region as she squirmed across; and for his part, he had to push his groin upwards to impart extra velocity to her motion.

When they were securely seated again, he reached across and switched off the autopilot. The airplane bucked but Tantra remained calm and she handled the joystick with a light touch, never yanking it too hard; she was a natural, he decided. Born to soar.

But Professor Crinkle was still determined to be critical. "She must be doing it wrong, Stringy. The revs are too high for the speed we're doing. I think she has lowered the landing flaps by mistake. The engine's fighting against a strong restraining force."

Stringent checked every dial. "No, doc, Tantra's handling it like a real professional, almost like a veteran. She's a Pink Baron in the making! But I agree there's too much drag. Feels like we've been hooked by a gigantic fishing line. Let me take a look." And so saying, he opened the passenger door and leaned out into empty air, peering back. Then he righted himself and slammed the door. "Goddamn!"

"What's the problem, Stringy? A tractor beam?"

"Nope, doc. We're trailing a huge commercial banner behind us. FOR ALL YOUR KITCHEN SINK NEEDS WHY NOT VISIT LUKE DISH-WASHER'S EMPORIUM TODAY, is what it says."

The professor nodded. "This must be because the last advert was cut short by the bomb in the garage. Those scoundrels certainly expect their money's worth! I'll cut it free with one of my tentacles." And he opened the window and turned the end of one of his arms into a knife blade. He then ex-tended this arm and severed the cords holding the banner. Almost immediately the Crisp accelerated.

"Glad to be free of that encumbrance, doc!"

"Yes, dear boy, and now we don't need to worry so much about fuel. I think we might even cross half of Africa before the tanks run dry. At last things are going smoothly for us!"

Stringent scratched his head. "You want to fly right into the interior of Africa? And that's our ultimate destination? I don't share your confidence we can hold out for quite that long."

"Maybe not with just a normal tank of fuel, Stringy, but this particular model is equipped with two spares under the wings. I noticed them earlier and did the mental calculations. There should be enough high-octane gas in them to get us to the Cameroons."

"So *that's* where we're headed! Gee, thanks, doc!"

"I didn't plan to tell you until we arrived, because I don't want to spoil the surprise for the reader." He twisted his metallic mouth. "Assuming we actually have any readers, that is!"

Stringent examined the console and found a lever. "This is the one that controls the spares. I wonder what will happen if I pull it?" With a sharp crack, something fell off the aircraft. The apeman craned his neck to peer down. Two torpedo shaped objects were growing smaller directly below. The professor uttered a deep groan.

"You've jettisoned all our extra fuel, Stringy!"

"Oops, doc! I really am a monkey-spanking dunderhead at times! I'll make it up to you somehow, honest!"

"We'll have to land and refuel somewhere in the Sahara now! And we are bound to have adventures wherever we stop. You've single-handedly extended this novel by 10,000 words!"

Stringent bit his lower lip and said nothing.

But Tantra continued to fly south . . .

Although no one in the Crinkle Crisp would ever realize it, the banner that had been cut off the aircraft flapped away and landed on Malta, right on the head of a cruel tyrant who had taken over that island. It suffocated him while he was making a pompous and bellicose speech in a square in Valletta, the capital. As for the fuel tanks: one of them smashed a hole in the hull of a pirate ship, sinking it instantly and drowning the nasty crew, while the other brained a hungry plesiosaur who was surfacing to devour some earlier victims of the pirates who had been forced to walk the plank. Mistakes are sometimes beneficial.

"Soon we'll reach the coast of Libya," said the professor, "and I admit I'm a little apprehensive about what we might find there. The colony that was founded by Signor Balbo many years ago ceased all communication when Bronson Bravo showed up. If we still had the spare fuel, we could take a detour around the country, but now we're compelled to fly directly over it. I have an unsettled feeling."

"What kind of unsettled feeling precisely, doc?"

"An extra vague one, Stringy."

"Can't you discover what perils are waiting for us in Libya with your psychic powers?" asked Stringent.

"I don't want to, dear boy, but I guess I could."

"Go on, doc! It makes sense!"

Crinkle sighed and he clutched his bell jar in several tentacles and concentrated as hard as he could. He felt as if spiral energy was radiating from the deepest part of his mind. This energy could gather information about anything it flowed over, and return that information to the sending brain. But as he continued to transmit the spiral, he felt another helix of similar energy interacting with it. This other helix was stronger than his and not human. Nor was it robotic.

The professor tried to disengage from it, but he was trapped. With an awful internal shudder he realized that a greater telepathic brain than his own was infiltrating his consciousness and trying to take him over. Mind control! He had given himself away to a vile hostile sentience and made himself vulnerable to some grotesque psychic predator that was roaming the astral plane. He fought to retain his identity, but couldn't keep hold of it. The other mind was too clever.

"Must obey my new masters . . . Must divert this plane to a landing in Tripoli . . . Must overpower the pilot with my tentacles . . . Must deliver us to the Plenipotentiaries of Zyra . . ."

None of the passengers heard these words. Nor did they notice that his tentacles were snaking forward like rigid lassoes, preparing to snare and restrict any opposing movement.

This behavior might have been reacted to by the HIPZIS, who could have tried to snap him out of his trance with verbal reassurance, but they were distracted by a new occurrence. And so was the apeman. Something had broken through the aerial junk clouds: an opalescent machine in the shape of a discus. It moved silently, disregarding the laws of flight like an anti-gravity simile or an extraterrestrial metaphor. It was several minutes before Stringent found his voice.

"Doc! What in the name of bishop-bashing?"

He pointed at the circular object that was skimming towards them and continued, "It looks like a crystal pizza! But I thought the Little Italians didn't have advanced technology!"

"I don't think it belongs to the Cosa Nostra Damus," said Nutloaf. "In fact I don't think it's Italian at all."

"That's a flying saucer, dude!" cried Moonwash.

"The Pectorals are, like, coming!" blubbered Quorn Joy. He groped for his packet of Arbeit cigarettes, fumbled with them and spilled reefers like jack-straws all through the cockpit.

"Who are the Pectorals?" demanded Stringent.

"The inhabitants of Bronson Alpha, man! They're alien beings, dude! They resemble human women but have much vaster bosoms. Firmer too. And they're all utterly sex starved!"

A beam of light emanated from the sharp edge of the saucer, scanning the occupants of the Crinkle Crisp.

This beam touched the professor for only a moment before passing on. It also barely grazed Nutloaf and Tantra; but it lingered for a few seconds on Moonwash and Quorn Joy; then it reached Stringent and fixed on him without deviating at all. Clearly he had been chosen, but exactly how was a question unanswered. He frowned.

And suddenly, with a pop, he vanished!

"Gone," commented Nutloaf.

"They've dematerialized him!" wailed Moonwash. "They'll reassemble his molecules back on their saucer and take him to Bronson Alpha, where he'll be forced to 'earn' his keep. In less than a week his groin chakra will be completely drained of energy!"

"The Pectorals never need a night off. I'm weeping like a squonk just thinking about it," said Quorn Joy.

"I'm sure Mr. Strange will cope," said Tantra.

They watched in amazement as the flying saucer suddenly zoomed up at a ninety-degree angle, scattering the aerial junk like chaff, disappearing in a mere few seconds. But the HIPZIS weren't given time to comment on this event. The tentacles of the professor looped around them. Tantra was pinned in the pilot's seat, but Crinkle moved her arms for her and worked the controls by proxy. Although he didn't know how to fly, the sentience that had taken him over surely did.

"I'm now in control of this airplane! We are going to land at Tripoli. Our new masters await us there. You must not resist the will of your new masters. You will submit! Submit!"

"Man, it's some kind of supernatural skyjacking!"

The Crinkle Crisp approached the North African coast. A city gleamed below in the light of late morning.

The professor put the plane into a shallow dive. Tantra struggled but it was no use. They circled a red castle that stood near the waterfront. With a skill not his own, Tobias Crinkle altered the angle of the turbine so that the aircraft would descend vertically.

Down into an open square it went.

It bumped on its wheels once. Then came to rest.

With one of his spare tentacles, the professor slid the canopy back and lowered the HIPZIS one at a time onto the ground. Then he eased himself out of the back seat and joined them.

Instantly his mind cleared. He was himself again!

An unwelcome welcoming committee had assembled to greet them, or possibly eat them. Half a dozen tyrannosaurs and a couple of triceratops stood next to the plane. The tyrannosaurs wore red fezzes, that conical hat with a dangling tassel that keeps flies off; but the triceratops wore turbans and veils that concealed their horns.

One of the tyrannosaurs gave the professor a long slow wink, but this wasn't a signal of complicity. It was a physical reflex that accompanied a transmission of a telepathic message. That's how these beings justified the title of this chapter. They were the Telepathic Winking Dinosaurs of Bronson Bravo, but in fact they called their own planet 'Zyra.' The nation once known as Libya was now a colony of theirs, indeed the only colony they had established so far on Earth.

Words entered the professor's head, and even though he hadn't spoken them, they were in his own accent.

"My name," they said, "is Grkkghj and I'm the Chief Plenipotentiary's gamekeeper. These are my assistants: Hgggru, Lushdjiis, Udhdjklsjdhoik, Qdlkjjkdwj, Ndgdgdgs, Saaailjkdnk and Bubba. You are now our official property. Do not attempt to resist."

The cyborg relayed this message to his friends.

"What do they, like, intend to do with us, man?" gasped Moonwash as he hid behind Nutloaf and Tantra. Meanwhile, Quorn Joy was attempting to hide behind *him* while lighting up another joint at the same time. With a grin that displayed his vicious teeth, the tyrannosaur turned his massive skull in the direction of the HIPZIS.

Then he winked again. And Moonwash heard the words, "Dude, we're going to use you in our, like, games."

"Why, that's not so bad!" gasped Moonwash.

"Yeah, we enjoy playing games, especially chess and checkers, but not backgammon, because of the owls," added Quorn Joy, as he blew rotating smoke rings out of his nostrils.

The dinosaurs opened their mouths and began laughing, but nothing of this mockery could be heard until they started winking too. Then giggles appeared in the minds of the prisoners. Grkkghj directed a new wink at all of them and sent this explanation:

"We were referring to our gladiatorial games."

"Bad vibe!" said Moonwash.

THE PLANET OF SEX STARVED WOMEN

Stringent found himself standing on the deck of the alien spacecraft in the middle of a dozen curvaceous women who were caressing him with soft but vigorous strokes of delicate but experienced hands. He blinked shyly and rubbed his eyelids with his knuckles, but the interior illumination was soothing and seemed to radiate from no single source. It was ambient. He couldn't think of any remark to make.

"Don't be frightened," said one of the women.

The apeman frowned deeply and regarded her carefully. She was like all the others: dressed in skimpy silver foil knickers, a transparent space helmet and a brassiere that was also transparent, consisting of two glass domes hermetically sealing each breast. Her vital statistics were enough to give a statistician a cardiac arrest or at least a police caution. Stringent felt weak and looked for a place to sit.

"Try these cushions," said a different woman.

He collapsed gratefully on a yielding pile that had been plumped up in the center of the circular room. All around him were flashing crystals and glinting jewels. It seemed that all the machines on this saucer were made from varieties of quartz. The woman who had spoken first stood over him and Stringent found himself looking up at a pair of athletic smooth thighs that could undoubtedly juice oranges.

"My name is Tolrah and I am Queen of Bellus."

"Pleased to meet you—I think."

She smiled. "Bellus is better known to you as Bronson Alpha, after the man who discovered it, Jiggery P. Bronson. The 'P' stands for Pokery, by the

125

way. All the Bronson worlds have their own names. Bronson Bravo, as your friends have learned in a different chapter, is actually called Zyra. As for Bronson Charlie, we never communicate with its denizens but we have reason to believe they refer to their own world as Harmonica. These three worlds periodically enter this solar system and fall into orbit around the Earth, only to drift away later."

Stringent gasped, "You mean to say that all this has happened before? How many times? And when was the last occasion? Maybe it explains the sinking of Atlantis and Lemuria!"

Tolrah continued to smile. "It's unusual for all three planets to arrive in Earth orbit at the same time. Usually it's just one or two. The last time the alignment took its present form was during the Permian Extinction, which wiped out more than ninety-percent of your fauna; but other factors were involved back then and it's unlikely the effect will be so catastrophic now. Anyway, that's the background."

"Are you taking me to Bellus against my will?"

"I'm afraid so. We need you."

Stringent shifted his position. "What for?"

"Basically, we want you to give us a damn good seeing-to."

"Every woman on the saucer!"

"No, my lusty fellow, every woman on our entire planet . . ."

"Holy testosterone!" he cried.

And the other girls giggled and cast seductive glances at the test pilot. A smile flickered across Stringent's face as he contemplated the prospect of spending the rest of his life as the slave of these rampant females, but he also felt twinges of guilt. What about Professor Crinkle and his HIPZI friends? He had a deep affection for all of them. Could he really abandon them and the rest of his world to the evil intentions of the pandimensional being called Rush and his acolytes?

"If I satisfy all of you, will you return me to Earth?"

Tolrah considered this proposition. She took advice from several other girls and finally nodded. "Very well, that seems fair. Success in satiating us will result in your freedom; and we will even return you to Africa, the same continent over which we abducted you. Never let it be said that the nymphomaniacs of Bellus are unjust."

Stringent replied, "Then I'm happy to come with you."

"I hope you'll come *over* us too . . ."

126

"Certainly I'll agree to that!"

Tolrah smirked. "Even if you didn't, my virile fellow, you would have no choice." And she picked up a weapon from a rack and aimed it at him, just as a reminder of their true relationship. This weapon was a gun but it was a design the apeman had never seen before: a ribbed purple cylinder with a bulbous slitted head. Two spherical magazines under the barrel fed some form of plasma energy to the firing chamber. These magazines were covered in short curly electrical wires.

Stringent held up his hands in mock surrender.

"Hey, don't worry about me, gal! I won't try to escape. How far would I get anyway? I may be the best test pilot in both hemispheres of my own world, but I doubt I could fly this crystal discus more than a yard without ditching it. I won't cause trouble!"

Tolrah lowered the gun. "Very well." Her nipples had visibly hardened behind their bosom helmets. "Are you hungry or thirsty? Is there anything you require before we reach Bellus?"

Stringent shook his head. But then he said. "Actually, I am wondering about the significance of wearing helmets on your breasts. It's something to do with atmospheric pressure?"

"You are very perceptive," said Tolrah.

He acknowledged the compliment. "Thanks. Information is what you can give me. Why don't you take the brassieres off? It must be stuffy for your bosoms inside such fish bowls?"

"The atmospheric pressure of Bellus is far higher than Earth's because our planet is much larger than yours. We are unable to breathe the air of your world without asphyxiating; and that is why we wear helmets that contain their own oxygen supply at the correct pressure for us. The same principle applies to our breasts. If they are exposed to the lower pressure of Earth, they swell enormously."

Stringent arched an eyebrow. "Oh yes?"

Tolrah nodded. "We deliberately maintain the internal pressure of this saucer at the Earth standard so that you (and any other males we wish to kidnap) are not squashed flat. It's easier for us to wear helmets in a lower pressure environment than for you to wear a reinforced suit in our higher pressure environment. Access to your groin would be severely hampered by even the most unobtrusive exoskeleton. There are perils for us in this system, of course: a single crack in the cup of a brassiere and the exposed bosom will inflate a thousand fold!"

Stringent stared out of the nearest porthole. In fact, the circumference of the spaceship was one continuous window. Earth was dwindling far to one side; the moon was nowhere to be seen; but Bronson Alpha was now enormous, dominating half the sky.

"But what happens when we land?" he asked.

Tolrah said, "We have installed nuclear-powered pumps that maintain our planet's atmosphere at a suitable number of bars for your physiology. The cost was staggering, but we deem it worthwhile. We are very randy, you see, and haven't been serviced properly for a long time. Personally I expect at least a hundred orgasms."

Stringent scratched his nose. "A suitable number of bars, you say? Do you intend to get me drunk first?"

Tolrah sighed. "A *bar* is a unit of pressure; and your pun wasn't good enough to pass quality control, so I'll ask the editor of this book to delete it. If he doesn't, it's because he wasn't reading as carefully as he should. I imagine he was distracted by his own mental images of vast bosoms. I'll go further and state that the majority of your male readers are now staring into space—and I don't mean outer space—and daydreaming about large bosoms. I'm afraid it's inevitable."

"I once knew a Protogruppenführer who used excessive bosoms as a safeguard against aerial attack. They are special things, for sure. I do like big ones, I'm forced to confess . . ."

Tolrah pointed at the planet Bellus. "See how swiftly it grows vaster, its hemispheres swelling until they dominate our vision? If my brassiere broke, you would think that two new worlds had entered the solar system. How about that for a comparison?"

"Evocative," agreed Stringent, "but not wholly accurate."

Tolrah scowled. "Why not?"

The apeman calmly explained, "Because your nipples would spoil the illusion. Planets have poles but they don't have nipples. Your bosoms are the converse of that rule. I don't see any poles on either one, but I do see nipples of extraordinary firmness and ripeness—or to be poetic, luscious russet nipples with autumnal aureoles."

"I think we have chosen you well, Mr. Strange!"

Stringent frowned to hear Tolrah speak his name, but then he recalled that he had introduced himself to her in a paragraph not included in this book for the sake of saving space.

By space I mean room—not interplanetary space.

The saucer suddenly shuddered.

"Turbulence?" cried the apeman. "In a vacuum?"

Tolrah rushed to a crystal console and fiddled with buttons that looked like gems. She leaned over to read a monitor, displaying her perfect rump to best effect. "Space between the Bronson Worlds isn't actually a perfect vacuum," she explained. "The atmospheres of the planets have mingled to a certain degree because of the complexity of the gravitational fields. The upshot of this is that there are numerous air pockets that move chaotically in the gaps between the worlds."

The spacecraft vibrated more violently.

"Are we in an air pocket now?" Stringent asked.

Tolrah turned to face him and nodded. "Indeed so. Prepare yourself for a rough ride, almost as rough as the one you'll get on the surface of Bellus when we mount you passionately."

Stringent rubbed his chin. "There's something I need to tell you. I can only perform if I'm allowed to pay for it. I hope you have money on your world—otherwise it's no can do!"

"Fear not, my fine hybrid. We have planned for every eventuality. We stole a human printing press many years ago and any type of currency can be forged on it without difficulty."

"Fantastic! In that case, I'm ready to go!"

"We'll advance you the sum of $1,000,000 to start with; but that won't last you more than a few weeks."

"You speak good German, by the way!" said Stringent. It had only just occurred to him that his author had forgotten to tackle the difficulties of mutually unintelligible languages since the scene set in Goodvibe. Tolrah seemed pleased by the observation.

But before she could respond to it, a lurch sent her reeling against one of the other women. The two brassieres collided with considerable force and Tolrah's cups shattered. She lifted her arms to restrain the inevitable expansion but she was too late. Like universes in the instant after the Big Bang, they ballooned tremendously.

She was facing Stringent now and the apeman jumped up to offer his assistance to her, so it turned out he ended up standing engulfed in her cleavage, globes of sweet lady flesh on both sides squeezing tightly and holding him firmly in place. He sighed and undulated his head from side to side, making blubbering noises.

So that's what perfect happiness felt like . . .

THE LITERARY GLADIATORS

The ancient red castle to which Crinkle, Moonwash, Nutloaf, Quorn Joy and Tantra were forced to march at unsheathed triceratops horn point by the Telepathic Winking Dinosaurs was none other than the Al-Saraya al-Hamra, which had once housed the Jamahiriya Museum, one of the best collections of classical art in the Mediterranean area. In fact the museum was still there, but the antique weapons had been removed and conveyed to the nearby site of Leptis Magna.

Despite the plesiosaur that had been killed by the falling fuel tank just offshore, there seemed to be only two species of dinosaur on land. It was a mystery as to why each tyrannosaur wore a fez; and as for the headgear favored by the triceratops, a minimal amount of research reveals that the turban and veil combination is called a *tagelmust* and is dyed with indigo. At no point did the prisoners ask for an explanation about these hats, for they had other things to fret about.

The tyrannosaur named Grkkghj explained that it was his duty as the official gamekeeper to secure new contestants for the arena. Gladiatorial battles were held every Tuesday—*Chewsday* in their own language—in the amphitheater that was one of the most impressive things about Leptis Magna. They were currently short of trident-fodder and thus very happy to host visitors from abroad. He promised that combat training would be available before the next massacre.

"But we're pacifists, man!" objected Quorn Joy.

Grkkghj winked in reply, "In that case you will be, like, booed by the audience while you expire, dude."

"Can't we opt out of the games?" asked Tantra.

"Afraid not. We have a low regard for humans, I am sorry to say, and you have absolutely no rights here."

The professor spoke up. "Technically I'm not a human but a cyborg. I assume it may be possible for me to formally apply for Zyran citizenship and avoid a messy death that way?"

"Nice try," said Grkkghj, "but your brain is wholly human and that's enough to condemn you. I do believe, however, you might stand a chance of winning all your fights. Looking at your impressive array of arms and the strength of your body, you could easily end up as a champion, or even as the champion of champions, or conceivably even as a champion of the champion of champions. Indeed."

"But I'm squeamish and hate bloodshed!"

"Well, you have precisely five days in which to alter your attitude on that particular point. Don't try and escape: my telepathic powers will bind you in an unbreakable astral web."

"You cold blooded monster!" growled Crinkle.

"Actually," said Grkkghj with only a faint trance of annoyance, "we're warm blooded, just like mammals."

"Perhaps so. But you're a bunch of terrible lizards to me!" retorted the professor with an anguished sob.

The tyrannosaur bowed low with exaggerated ironic politeness, but his fez didn't fall off; perhaps it was glued to his head. Then he turned to go, closing the door of the cell behind him. This time there was no guard with a bunch of keys standing outside in the corridor. And the heavy iron door was even more bear-resistant than the one in Little Italy. They were truly stuck. Moonwash collapsed in a corner and began crying. Nutloaf did her best to provide comfort with kisses.

As for Quorn Joy, he lit two joints at the same time and puffed on both of them like some insane organic chimney. Tantra examined the walls of the cell, searching for weak points.

But there were none. This castle dated from a time when builders took a special pride in their work and designed structures to last for centuries. Its outer wall formed part of the wall of the Medina, the old town that had been erected shortly after the Ottomans occupied Tripoli in 1551. With a frustrated growl, the professor moved to the window, a filigreed opening that looked more fragile than it was. Forcing this might have been within his capabilities, but was pointless.

Because it led *into* the Medina, which was sealed from the rest of the city.

The drop from the cell to the ground was too high for the strongest cyborg to survive, let alone a group of HIPZIS. He sighed and surveyed the whitewashed buildings and narrow twisting streets. Directly opposite his window stood the impressive Ahmed Pasha Karamanli Mosque, with its octagonal minaret and five decorated doorways. He knew this was its name because his psychic powers told him so. His Psi-Suppressor Cluster was truly dead now, every last cell.

The realization of this made him pout, but then he paused and resolved to use his powers to improve their situation, if such a thing was possible. So he fully opened his inner eye to the spectral reality that exists behind the grosser material counterpart in which we do all our basic living. The spectral reality is the spooky one.

Images flooded his mind, and they brought hope as well as gore. With a little skip, he clapped ten hands.

"We don't have to worry about fighting!"

Moonwash had stopped weeping, but his cheeks were damp with tears and his eyes were bloodshot. "What do you mean, man? You heard what the tyrannosaur gamekeeper said!"

The cyborg extended his technetium tongue, but without any intention to belittle the HIPZI; it was merely an expression of relief. "I sent out the extrasensory part of my mind to investigate the surrounding regions. The ruins of Leptis Magna, where the games are held, are located less than 50 miles east of here, and I probed the place where the spirits of all the dead fighters spookily swirl and congeal."

"The cemetery, you mean, man?"

"No, my friend, the kitchens. For the Telepathic Winking Dinosaurs of Bronson Bravo feast on the losers!"

"But triceratops are herbivores!" cried Nutloaf.

"Yes, that's an oversight, it seems. Maybe the triceratopses get to keep the devoured men's possessions?"

"Are you, like, sure that's the right plural!?"

The professor ignored the criticism. He didn't give a hoot, snort or roar what more than one triceratops should be called. "One thing is certain: the tyrannosaurs *do* eat meat," he said, "and we are meat! The spirits weren't talkative; I don't conclude they are sentient souls, but spiritual echoes that have been recorded on the fabric of spacetime, fixed into place by trauma, namely the violence of their ends."

"That theory of ghosts is called Residual Haunting," said Tantra. "Also known as the Stone Tape Theory."

The professor nodded gratefully. "Anyway, these attenuated phantoms managed to convey an interesting fact about the 'games.' Only writers are allowed to fight. Not normal people!"

"Are you sure? That seems an eccentric rule."

"Yes, it does, but that's not my fault. It seems that Signor Balbo set up a colony with high cultural ambitions. Libya became a sort of laboratory of literature; and more books were published here every year than in any other country. But when Bronson Alpha made its first pass, the governors realized that their experiment was in danger of being annihilated, so they decided to take action. They instructed agents—secret agents, not literary ones—to kidnap the finest writers in the world and convey them to Libya, where they were frozen in cryogenic suspended animation until such time as it was safe to reawaken them."

"Man, that was an ambitious program!"

The professor smiled. "Indeed so, Quorn Joy. And it may have worked if Bronson Bravo hadn't also gone into Earth orbit. The inhabitants of that second rogue planet happened to choose Libya to set up their own colony. They wiped out Balbo's descendants and discovered the hidden cache of frozen writers. Since then, they have been thawing them out periodically and urging them to kill each other."

Tantra said, "So if we just explain that we're not writers, they'll let us go free? It seems too easy to me."

"Yeah, dude, there has to be some catch!"

The professor shrugged. "If there is, I can't guess what it is. None of us have ever written a book, have we? No! That's pretty clear and if we take care to stress this point to our jailers, I'm sure they'll see reason and allow us to walk out of here and resume our quest. So like I said earlier, there's no need to worry about our safety."

The bolts on the door were thrown back and Grkkghj entered, but this time his fez was at an angle. "I heard all that telepathically," he said, "and it's my duty to correct several errors you have made in your suppositions. We *do* regard you all as writers."

"No, dude, we're characters!" countered Moonwash. "We didn't write this tale, we're just starring in it."

"Yeah," added Quorn Joy. "The man who invented us is the one you're really after—he's lurking somewhere outside this page; but I don't suggest you reach out to pull him in, because you might end up snaring the reader instead and there'll be a lawsuit."

Grkkghj winked languidly. "Characters that act like characters do have protected status and aren't eligible for the games, true enough, but when it comes to characters who are openly aware of their fictional status . . . Well, that's quite a different matter. Metafictional characters should take at least *some* responsibility for the way the plot develops; and in fact we say you are active collaborators in this novel. The collaborator of an author is also an author; thus you are writers."

"Man, he has doomed us with, like, logic!"

"It's not good logic but sophistry," spat the professor. "Nonetheless it's clear our fate is to bleed to death in the sand of the barbarian arena. These neo -prehistoric villains won't ever be dissuaded from pitting man against man, and cyborg against man, until the human race is extinguished. All in the name of saurian entertainment!"

Grkkghj smiled. "It's what we do best."

He turned to leave again, but on the threshold he glanced back over his shoulder and added, "It's a special occasion next Chewsday, for the Chief Plenipotentiary is celebrating his sixty-five-millionth birthday, and I have promised him a really good show, so please take care to die spectacularly. Have a good evening. Goodnight."

The door was locked again and the light of the setting sun through the window colored the room a rich arterial red. Moonwash and Quorn Joy squatted on the floor and clutched their heads in their hands. Nutloaf and Tantra were less intimidated but equally depressed. The professor hissed. He punched an open palm with the fist of another hand. "If only Stringent Strange was here! That blessed son of an ape would know how to act. But he's sowing his oats on a far world . . ."

The cell lacked artificial light, so when the sun went down, it was time for them to go to sleep: there was nothing else to do. The night proceeded slowly, but all the sounds from outside were exotic and alluring. Tripoli at night was probably a magical place; it was just a shame that they would never get to experience it properly.

The professor had a dream that was certainly clairvoyant. He saw odd figures approaching the wreck of a peculiar aircraft. They dismantled the wreck and dragged away the most important part of it. The leaves of very tall trees rustled melodiously. Soon the figures had vanished again, back into the under-growth of the forest.

At the first hint of dawn, the bolts were withdrawn and the head of a triceratops appeared in the doorway. "Anyone who wants to learn about hand to hand combat, follow me!" he winked. And Nutloaf, Tantra and Crinkle blinked sleepy eyes but went meekly with him, while Moonwash and Quorn Joy remained behind. The triceratops was called Bubba and it was his duty to ensure that new gladiators put on a noteworthy show. He led them to an Ottoman mansion.

"This building is the Old British Consulate on the street named Sharia Hara Kebir; we are near the northern edge of the Medina. Inside there's a courtyard and that's where you'll be doing your training. You are allowed to choose between three different sets of weapons: trident and net; shield and sword; or two throwing axes."

"Are there no other options?" cried the professor.

Bubba winked in the negative. "Not now. A few years ago we unfroze a writer called Piers Anthony and he insisted on using a rope, just a rope on its own, but he was amazingly successful and ended up ruining all the betting for us; so we passed a rule and formalized the choice of weapons. Nothing unorthodox is permitted."

They passed through the building into the courtyard. Sand covered the ground. Bubba indicated a rack of weapons and asked them to make their selection. The professor went for the axes; Tantra favored the shield and sword; Nutloaf seized on the trident and net. Bubba showed them various techniques of attack and defense.

Crinkle was a wonder to behold, for his numerous tentacles and ability to change his hands into any shape gave him an element of surprise that no human warrior could ever be expected to match. And his metal body provided superb protection. But the HIPZI girls also proved to be natural adepts, supple and very athletic . . .

Grkkghj came along later in the day to see how things were going. He expressed pleasure at the performance. "But where are the two men who were with you? Did you kill them?"

And he glanced around, well aware that some gladiators were always lost in these training sessions. But Bubba winked a chuckle and Grkkghj realized the truth and laughed back.

"I'm afraid they are incapable of learning the arts of war," said Nutloaf as she twirled her trident skillfully.

"Ah well," winked Grkkghj unhappily.

"They are so gentle, they can hardly tolerate the death of a fly," added Tantra, spinning her sword expertly.

"That's unfortunate," said Grkkghj ironically.

The professor sighed. "No more sentences ending with the letters 'ly' if you please!" he pleaded pedantically.

The training session was concluded and Bubba led the three gladiators back to their cell. Thus ended the first full day of captivity. Another night passed and Bubba reappeared in the morning. Once again, the professor and the HIPZI girls were led to the courtyard and given instruction by the triceratops, a routine repeated every single day until the dawn of the fifth, when Grkkghj appeared at the cell door and said, "There's no time left for Bubba to teach you anything new."

"The games are today," muttered Crinkle.

"Indeed so!" winked Grkkghj.

"Chewsday, man, the day we become, like, dinner!" wailed Moonwash as he tried to duck behind Quorn Joy; but Quorn Joy was simultaneously trying to duck behind Moonwash, so they went round in pointless pacifist circles until they were exhausted.

"Come, your transport awaits," said Grkkghj.

He led them along the corridor.

Outside the red castle stood a battered old bus. The tyrannosaur sitting in the driver's seat was the one called Lushdjiis and he considered himself something of a comedian. "I'm looking forward to having you all around for supper later," he quipped, but the girls groaned so discouragingly he mumbled an apology and promised to make his next joke more original. When all the captives were aboard, he started the badly tuned engine and released the stiff handbrake. Off they lurched and the bus bounced along the coastal road that heads eastwards out of Tripoli towards Leptis Magna. The professor whistled confidently as they went.

"No need to rub it in, dude!" sniffed Quorn Joy.

"Sorry, dear boy," said Crinkle.

"Don't worry," winked Lushdjiis, "I'm a vegetarian."

"Man, are you, like, serious?"

Lushdjiis nodded. "Yes, I never eat carnivores!"

Grkkghj, also at the front of the bus, slapped his chest and shook with mirth. Lushdjiis made similar motions but kept his claws on the steering wheel. Their telepathic laughter re-echoed loudly in every mind but didn't muffle Quorn Joy's screams at all.

THE MOST EXHAUSTING CHAPTER IN THIS BOOK

The cities of Bronson Alpha were full of hemispherical buildings with a stubby pinkish spire on top. Sometimes these buildings wobbled and the spires stiffened, but Stringent didn't have time to form an opinion on the indigenous architecture, nor on most other aspects of Bellusian life. He was too busy pleasuring women.

Tolrah was the first inhabitant to be completely satisfied by his efforts. Even before the saucer had landed he had done his best to give her twelve orgasms, although it had taken his full primeval strength to compress her bosoms back to practical dimensions.

When they reached her capital city, that ancient crystalline metropolis known as Erohw of the Kumons, he had given her the extra eighty-eight orgasms over a period of three days.

Then he gave her a free one for good measure.

His obligation to her discharged, he tackled some of the other women, responding to their needs with virility and determination. The money that Tolrah had given him helped not only to arouse his ardor but maintain it at maximum level, and the instant he ran out of cash his funds were fully replenished, so he remained in a permanent priapic state of readiness for horizontal rumba action.

Somewhere in the subterranean sectors of Erohw, a printing machine was working overtime, and the dollar bills it produced were being spent as fast as they appeared. The risk the apparatus might overheat and melt was very real; but it held together.

So Stringent toured the planet with his erection, discharging it and his duty at every available opportunity.

Five years he remained on Bellus, but a truly curious effect took place during his stay that confused the issue of subjective versus objective time. The nuclear-powered pumps that kept the atmospheric pressure low were responsible for flooding the planet with *chronons*. These particles rushed into the atmosphere from surrounding spacetime in a mistaken attempt to restore environmental equilibrium.

Take something away from somewhere and you can be sure that some other thing will end up falling into the gaps. That's a cosmic truth, but the sex-starved women hadn't considered the possibility. They were too eager to get themselves lustily serviced.

When a local reality has too few *chronons*, time accelerates as they are devoured more quickly; but when there are surplus particles of time, more things can be accomplished in the same number of seconds, because local time will seem to pass more slowly.

All relative to the outer universe, of course.

Less air molecules on Bellus meant a big influx of extra *chronons*, and thus the half-decade experienced by the apeman was no more than two or three weeks to his friends on Earth.

This is a significant point because it resolves inconsistencies regarding the timeframes of the two divergent plotlines. There's no way the apeman could hump a planetful of women in two or three weeks; and if you aren't convinced he might do it even in five years, please bear in mind the fact a Bellusian year is lengthier than ours.

When Stringent finally finished his task, Tolrah completed her side of the bargain by returning him to Earth in her saucer. Landing on a beach in Africa, she blew him a farewell kiss as he limped off along the sands. He clutched a bundle of banknotes totaling $50, all that remained of his vast forged fortune. It would be enough.

Not until Tolrah's saucer took off and vanished through the clouds of aerial junk did Stringent realize that he didn't know where he was. Africa is a very large continent: he could be anywhere! How would he get to the Cameroons now? It was a problem.

THOSE WHO ARE ABOUT TO DIE

The amphitheater at Leptis Magna was full of shouting spectators, and in a special pavilion halfway up the circular rows of seats sat a withered old tyrannosaur who wore green sunglasses made from carved emeralds. This was evidently the Chief Plenipotentiary himself, a monster of malevolent manners and perverted principles called Yyyshk. Also in the pavilion sat Grkkghj, Lushdjiis and Saaailjkdnk.

The professor and the four HIPZIS could hear everything from the pen under the arena where they were being kept in readiness, but their vision was restricted to a narrow grille that showed only the feet of any gladiator who happened to stride close enough.

They were guarded by another tyrannosaur named Ehkjgslsjhb and he had provided them with a typed schedule. For some reason they were the star attractions and therefore on last, and the only explanation Crinkle had for this state of affairs was that they were new. Maybe the audience were bored of the familiar combatants and welcomed any change to the list of participants? But it was odd anyway.

To learn exactly what was happening above, the professor reluctantly agreed to utilize his psychic powers.

He gave a running commentary to the others.

"Gertrude Stein has just been sent out to fight John Steinbeck, but she doesn't know what to do with her weapons and the crowd are jeering her. She's shouting something. An axe is an axe is an axe! I don't know what that's supposed to mean! Now Steinbeck has slashed at her with a sword and she's down. The audience are going wild! A triceratops has been sent into the arena to drag her body off."

Moonwash and Quorn Joy trembled at this news.

Tantra checked the edge of her own blade. It seemed sharp enough. As for Nutloaf, she was inspecting her net for any weak points. The professor continued to deliver his commentary.

"Mikhail Bulgakov, the Russian author, is being attacked by a bipedal feline; but this cat seems to be real, rather than a Debonair Werewolf in a costume. Clearly it's not just a case of one writer fighting another, but of a writer fighting *anything* the Telepathic Winking Dinosaurs care to send against him. This makes the situation more dangerous for us. I don't think our captors are genuine sportsmen."

More cheers from the crowd, more blood on the sand. Moonwash and Quorn Joy pressed hands to their ears and squeezed their eyes tight. They wanted no part of the bloody travesty.

The games continued. And they became odder. Philip José Farmer did battle with his evil anti-matter twin, Philip José Industrialist. Weapons of choice: sickle and hammer. This contradicted Bubba's assertion that only three sets of armaments were allowed. Clearly these interplanetary beasts weren't sticklers for consistency; which saves me the bother of having to do any rewriting, so I don't complain.

The morning turned into high noon. Thomas Pynchon dueled with his own reflection, which was imprisoned in a mirror that trundled after him on wheels wherever he went. He soon went mad and sank to his knees in defeat; but so did his reflection, and the judges declared the bout a draw. He was reprieved for the next games.

Win Scott Eckert went up against John Updike and literally wiped the floor with him, piling the sand up at the circumference of the arena; some spectators speculated that 'Win' was a description rather than a name, for his fights were foregone conclusions.

Dinosaur assistants ran on with buckets of fresh sand to replace what had been swept aside. This new sand contained broken shells that would add to the hazards of the duelists.

Ernest Hemingway was sent out with a shotgun to fight Noel Coward, but when the bearded savant aimed this weapon and squeezed the trigger it turned out to be a harpoon gun that couldn't be reloaded. The projectile missed its target and Noel seized the opportunity to belie his surname and tenderize his opponent with a flail.

Kevin J. Anderson fought a trio of giant sandworms, an example of a *melange à trois*, but the worms weren't really big because the sand in the arena wasn't deep enough. In fact they turned out to be three other writers inside costumes, Keith Laumer, William Tenn and Mercedes Lackey, and Kevin won by hooking them on a fishing rod.

The professor heard a nearby rustling . . .

Someone was occupying the adjacent pen. He was a human male who had remained quiet until this moment, but now he grasped the bars of his cage and hissed, "Hey! Over here!"

The professor trundled closer. "Who are you?"

"My name is Felipe ¡Que Dick!" returned the man, "and I'm on next. I thought they were going to send me against a herd of electric sheep, but it was just a joke and I'm actually going to have to battle a man whose teeth are all exactly alike. I think he must therefore be an android, a replicant of some sort, and I doubt I'll survive."

"That's too bad," sympathized the professor.

"Listen carefully to me," continued the man. "I've been here for a long time and I've survived everything they've hurled at me: gargoyles, paranoia whales, congealed clouds of pink light, Stanislaw Lem, lasers. You name it, I've seen it! But I fear my time's up. It doesn't seem I'll get a chance to put my escape plan into action."

"Escape plan? What do you mean?"

Felipe lowered his quiet voice even more. "As I'm sure you are aware, Leptis Magna stands next to the sea. Well, anchored offshore is a working seaplane! It has been there since Balbo's day and somehow survived the upheavals and all the erosion. It's fuelled and ready to fly. If you flee the arena and reach it, you'll be free!"

Crinkle stroked his chin. "What kind of seaplane?"

"It's a Savoia-Marchetti S.55."

"With 880-hp Isotta-Fraschini Asso 750V engines?"

"That's right, two of them, one pusher, one puller, mounted in a rather unusual configuration back-to-back on pylons just above the wing center-section. Balbo himself flew a large formation of these aircraft from Rome to Rio de Janeiro, and also from Rome to Chicago. I think the one outside was caught in a convenience loop!"

The professor frowned. "What's that?"

"When an author can't think of a more plausible way of extracting his characters from a tight situation, he'll introduce an item of machinery into the tale that can't possibly be (but miraculously is) still working! The way these items of machinery are protected from the ravages of time and logic is by being held in a convenience loop, a sort of metafictional maelstrom that shields them from all damage."

"But not from the criticism of readers, surely?"

Felipe smiled. "Not from that, no."

A triceratops came to unlock his pen and lead him to his doom. The professor managed to switch off his psychic powers at this point: he had no desire to witness the brave fellow's death. But in fact there's a chance Felipe ¡Que Dick! actually won his fight. But that's not a story I intend to tell. Do it yourself, if you like . . .

The loser was dragged off amid applause.

Now there was a brief interlude and a saurian brass band played weird Zyran music and the audience stamped their feet and lashed their tails in time, making the amphitheater shake and even toppling a column or two somewhere in the Hadrianic Baths.

During this interlude, a commercial break took place in which Yyyshk promoted KROK FOSSIL'S CRYPTOZOOLOGIC MOUTHWASH by breathing straight out of this page into the reader's face, in other words directly into *your* face, without creating nausea.

"Gargle once an era before bed!" he winked.

The interlude was quickly followed by an event intended to highlight and remedy the neglect of various "forgotten masters" of the early science-fiction age. S.P. Meek, Ray Cummings, Neil R. Jones, Charles R. Tanner, Raymond Z. Gallun, Henry Hasse, and maybe half a dozen others, fought each other all at the same time. At the inconclusive climax of this event, the audience threw squashed fruit at the survivors, but this gesture wasn't planned as an insult. On the contrary, it was merely a literal appreciation of the "pulp" origins of those writers.

I'm convinced the editor will insist I remove that scene.

He'll say it's just a little too silly.

And I'm sure it is, but that's not my fault. It's the fault of the Telepathic Winking Dinosaurs. I am innocent!

Yyyshk now raised his little arms and silence settled over the crowd while he cleared his throat. It seemed he intended to make a speech, so everyone listened carefully. "As you know," he began, "it's a special day for me today; but even though all birthdays are special days, one's sixty-five-millionth is *extra* special. Therefore I have decided to give you all an extra special treat. That's symmetry for you."

The crowd chuckled politely. Yyyshk continued, "Also, for the first time in the history of these games, I've permitted a few human spectators to sit on the amphitheater steps at the rear and enjoy the show. Who are they, you ask? Well, they are those readers who were good and wise and kind and rich enough to pre-order this book instead of waiting for it to be published before parting with their cash."

There was a murmuring as the dinosaurs in the audience turned their heads to squint at the back row of seats.

"Don't strain your necks!" cried Yyyshk. "If you want to know who they are, simply turn to the end of this novel and you'll find their names listed in the order in which they are seated."

Some of the dinosaurs began turning unseen pages, making a rustling sound that caused Yyyshk to frown and shout, "If you do that now, we'll fall over. We stand on some of those pages! Anyway, that's not the treat I mentioned. No, I have something more unusual in store. We like to bend the rules here, so prepare yourself to behold the desperate mortal combat of seven readers snatched from outside this book! That's right. Plucked from their safe chairs and into this novel . . ."

Yyyshk didn't bother explaining that those seven readers had entered an auction to appear in this very section of the book and that a percentage of the proceeds from their combined bids were destined to be donated to charity.

Perhaps the Chief Plenipotentiary was shamed by their generosity and wanted to downplay it. Or possibly the choice of charity irked him, for it was one concerned with animal rights and no amount of reform in that field could be of much use to dinosaurs, neither those of Earth nor Zyra. Or maybe he just enjoyed being spiteful.

At any rate, he preferred to maintain the illusion that the chosen seven had been kidnapped against their will, innocent humans abruptly yanked into the body of the text they happened to be reading. As has already been mentioned, Yyyshk was a creature of perverted principles. Throwing his head back he cried, "They have been permitted to choose the writers they will fight and also their own weapons."

The dinosaurs roared their approval of this novelty; and so did the few human spectators, safe from being slaughtered and very glad they hadn't entered the auction: for what had seemed like simple fun when mooted as a publicity stunt was now revealed as a grisly business indeed. Which is the way it should be, of course. Metafiction always has the potential to be more visceral than ordinary fiction.

That potential shouldn't be wasted. Anyway . . .

"Bring on the first contestant!"

I ought to stress that these charity bouts are going to be conducted in reverse order. This was the publisher's idea, not mine, but I adopted it in order to heighten the tension. And so . . .

Yyyshk waved a vicious claw and assistants opened a metal gate in the floor of the amphitheater. Adjusting the emerald sunglasses over his eyes, the Chief Plenipotentiary bellowed:

"Let the carnage begin! No quarter! AND FOR ALL YOUR CUTS AND ABRASIONS WHY NOT TRY TUMBLEWEED'S BAND AIDS? WATERPROOF AND STYLISH TOO. Slaughter ahoy!"

Oh yes, I almost forgot to say . . . Feel free to skip the next chapter, as it doesn't move the story along, but it was great fun to write! In order to skip it, hold the beginning in one hand, the end in the other, swing it over your head and under your feet. Keep jumping.

THE MUNIFICENT SEVEN

From the dungeons in the bowels of the amphitheater, up the rusty ladder, each rung flaking under his feet, stepped into the bright light the first of the seven readers, the lowest bidder.

(7) Tim Love. Who had armed himself with a hockey stick, for when he was younger he had played that sport with skill and success and thus knew how to handle such an implement, whereas the hefting of a bladed or spiked weapon was unfamiliar to him.

He had chosen to fight Thomas Ligotti and Tim Lebbon, the reason being that they had stolen his initials and he wanted them back, but this was surely a joke. Initials aren't like that.

He strode forward, nodding first to Ligotti, then to Lebbon, who were armed only with long lassoes but who had clearly decided on a strategy before entering the arena. They parted and moved to either side of Tim, who was now unable to engage both at the same time. He knew he had to choose one of them to rush. But who?

While he dithered over the decision, Ligotti and Lebbon set in motion their lengths of rope with the nooses on the ends, describing figures of eight in the whistling air. Suddenly one of the spectators threw something into the arena. An egg, a symbol of derision. Conditioned by instinct, Tim Love ran to meet it, hockey stick upraised.

He struck it with as much force as he could muster.

An explosion of yolk should have followed, and the outraged shriek of some mother saurian deprived of her future offspring. But it was the hockey stick that shattered, into a thousand splinters, and the rascally beast who had lobbed it laughed manically.

147

"A fossil egg, not a recent one! It was the unhatched brother of one of my ancestors. What a jest!" he explained.

All eyes turned to Yyyshk, to gauge whether he would halt the fight at this point in order to give Tim Love another hockey stick, for audience participation was against the spirit of the games, but he merely shrugged and beckoned for the combat to continue.

Tim now stood without a weapon, while Ligotti and Lebbon cast their lassoes simultaneously, snaring his wrists. The nooses instantly tightened and cut off the circulation to his hands.

They leaned back, heaving with all their power, trapping Tim between two taut ropes. They continued to pull and both arms abruptly dislocated, popping out of their shoulder sockets like baguettes out of a not-properly-planned simile. And Tim Love screamed.

His assailants didn't heed his shrill pleas for mercy; they tugged even harder and blood sprayed in little jets from both arms at the points where the tendons were ripping from the shoulders.

With a not unmusical twang the arms came completely off! Ligotti and Lebbon fell backwards, then righted themselves.

"Stop the fight. I'm unarmed!" begged Tim Love.

This was asking too much. His arms were still gripped by the lassoes, and Ligotti and Lebbon started swinging them through the air, turning the bloody limbs into a type of weapon known as a meteor hammer, basically a rope with a simple weight on the end.

With perfect coordination, they violently slammed the loose gory arms against the sides of Tim Love's cranium, striking him on his right and left temples at precisely the same instant.

He blinked and drooled but didn't collapse, because the opposite and equal blows stabilized him. A second time, his opponents struck him on the head with his own arms. And again.

Every pair of blows hit the same place. Soon something strange and horrid became apparent. Tim Love's head was being elongated, its shape changing under the repeated impacts. Finally his eyeballs burst, his brain poured out of his nose, and he expired; but he died standing and remained there like a very poorly executed statue of himself with a sculpted head that was all wrong, for the rest of the day . . .

(6) Steve Mattsson. He bounded up the ladder and into the scrutiny of the spectators like a ninja kangaroo, proving he was no stranger to the arts of

fighting. To his leathery palms were strapped a pair of brass cymbals and behind him padded a stealthy jaguar.

The dinosaurs murmured appreciatively as Steve clashed the cymbals together and in response the jaguar roared.

Groping his way through an opened door in the side of the arena came his opponent, a decrepit blind bald man . . .

The dinosaurs set up a telepathic commotion. "What's the meaning of this? Has the bout been fixed?" they cried.

Yyyshk explained, "That old man may appear harmless at first glance but in fact he's none other than Jorge Luis Borges and therefore mustn't be underestimated by anyone."

All eyes returned to the unfolding drama below.

Steve's square jaw caught the light heroically and reflected it over the wild animal by his side. With cymbals he could control the beast, make it tear out the throat of anyone he disliked.

Borges shuffled to a stop and stood with his head at a slight angle as if listening to something. Then he smiled.

His smile seemed to radiate the beauteous despair of infinity and Steve was forced to shield his eyes against the glare. The jaguar whimpered and Steve knew that if he didn't act immediately he would lose the advantage of his superior strength and stamina.

He clashed the cymbals and growled, "Kill!"

The jaguar sprang at Jorge Luis Borges, who casually hurled down a handful of sand grains before the beast . . .

And the jaguar and Steve were inside a labyrinth that had risen from nowhere. No, not from nowhere, for the walls of the maze were made of sand, the sand that had covered the floor of the arena. Somehow it had reformed into walls. Steve kicked a hole in the nearest wall; but the grains shifted and repaired it instantly.

"Curse that magical master of fabulation!" yelled Steve as he hurried through the passages of the labyrinth, seeking the exit. The jaguar loped after him. Then Steve had an idea.

He reasoned that if he ran with sufficient velocity at a wall, he would penetrate it with the inertia of his muscular body and pass through to the other side before it had time to reform.

At the next turning Steve continued running straight ahead. He felt the abrasive clawing of the sand on his tanned flesh. Then he broke through! And yes, the jaguar was with him!

But he was still in the labyrinth . . . The walls had flowed and reformed around him. He stopped and considered his options. An outdoorsman, a fellow who had experienced danger many times, he wasn't fazed by his present situation; at least not to the point of being rendered unable to take sufficient action to save himself.

He decided to climb the walls instead of bursting through them. With a deep breath to steady his nerves, he commenced scaling the vertical face of sand, using the cymbals on his wrists to gouge out handholds; but the wall curved inward as he climbed, becoming an impossible overhang, and finally he lost his grip and fell.

A cackle of laughter reached his ears.

Borges was laughing at him! He regained his feet and set off in pursuit of the chuckle. The jaguar needed no prompting to follow. They turned innumerable corners, ducked down a plethora of passages; sometimes the laughter grew louder, other times fainter.

Finally they turned a corner and found themselves in a wider space at the center of the labyrinth. Jorge Luis Borges stood there, but he had the body of a bull, an inverse Minotaur.

Displaying his horns, he charged and gored both Steve and the jaguar with a single toss, hurling them into the air.

The walls of the labyrinth collapsed and everything was normal again, the corpses of Steve and the jaguar leaking into the sand at the far end of the arena while the old blind man trotted his way out of the limelight and back through the door in the wall . . .

(5) Tim Uhl. He had elected to fight Pierre Menard, a fictional author rather than a real one, who in fact was a creation of the author that had fought the previous bout, Jorge Luis Borges.

Whether the dinosaurs were keen on intertextuality or not, they didn't object to this unorthodox request.

So Tim appeared at the top of the ladder armed with an umbrella. The spectators instinctively looked up to see if rain was expected, but no, this was merely one of Tim's peculiar jokes.

He knew that he was going to lose, that the outcomes were fated and couldn't be altered; so he had decided to make his death amusing not only to the dinosaurs but also to himself.

Opening the umbrella he walked out into the arena.

And bowed rather elegantly.

Pierre Menard stepped out from the shadows, which was odd because there were no shadows here, and approached Tim Uhl. In his right hand he carried a forking path shaped like a bolt of lightning that crackled and hissed like an electric serpent; in his left he bore a lottery ticket with a winning set of numbers embossed on it.

But the prize was a hideous death by slow torture!

He offered the ticket to Tim, perhaps hoping that it would be taken in a reflex gesture; but Tim shook his head.

Pierre Menard said, "I intend to duplicate the worst death that has been ever experienced by anyone in this amphitheater but without recourse to knowing anything about it. And so—"

"I don't want it," answered Tim, spinning the umbrella hypnotically in front of Pierre Menard's eyes like a mandala on a stick. Pierre tucked the forking path under his armpit and proceeded to fold the lottery ticket into a paper dart with short wings. Then he aimed it at Tim, seeking to send it gliding under the defense of his umbrella.

Tim guessed that if any part of the lottery ticket touched his exposed skin he would be forced to undergo the hideous torture hinted at by Pierre Menard, a torture that involved being slowly grilled by a fire until he was cooked but still alive, and then set upon by famished infants with wonky milk teeth who would bite and chew the steaming flesh from his bones with excruciatingly childish imprecision.

It goes without saying that Tim Uhl planned to evade such a grotesque destiny to the best of his considerable ability.

At last Pierre thought he saw an opening and he hurled the paper dart. It swooped and looped on a complex flight path, but Tim was ready with his umbrella and deflected it with ease.

Pierre Menard gnashed his own molars, which seemed to be made out of paper stiffened with many coatings of glue, with writing on them in a minuscule script. As the tip of his tongue lightly touched each tooth they sang musical notes analogous to whatever was written on them, but none of it made any sense; they were random letters forced into pseudo-words, passages from the texts of the most useless volumes in some hypothetical but ultimately terrible Library of Babel.

"So you have escaped the lottery ticket!" he snarled. "Then you shall have to face the forking path instead!"

And like an ancient storm god he flung the bolt of lightning at Tim's face. Tim raised his umbrella in time but the missile went through the fabric, setting it on fire as it did so, sending sparks rushing up into the already over-heated air of the amphitheater.

The forking path impaled itself in the center of Tim's forehead and discharged its entire energy into him.

He stiffened and then every muscle in his body experienced a spasm and his lips quivered. He wanted to open his mouth to scream but he had no control over any part of his own body.

Pierre Menard turned away in abstract disgust.

And Tim Uhl finally understood the awful secret of the forking path. It discharged into him not only the ordinary death that any pronged weapon might give a man, but all the other possible deaths that a gladiator could experience in this arena. And so Tim died in a million billion different ways, most agonizing, a few pleasurable; and one of those ways was the death promised by the lottery ticket . . .

(4) Anthony Cardno wasted no time taking Tim's place. He carried a tomahawk and a corvo. A corvo is a cross between a machete and sickle that opens deep wounds but is difficult to use properly, its peculiar shape making the weapon tricky to balance correctly. With a bass growl and gleaming eyes, Anthony dropped into a crouch and prepared to meet the two gladiators who squared up to him.

One of these gladiators was Neil Gaiman and his dreaded specialty was to fling sand in the eyes of his opponents, blinding them long enough for his partner to deliver the killer blow. For this reason his nickname in the arena was simply "The Sandman."

His partner wore no armor, just a large green carnation in place of a fig leaf, but he was armed with a bullwhip and protected by a wooden shield with a pig iron spike protruding from it. He sneered, "I am Oscar Wilde. Prepare for a flippant death!"

Anthony adjusted the chinstrap of his helmet and waited for Neil and Oscar's onslaught. They circled each other like moths around a cliché or rival literary critics around a contrived comparison. Suddenly the tip of the whip cracked like a hornet's quip.

Anthony howled. His right thigh had been neatly sliced open and the blood surged like thick sauce. "Argh!" he yelled. Oscar struck an ironic pose, still the perfect champion of *argh for argh's sake*, Anthony thought bitterly as he felt waves of pain shoot up his leg into his abdomen. But adrenalin surged into him. He laughed.

"Just a flesh wound," he snorted, and he kept his eyes on the whip, as they continued circling, poised on their toes, almost dancing a slow and deadly dance, a termination tango.

"One can survive anything these days except death," crooned Oscar, his carnation undulating hypnotically, and Anthony roared back, "You're plagiarizing yourself now, dear boy . . ."

Oscar cracked the whip again, cutting open Anthony's cheek. Tears poured from his eye into the flesh crevice, stinging the inside of his face and forcing him to jump back a few steps. He still hadn't got the range of that cursed bullwhip! If only he could snag it on the sharp inner edge of his corvo the next time Oscar lashed out, then it would be shortened and present much less of a danger to him.

He licked his lips. His instinct was to back away but he knew that if he did that, Oscar Wilde would simply follow him around the arena, lashing him to pieces, flaying strips of his flesh off his bones until he was nothing more than a stumbling skeleton oozing with gore and gristly gravy. The best course of action would be to rush forward and get inside the whip's effective range, slashing simultaneously with tomahawk and corvo at the renowned aesthete, severing his neck.

Gathering his strength, he ran at Oscar at high speed, but the whip was faster, shearing through Anthony's wrist, whistling through flesh, veins, nerves and bone, leaving only a few tendons connected, so that his hand flopped loosely and uselessly like the lid of an open bread bin. Blood and marrow sprayed out and the corvo fell into the sand, glinting pointlessly in the torrid African sunlight. Another crack of the whip and the entire hand came off, plopping like a deformed spider next to the corvo. Oscar gazed at the hand and covered a yawn.

"Shall I get you a bag to put it in?" he mocked.

Anthony was baffled. "A handbag!?"

Oscar smirked. "You took the words right out of my mouth."

"How dare you?" howled Anthony.

"I have nothing to dare but my genius . . ."

Anthony shrieked and launched himself at the playwright, heedless of the danger, caring only that the sneering fin-de-siècle bohemian dandy should not live to greet another morning. But Oscar was ready. He raised his shield and thrust it with all his strength at Anthony. The pig iron spike went through Anthony's left eye with a hideous squeak and a crunch, and emerged from the back of his helmet.

Anthony collapsed to his knees, drool cascading down his chin. Oscar stood with his hand on his hip and blinked.

"I wish I could die like that . . ."

"You will, Oscar, you will!" gasped Anthony Cardno, as with his last breath he flung the tomahawk at the ironic playwright. It span through the dusty air like a propeller without an engine, or more accurately not at all like that, and the wedge of the blade buried itself in Oscar's skull with the solid thunk of a piece of wood being chopped. Oscar folded to his knees, gaping his mouth like a fishy metaphor.

His witty brains, as grey as those of any normal man, trickled and then poured down his face, into his eyes, over his cheeks, onto his protruding tongue, and he swallowed them without meaning to, and bubbles of mind goo popped out of his nostrils, but there was still just enough grey matter left inside his skull to power a final *bon mot.*

"Murder is always a mistake. One should never do anything that one cannot talk about after dinner . . . Urgh!"

Anthony giggled in triumph, but he had forgotten about Neil Gaiman, who suddenly pounced and forced fistfuls of bloody sand into his mouth, clogging his throat until he choked to death . . .

(3) Marty Kardon wore a cape that billowed behind him but nothing else apart from a wide belt, from which dangled a cheese grater. In his right hand he held an eight foot long oak spear with a wide bronze head; in his left he carried a big bucket of water.

His opponent was the objectivist philosopher Ayn Rand.

She wielded a curious implement that turned out to be a large dollar sign made from gold and sharpened on a grindstone. She opened her lips to make a speech, but Marty was prepared.

He ran forward and knocked her down with the reverse end of his spear. Then he sat on her heaving chest.

"But you haven't allowed me to recite a monologue against socialists and liberals yet!" she wheezed in anguish.

Marty didn't reply. He simply rammed the edge of the full bucket into her mouth and began pouring. Ayn Rand's eyes widened but she couldn't escape from under him. Marty dropped his spear and pinched her nostrils to prevent the water escaping that way.

She had no choice but to swallow the liquid!

Soon her stomach noticeably bulged and her face went blue.

Finally the bucket was drained.

Ayn Rand lay motionless, unable to stir.

Bloated beyond belief, she was nonetheless still alive and conscious as Marty leaped high into the air and landed on her, both his feet connecting with her bulging stomach. The consequences of this action were extreme. Ayn Rand's jaw clacked wide and a pillar of water mixed with blood and parts of her stomach lining shot up.

"I call this tactic 'The Fountainhead'," explained Marty.

And yes, briefly, her head really did resemble a fountain, a horrid and very unhygienic example of the type!

Something, or perhaps many things, had ruptured deep inside her and she suddenly convulsed and expired . . .

Marty Kardon stood and paraded around the arena.

The dinosaurs in the audience went wild. They were outraged, for this was against the script of the day. The authors were supposed to win! They might have rushed down into the arena and killed Marty themselves if the Chief Plenipotentiary hadn't intervened.

"Calm down, my friends! So something unexpected has happened! Is that such a big deal? I will simply send another author against this upstart gladiator. That's surely the best solution."

And before Marty could protest at the injustice of this, another figure bounded into the arena. It was Sun Tzu, author of *The Art of War*, one of the greatest military treatises ever written.

Marty stooped to retrieve his spear, then he whirled to face Sun Tzu, his hand reaching for his cheese grater.

Sun Tzu's expression was impassive. He said, "If you know your enemies and know yourself, you will not be imperiled in one hundred battles; if you do not know your enemies but do know yourself, you will win one and lose one; if you do not know your enemies nor yourself, you will be imperiled in every single battle."

"I know myself well enough," Marty snapped back.

"But do you know me, grasshopper?"

"Well, I've read your book, so I guess I do . . ."

Sun Tzu shook his head. "My book? You think I only wrote one? The others have been lost to history. One of them was a book of recipes and contained a famous lesson, namely do not use radish sauce on cucumber if you seek not to offend your guests."

And he displayed something that he had somehow managed to conceal behind his back even though it was taller than he was. A nine-foot long cucumber greased for its entire length in a radish sauce. Marty compared it with the spear he held. He had the strength of materials advantage but Sun Tzu had the length and flavor advantage.

"I know myself and I also know you," said Sun Tzu.

"How do you know me?" sneered Marty.

"I did some research on the internet," answered Sun Tzu. "Therefore it seems that I am certain to win this fight."

"Only according to your own wisdom," pointed out Marty.

Sun Tzu bowed. "That's good enough for me." Then he charged with the cucumber cradled under his arm.

Marty's spear wouldn't help him now unless he threw it, but that was a risk he wasn't prepared to take: if he missed he probably wouldn't get it back. So he held up the cheese grater instead.

The tip of the cucumber connected with the grater and Marty started moving it back and forth as fast as he could.

Shreds of cool cucumber flew everywhere and the length of the evil vegetable was reduced by many inches.

"It's not the length that counts but the quality," said Sun Tzu, his face not changing its expression for an instant.

"I concede that this is a very fine cucumber." But Marty didn't stop grating it. In fact he redoubled his efforts. Cucumber spattered his face and he found himself enjoying the taste.

"But I forgot to mention one thing," Sun Tzu said.

"What's that?" gasped Marty Kardon.

"The radish sauce is poisoned. You will die shortly."

Marty retched, tried to spit out the shards of cucumber that had entered his mouth. But it was too late. He had absorbed them into his bloodstream and now felt dizzy and weak. "Cheat!"

Sun Tzu seemed genuinely offended and his expression changed for the first time in centuries. "I resent that accusation. Any means that helps to win a war or a battle is justified."

"Maybe you're right. I'm too ill to argue," gasped Marty as he keeled over and his heartbeat grew irregular and then stopped beating altogether. Sun Tzu shrugged and then left the scene . . .

(2) Adrian Chamberlain. He flounced up the ladder dressed only in a

leather thong; but he had serious weaponry at his disposal: a recurve bow and a Franchi SPAS-12 combat shotgun.

"Come and get me bitch!" he lisped in defiance.

Striding forward to meet the challenge, armed with a sword and a seax and protected by a wide kite shield, came Bernard Cornwell, the writer of historical adventure stories. A seax, incidentally, isn't a Saxon axe, as I originally assumed it was, but a particular kind of knife, long with a deep blood gutter running down the middle.

"I will indeed come and get you, by Woden's spare ravens!" growled Bernard Cornwell, rattling his sword against his shield. Adrian loaded a cartridge into his shotgun, aimed and fired.

But Bernard ducked down behind his shield, which was broad enough to cover his entire body; and the seasoned English oak banded with iron and toughened by immersion in mead vinegar deflected most of the tiny steel pellets as if they were seeds spat from a peashooter. Adrian knew at this point that modern weaponry wasn't superior in every situation but he didn't allow his disappointment to show.

He watched as Bernard advanced, crouching behind his shield, waving his sword above his head, the blade catching the light and turning mellow with the cruel deceptiveness of optical illusions. There was nothing nice about Bernard Cornwell's length of death.

Adrian discharged another shot, with the same effect.

He now had only six cartridges left.

In the quiver he wore over his shoulder were ten arrows.

Perhaps they would have more penetrating power? And if there was one thing Adrian wanted more than anything else in the world, it was to penetrate Bernard Cornwell. So he set down the shotgun on the sand, strung the recurve bow and nocked an arrow.

Such bows tend to be more powerful than the ordinary straight bows favored by ancient knights. Adrian pulled back the string and aimed at the center of the shield. He found using this weapon more exciting than the shotgun. The swelling in his leather thong could prove this fact, but it's best not to dwell on such details.

With a gasp of delight, Adrian discharged at Bernard.

The arrow hit the shield and bit deep.

Indeed, as evidenced by the howl of rage from behind it, the point must have gone clean through the oak and punched a hole in the torso of Bernard

Cornwell. But it wasn't a mortal wound by any means, for the shield began moving forward again.

Adrian nocked another arrow to his bow.

This time his shot struck the shield at a slight angle and was deflected without puncturing the oak. Bernard shuffled even closer, groaning as he did so from the pain of the first injury.

Adrian retreated at the same speed, firing a third arrow that completely missed the target. Then he realized to his alarm that he had forgotten the shotgun. It now lay exactly halfway between them. Adrian saw Bernard peering from over the top of the shield.

They both ran forward and collided directly above the shotgun. Adrian was hurt by the impact more than Bernard was; some of his ribs snapped and crimson froth flecked his lips. He regained his balance, fitted another narrow to his bow and attempted to draw the string back; but pain made this task impossible as the muscles of his chest were stretched and rubbed the broken edges of his ribs together.

Bernard planted his shield firmly in the ground.

Now both his arms were free.

He stepped from behind his protection, sword and seax ready. Adrian unslung his quiver and grasped a handful of arrows from it, holding them out as his only defense. Bernard snorted.

"And now, by Thor's tongs, I will perform the rite of the Blood Eagle upon you! Your back will be slit open and your lungs pulled through the gash to inflate and deflate with each agonizing breath like the wings of a mythical bird. What do you say to that?"

"I'm not entirely sure I fancy it myself," said Adrian.

Bernard kicked the shotgun aside; but this set it off and it fired, most of the pellets embedding themselves in him. He staggered and then with a monumental effort righted himself.

Grumbling and cursing, he started using the tip of the seax to dig out the pellets from his flesh. Adrian decided to seize the chance and limped forward, every breath like a spike of frozen fire deep in his sternum, his clutch of arrows proffered like a bouquet of cruel orchids. It was a very desperate stratagem and it totally failed.

Bernard waited until Adrian was almost upon him.

Then he swung his sword and severed a leg just below the knee. With a snarl of indignation, Adrian hopped back, swayed and gritted his teeth before resuming the attack. Instead of lopping off the other leg, Bernard merely angled up the blade of his sword.

Unable to stop himself in time, Adrian ran straight onto the point and slid down it; his momentum carried him all the way to the hilt. He sagged and Bernard took his weight but he didn't send him crashing to the floor. Instead he used the seax in his free hand to slice off Adrian's ears and lips and chin. This was done almost lovingly.

"Your books are wonderful," Adrian spluttered.

"What did you say?" demanded Bernard.

"I'm a big fan of yours, that's all."

"By the Fenris poodle I understand ye not! All I can hear is a hideous death rattle and a grotesque wheezing."

"Don't worry about it then," were Adrian's final words . . .

(1) Jason E. Rolfe. He had chosen to fight Beatrix Potter, not because he imagined she would be easy to beat but out of a combined sense of social justice and mischievous irony. A panel in one of the walls slid back and she jumped out to confront him.

They stood facing each other, the sand swirling around their feet. The crowd gasped telepathically when she raised her weapon, a vicious and improbable morningstar, a mace that is basically a spiked ball on a haft, but there was something peculiar about this example. Beatrix noticed the bafflement and turned to address the audience.

"Mrs. Tiggy-Winkle is what I call this. A hedgehog on a pole recreated in iron. Can bash shields and heads to perforated flatness, yes it can. Now watch carefully as I demonstrate its potency."

She spun it around her head but it was too heavy to make a whooshing noise. Yet she was very dexterous in handling the fearsome thing and her old-fashioned clothes, including the black hooded cape, lacy bodice, long drab skirt and prim buckled shoes didn't hamper her agility at all. As for Jason he lifted his own weapon in response.

A severed rabbit's foot. A giant rabbit's foot, hacked from no feasible bunny known to science. Mayhap it had been genetically bred by a mad meddler in some Canadian laboratory, for that country was the homeland of Jason. Did the Rushans have something to do with it? Beatrix scowled and with her free hand raised her skirt in mockery, displaying layers of petticoats like the petals of a nursery lotus.

"I feel that your furry meat club will be inadequate for the task facing you, good sir. You are fated to splatter."

Jason said nothing in reply. He merely grinned, for his rabbit's foot was not only a physical bludgeon but possessed the ability to bestow *luck* on whoever wielded it. That was his secret.

The crowd urged them to engage with each other.

Beatrix made the first lunge. She crouched and aimed a blow at his knees, but Jason hopped back and the spikes of the morningstar grazed his kneecaps, doing only minor damage.

He counter-attacked almost immediately, stepping forward and trying an uppercut with the giant rabbit's foot.

Beatrix jerked her head aside and the resultant blow glanced off her jaw, yet the force of it still knocked all her bottom teeth loose. She spat them out amid dribbles of blood and hissed:

"Mrs. Tiggy-Winkle will avenge me for that slight!"

Jason kept his eyes on the spiked ball of the weapon; and this was the opportunity for Beatrix Potter to attempt one of her unorthodox moves, suddenly reversing the mace and lunging with the shaft. Prepared only to dodge swipes, Jason was completely caught out by this thrust, which hit him in the abdomen and caused him to double over in pain. He felt bile boiling and seething in his numb stomach.

"Well done, Mrs. Tiggy-Winkle!" Beatrix crooned.

As she moved in closer to deliver the coup-de-grace, Jason looked up and unexpectedly projected a pillar of thick vomit into her face. Blinded by its acidity, she wailed and stumbled.

"That was a disgusting thing to do, wasn't it?" she chided. "I'm not very charmed by that, sir. I don't think we'll ever be friends now, oh no. In fact I think I might have to flatten you slowly, limb by limb, then your pelvis and chest, leaving your head for last."

She wiped her eyes with one of her fussy sleeves while Jason managed to regain his breath. They glared at each other. Green and black bile made her face shine like the facets of an undesirable jewel in the afternoon sun. Then they started to circle each other warily.

"You can't hold out for long, you know," she told him.

"I intend to do my best. That's all any of us can ever do," he replied. While she mulled over the wisdom of this cliché, he seized the chance to swing a blow at her hip. It made contact.

The force of it would have broken the pelvis of most females, but her many layers of petticoats protected her. She was knocked several feet to the side but somehow remained upright.

"You absolute rotter, sir!" she spluttered.

Jason shrugged. He couldn't allow himself to be tricked by her, the stakes were too high for this, and he could plainly tell that beneath her soft and charming exterior, under all the undergarments, burned the soul of a brutal barbarian. He congratulated himself on the fact that he hadn't for an instant been fooled by her seeming innocence and winsome smiles. She was evil, he knew that, and lethal.

"I can't honestly regard you as a gentleman and—"

While she was still talking, Jason swung at her again and hit her other hip. She was knocked back to her original position, but something had snapped beneath her skirt, some crucial piece of elastic or string, and all her petticoats fell down, puddling in the dust. She gaped at him in shock, her cheeks blushing like embarrassed plums.

"No man has ever removed those items of clothing before! It's simply not possible! How could you manage it?"

"With the assistance of luck," answered Jason.

"But luck is only an illusion!"

"Luck is my friend," he said, lifting the giant rabbit's foot to his lips and kissing it fondly, "but your doom."

Beatrix narrowed her eyes and for a moment it seemed she sagged in anticipation of defeat. A sigh racked her frame. "It's clear that I'm not dealing with any ordinary fellow. I have misjudged and underestimated you. Will they let me surrender, do you think?"

Jason shook his head. "Never. Nor would I, if it was my decision. One of us must die today. That is the law."

She nodded sadly and sighed again. Her damaged mouth quivered as she came to terms with her position. Then her eyes widened. She stared at something over his shoulder. "Squirrels!" she squealed. "Lots and lots of lovely little squirrels. What *can* they be doing here in this terrible place, this venue of spilled guts and death?"

And Jason made his fatal mistake. He looked back.

The next thing he knew, he was sprawled in the sand and his spinal fluid was leaking away, pooling around his neck. It was warm and not unpleasant. He blinked up in confusion into the leering and distorted face of Beatrix Potter, who towered above him. "Well, *really*," she was snarling, "how could a bright young man like you fall for such a simple and obvious tactic as that? Squirrels indeed!"

"Luck . . ." he croaked. His weapon lay some distance away. The force of the morningstar blow had caused him to somersault in mid air. His top vertebrae were crushed and the nape of his neck was riddled with holes where the spikes of the mace had entered.

"It ran out," she said, shielding her eyes and pretending to watch it vanish in the distance. "Too bad for you."

And then Beatrix Potter kept her dark promise.

She started with his feet and legs, hammering them flat, moving on to his hands and arms; slowly, very slowly, while all the saurian spectators stamped their feet in approval, she reduced him to the thickness of his shadow. The last word he said was, "Arrrrgh!" but any allusion to Jason and the arrrrghonauts must be discounted . . .

CYBORG AT THE CIRCUS

A nd now the seven corpses lay strewn around the arena.

The audience applauded rapturously.

The saurian brass band played a jolly march and Yyyshk basked in the warm appreciation of his subjects. Then he waved a claw and the normal program resumed. Paul Di Filippo fought A.A. Attanasio; Ian Watson and Brian Aldiss slugged it out; Fritz Leiber battled a tall broad barbarian and a small mousy thief while very drunk.

Meanwhile dinosaur accountants added together the bids of the seven generous gladiators and nodded appreciatively at the impressively high figure.

A few more fights took place before it was Tantra and Nutloaf's turn. A triceratops came to unlock the pen and lead them away. They emerged in bright blinking sunlight to a tumult of applause. Fortunately they didn't have to fight each other; the arena was roped off into two halves and they were required to tackle two enemies simultaneously: Norman Mailer and the appropriately named Gore Vidal.

The girls won easily. It was almost an anticlimax.

Tantra and Nutloaf didn't return to the pen. They were invited to share the pavilion of the Chief Plenipotentiary. This wasn't a privilege they had respect for, but as refusal would result in instant death, they obliged with good grace and seated themselves.

As they watched, Professor Crinkle was led out with Moonwash and Quorn Joy. The dinosaurs had devised a particularly fiendish battle: the cyborg against the two HIPZIS. Grkkghj turned to Tantra and winked a derogatory comment about the two men. Lushdjiis laughed and drooled and some of his spittle fell on her.

She seethed inside but remained silent.

Moonwash was attired as a *retiarius*, the same as Nutloaf, with a net and trident; while Quorn Joy was dressed like a *paegniarius*, with whip and club. Neither man seemed able to hold their weapons properly. As for the professor, he held both his axes in two random tentacles, but some of his other arms were busy elsewhere, burrowing under the sand like snakes and remaining unseen by anyone.

The order to start battle was given by Yyyshk.

Crinkle waved his two axes in complex patterns, deliberately missing his opponents by inches. Every time he got close enough to one of them, he hissed a little more of the plan that had taken shape in his mind. First he would tie together all the tails of all the dinosaurs on all the seats in the amphitheater. Then he would give a shout, and at this signal, the HIPZIS must start running towards the exit.

"But the exit is, like, guarded, man!" cried Moonwash.

"By a tyrannosaur!" added Quorn Joy.

"Indeed so," said the professor, "and because there's only one of him I can't tie his tail to anything, so we'll have to tackle him with our weapons. I hope the girls will understand what we're doing and join us. Apart from Jack Northrop and Philip José Farmer, they are the brainiest characters in this book, so I have no worries on that score. Just try your hardest to look like you really mean to be mean."

"Man, two uses of the word 'mean' in a single sentence! Do I, like, win any sort of prize for spotting that?"

"No," said Crinkle, dodging an inept lunge.

His unseen tentacles reached the circumference of the arena and began snaking up over the rows of seats, tying knots as they slithered along. The audience was so spellbound by the action taking place below they didn't feel a thing. It took almost twenty minutes to tie all the knots but finally it was possible to retract his arms.

"There's only one problem," the professor mused to himself. "Even if we succeed in getting on that seaplane and taking off, the dinosaurs will send out telepathic rays that sap my willpower and make me their slave. Then I'll be forced to return the aircraft and deliver us all back into their clutches. How to avoid this fate?"

The solution came to him immediately.

"Moonwash!" he hissed.

"Like, what is it, dude?" answered the HIPZI.

"Stab me in the brain with one of your trident prongs. I'm serious! It's essential you destroy the ESP Nerve Net that is located under my rotting Psi-Suppressor Cluster. If you don't permanently disable my extrasensory powers we'll never get out alive!"

"Don't ask me to do that, man! I'm squeamish!"

"Do it, dear boy! For the love of humanity! For the love of cyborgity! For the love of lentils! Do it!"

"No, dude, I can't. How can I? No!"

"DO IT, MOONWASH!"

"I don't know where to lunge, man!"

"Just to the left of the flechette wound, the scar left by that assassin's effort to murder me in Berlin."

"Yeah, but . . . Your left or mine, dude?"

"Mine, Moonwash, mine!"

"Well, if you insist!" gasped the reply, and the pacifist gladiator thrust his trident forward, closing his eyes tight and turning his head away at the same instant. The left prong (or tine) penetrated the ultraglass and entered the grey mass of quivering matter. Then the cyborg trundled back and out slid the cruel spike of the weapon.

The professor thrashed his tentacles and frowned.

Something didn't feel right.

"Um, I meant *your* left, my boy," he said.

Moonwash jabbed again; and this time the prong did the job intended for it, rupturing the designated cells and destroying the professor's ability to foretell the future, communicate cheaply at a distance with brainwaves, bend spoons, see ghosts and other stuff. Jerking free of the prong, letting the ultraglass reseal itself perfectly, Crinkle lifted both axes high. Then he emitted a loud mechanical shriek.

"Time to get out of here!" he cried as he sped on his castors towards the exit. There was immediate uproar among the audience. Tyrannosaurs and triceratops jumped up to give chase, but they instantly fell over, the tangle of their tails making movement in any direction impossible. If one tried to go one way, he pulled along his neighbor who might be attempting to go another. Chaos reigned. Angered and pained, many of them started biting or stabbing each other, forgetting the escapees in the arena. And now the professor hurled both his axes . . .

He flung them at the lone tyrannosaur guarding the exit. The beast had never expected that anyone would dare make this attempt and maybe had grown complacent or soft. He shielded his head with his little forepaws, a reflex that meant he couldn't see anything. He was evidently in shock. As it happened, neither axe hit its mark, but the professor and the two HIPZI males were able to skirt him and pass through the archway. "Head for the sea!" cried Crinkle as they puffed.

Tantra and Nutloaf observed this development with excessive interest. After the briefest exchange of glances, they instinctively burst into action, Nutloaf flinging her trident at the Chief Plenipotentiary and her weighted net at Grkkghj, while Tantra instantly thought better of tackling Lushdjiis and Saaailjkdnk with a puny sword and instead slashed the ropes holding up the canvas canopy of the pavilion. Down it came, ensnaring the horrid monsters; and with athletic leaps the girls skipped over the prone bodies of all the tumbled dinosaurs on all the rows, reached the arena and hurried around and past the immobile guard.

They caught up easily with the professor and the two men. Not far out to sea bobbed the seaplane; but just as they were about to plunge into the water and swim for it, an enormous adult triceratops came charging down the beach towards them at maximum speed, his horns lowered, his mouth open and booming, his little eyes furious. There was no chance of fleeing him and no chance of surviving the impact. The professor sadly regarded his friends and sighed fatalistically.

"So this is the end. Time to say goodbye!"

Just at that moment, two of the Bronson planets disappeared over the horizon, changing the pattern of gravity in this locale yet again. The junk in the sky found it harder to stay aloft and some of the less aerodynamic pieces began falling back to Earth.

Bent rivets and chain links rained in torrents.

Ball bearings clattered urgently.

These had almost no effect on the tough hide of the triceratops, but in the split second before his horns connected with the professor, a massive iron object fell directly on his head, powdering his skull and burying his front half in the ground. This object had the shape of a truncated pyramid and 100 TONS was written on it in white letters. It seemed out of place in the world of authentic phenomena.

"My goodness!" cried the professor. "I haven't seen one of those since the

1930s. It must have been circulating up there for all that time, nobody knows how or why, just waiting to flatten this deadly triceratops and save our novel from a premature ending."

"What is it, man? Where does it come from?"

"It's a comedy weight, dear boy, and it is a typical product of a race of beings known as the Slapstickians."

"Who are they, dude? And where's Slapstickia?"

"It's not a place but a style."

Moonwash, Quorn Joy, Tantra and Nutloaf all looked questioningly at the professor. He sighed and said:

"They lived a long time ago, when I was a boy, and went extinct many years before Yellowstone erupted. Some say they were finished when the movies acquired sound, but that's not for me to deny or confirm. I can see I've confused you. Let's not worry about such matters; we should just get the hell out of Libya while we can!"

They ran down the beach and into the sea.

SLEDGING TO THE CAMEROONS

Stringent Strange felt good as he walked up the beach towards the forest and he realized that Africa was in his blood, that he belonged to this huge mysterious continent, that his genetic heritage was rejoicing deep inside him to breathe tropic air again. But his conscious mind was unhappy, for he still didn't know where he was.

But now he saw a man sitting under a parasol. The man was dressed in modern casual clothes and wore a brightly colored woolen hat. He rose to greet the newcomer. "Welcome to Gambia! How are you today? Want to see the monkey park? Want some fresh juice? Mango and lime! Come to my restaurant, taste the best fish, the freshest fish, not even caught yet! Need a taxi? Where are you from?"

Stringent was flabbergasted. "Is this really The Gambia? But you sound and look exactly like a Jamaican!"

The man laughed more loudly than was strictly necessary. "It's all the same, we're brothers together, black and white, human and gorilla. You want a necklace for luck? Cowrie shells against bad juju! Need a guide for the monkey park? Very few tourists today. They eat peanuts out of your hand, very funny. So do the monkeys. Bijilo Forest Park. Rather dangerous without a guide. You are English?"

"I'm from Germany. Well, the USA actually. To be honest, I'm from the past. I'm not a tourist but a hero . . ."

"The past! I have a brother who lives in the past! He's studying ecology at college there. I'll guide you to the monkey park for a special price. Then we can visit my restaurant later."

"I'm not very hungry and I don't have much money. I need to get to the Cameroons as fast as possible."

The man shrugged. "If you head east, you'll get there eventually. Come back one day, won't you, brother?"

Stringent nodded. "If I ever do, I'll buy your juice and eat your fish and let you guide me anywhere at all."

The Gambian laughed and sat back down.

Stringent walked onwards. He knew where he was now. On the coast of West Africa, not more than two-thousand three-hundred miles short of his destination. How might he cover that distance with only $50? West Africa is a lot more expensive than people think. I was surprised by this fact when I went there myself a few years ago. You'll be lucky to get a glass of fruit juice for less than $3. For budget travelers, East Africa is a better bet; but Stringent didn't have that option.

He wandered into the forest, following a clearly marked trail. Monkeys in the trees chattered encouragingly at him as he passed; maybe they felt a remote kinship with the part of him below his neck. Then something in the bushes caught his attention. Three or four shining globes. Eggs? But they didn't resemble those of any bird or reptile he had ever read about. As he stooped to pick them up, a frenzied blue monkey screamed and launched itself at him. Reluctantly, Stringent swatted it away, and it landed dazed in the undergrowth. He walked on.

As he walked, he held the eggs in his open palm and examined them. It was while he was maintaining this stance that he encountered another man coming along the trail in the opposite direction. This man was European; a fedora hat shaded a bearded face.

"Good heavens!" he cried. "Are those . . . ?"

He seemed unable to speak; he merely jabbed at the eggs with sunburned fingers and did a little odd dance.

"Are they what?" spluttered Stringent.

"Monkey eggs!" cried the man.

"Monkeys don't lay eggs; everyone knows that!"

The man removed his fedora, fanned himself with the floppy brim, and then he said, "Yes, they do. Some do, anyhow. The rarest kind of monkey, in fact. The Gambian Gibberer."

"I've never heard of that kind of simian."

"Because almost nobody has ever seen one! They are bright blue! Let me introduce myself. My name is Captain Kettle and I have been looking for monkey eggs for ten years."

"Are they worth anything?" asked Stringent.

"Are they?" gasped Captain Kettle.

"Yes, that's what I asked."

The explorer replaced his hat and puffed out his grizzled cheeks. "The smallest of the four examples you hold in your palm is worth maybe sixty thousand pounds. The largest might be valued at £400,000 or even more. You are a rich man now, sir!"

He cast his eyes to the forest floor and his face began to redden. It was clear he was only keeping himself under control with an immense effort. It occurred to Stringent that this man might soon become an enemy, and even though the ape-man had confidence in his own strength, the explorer clearly wasn't a softie. In fact he was Welsh, which meant he was unpredictable as well as hot headed. Stringent saw no proper reason why he shouldn't share his good fortune with this fellow.

"Here you are: the two midrange eggs."

Captain Kettle rubbed his beard furiously but he took the proffered gift anyway. "You have given me quarter of a million pounds. That was both generous and sensible of you."

Stringent laughed. "I thought as much. But value is a concept that can't achieve anything until it has been converted into hard cash. I guess that I ought to take them to the nearest market and sell them. Let's see. The main town in these parts is Serekunda?"

"Heavens, boyo!" exclaimed Captain Kettle, rolling his eyes and flaring his nostrils. "Take them to a human market and you'll get a poor price for them, and you may be robbed and killed too, even though Gambia's a safe country indeed; but monkey eggs have that effect on people. No, I don't recommend selling them that way."

"Well, who should I sell them to if not humans?"

"Why, to monkeys, of course!"

"You mean, sell them back to the Gambian Gibberers? But isn't that a form of ransom? You make me sound and feel like a kidnapper. I'd feel a little uncomfortable doing that . . ."

Captain Kettle shrugged. "It's a standard procedure. The monkeys are aware of how it works, indeed they set it up in the first place. Keep going through this forest for another five miles and you'll find a clearing where the monkeys are open for trade."

Stringent opened his mouth to continue the conversation, but Captain Kettle moved off into the undergrowth and the apeman was left alone. He realized he had no choice but to take the explorer's advice; and so with a swirl of mixed emotions coursing through his soul he continued his stroll along the path. Eventually he came to the promised clearing. Dozens of blue monkeys had set up stalls here and they chattered and gibbered with unfettered animation. Like cartoons.

Not like that really, Stringent decided as he entered the clearing. The monkeys stopped speaking and stared at him. He approached slowly, one egg in each hand, holding both up.

Several monkeys began clapping their hands.

One monkey pulled him by the hairs that sprouted from his kneecap and led him over to the nearest stall.

The monkey that squatted on a tree stump behind this stall screwed a magnifying lens into his right eye and studied the eggs carefully. Then he rapidly worked the beads on an abacus. These beads were nuts. With an elegant smacking of the lips he finally arrived at the sum of £420,000. The apeman knew he was being swindled, that the price should be forty grand higher, but he didn't care to haggle.

He nodded and the cash was counted in front of him.

The transaction completed, he turned to leave, but then he stopped with a frown. Maybe these monkeys could help him with his mission? Although the language of monkeys and gorillas is utterly different, he did his best to convey meaning through gestures.

"Take me to the Cameroons . . . Fast as feasible . . ."

A monkey plucked at his elbow and said in German (futuristic German, which is identical to English, remember) that he was just the simian to aid the hero in his quest. "Follow me."

"Where did you learn to talk human?" asked Stringent.

"In the Simian-ary," came the reply.

"What's that?" said Stringent.

"An awful pun on the word 'seminary' but it's also a genuine school for monkeys of a religious persuasion."

"Do you praise Zumboo? Does he exist?"

"Zumboo is my chief god, yes, but I also worship Thomp, Spanko and Basha. I don't believe they have the form of primates, as we were taught by the Arch-Baboons, but I do believe there *is* something very hairy out there. What about you? Are you an atheist?"

"Apparently I'm under the control of a god called 'The Author,' but I've never seen, heard or smelled him, and lately I've been plagued with doubts about the meaning of this Book."

The monkey sneered. "I've heard of him. He's just a normal man and is often incompetent. Can you believe that he even forgot to give me a name! So now I'm just 'The Monkey.' Bah!"

"Why don't you give yourself your own name?"

"That's not a bad idea. Sure."

"Have you decided what it will be?"

"Yes. Call me Malcolm."

Stringent and Malcolm walked across the clearing to an area that was obviously a transport terminus. Sledges lay in readiness for departure and strong monkeys lounged around waiting to be harnessed up for journeys. These sledges all looked rickety but Malcolm assured the apeman that they were strong enough for the purpose.

"Certainly they will last all the way to the Cameroons."

"In that case, I'm ready!" cried Stringent.

"This mode of transport is called Latitude Cars. Just as cable cars only run on the cords they are suspended from, so these sledges can only travel along lines of latitude," said Malcolm.

"That's rather peculiar," commented Stringent.

"Yes, it is," concurred Malcolm.

"And why should this be so?" pressed Stringent.

"I have no idea," said Malcolm.

And he really didn't, he wasn't monkeying around. So Stringent sat in the nearest sledge and eight monkeys instantly jumped to attention, fitted themselves into the harness and spat out the gum they were chewing. The apeman made himself comfortable.

"Payment in advance!" insisted Malcolm.

"How much?" asked Stringent.

Malcolm performed careful calculations on his fingers; when he ran out of fingers he continued his sums on his toes; when he ran out of toes, he used the apeman's toes; and when he ran out of those, he used his fingers, not forgetting to make adjustments for the different number of digits that our hero possessed, so far the only one of his abnormalities known to him. Finally he arrived at a specific price.

"Exactly £420,000 for a one-way trip."

"You must be joking!"

"Plus $50 insurance, of course."

Stringent's lips curled. He handed over the cash and the monkeys in the harnesses jerked. He was off!

Before this novel began, Stringent had memorized a map of Africa that his author had given to him. So he knew exactly where he was going. You may sneer at this and utter the deadly accusation, "Contrived!" but I did do that, honest. Look, here's the map. I would hardly be able to produce a map at such short notice if I wasn't telling the truth, would I? Exactly! Now stop accusing me of any impropriety . . .

The sledge rushed through the forest at incredible speed. And yet while they pulled it, the monkeys didn't seem troubled by the effort at all. Some of them conducted conversations; others played the Jew's Harp or flute; a few even managed to start a poker game, though most of the cards ended up being snatched by the wind.

Due east along the 13th Parallel, which is the latitude of Gambia, lay the famous Lake Chad; and the southern shores of Lake Chad were part of the sovereign territory of Cameroon.

Stringent was satisfied to know this!

But he didn't yet know which part of that vast country had been decided upon by Professor Crinkle as their original destination. Still, it would be a very good start to get anywhere within its borders. The question was: how many long weeks might it take?

He got to learn the answer to that question.

He learned it the hard way.

They pushed deeper into the interior of Gambia. The forest thinned out and the trees and bushes became smaller and the soil more parched. As the sun went down, Stringent wondered how the monkeys would proceed over the rough terrain without overturning the sledge; but in fact they stopped at the base of a massive boulder and made camp. One monkey lit a fire while his companions went to gather berries. Then a weird fruity soup was made in a cauldron. Bats flittered above.

The monkeys chattered long past midnight, played hairy songs on flutes and yawned. It was time for bed.

Stringent stretched at full length on the sledge and fell asleep. An hour before dawn he felt cold, reached out for the nearest monkey and pulled it over him like a small fur blanket.

The sun rose and it was time to be going.

They travelled like this for several days before reaching the border with Senegal. They didn't cross at an official border post. The country here was almost identical to that of Gambia but as they proceeded eastwards the soil became even more baked and the landscape less fertile. A week passed and they entered Mali, a magnificent country of incredible music, but Stringent didn't get the chance to hear any.

The hot sun beat down on his head; but irregular shade was provided by the Bronson worlds. They slid over semi-arid scrub savannah, and he knew they had entered the Sahel, that vast region of sub-Saharan Africa that isn't quite desert but isn't fertile land.

Two more weeks went by and they crossed into Burkina Faso, possibly the most politically interesting of all the nations in the region, for this was where a man named Thomas Sankara established a government that fought corruption and won, something almost unheard of in West Africa. But that was back in the 1980s, one hundred and twenty-five years before now, and Stringent knew nothing about it.

After Burkina Faso they entered Niger, a real desert land, and the dunes proved troublesome for the monkeys; it took a further four weeks for them to reach the northern shore of Lake Chad. The apeman disembarked at the final stop with a tear in his eye, waved farewell to the trusty creatures and started walking along the shore.

He entered Cameroon a few days later.

Something white and oddly shaped gleamed on the water. Some sort of seaplane? A Savoia-Marchetti S.55! What was it doing here? The apeman decided it must be a mirage. Such things could not exist in the year 2112. Maybe he was suffering from sunstroke or heat exhaustion? He continued gazing at the object as he walked.

He crashed through a clump of reeds into a clearing. Huts stood around a central firepit. As he approached, a naked man looked up and confronted him. But he wasn't a native of the locale. His skin was fair and his pubic hairs were blonde and he wore a helmet on his head, a helmet identical to that of a mediaeval knight; but the visor was open and there was nothing inside! He slammed it shut angrily.

Although nude, he was wearing a broad belt.

Hanging from this belt on his right side was a holster. He reached for it and withdrew a peculiar gun, not an automatic pistol but something snub-nosed and shiny that bristled with aerials. Stringent thought it looked familiar and took one step forward.

This was an error of judgment. The naked man discharged his weapon at the apeman's jaw. Blue sparks leaped and danced about his teeth and he collapsed like a sack of doughnuts, the ones without cream in the middle, yes, still the toroid ones, I'm afraid.

Tarotplane to Harmonica

Stringent blinked up at the face of the professor, then sat up on his pallet bed of reeds and gripped one of his stepfather's tentacles in his hairy but tender hands. "Doc! Is it really you?"

"Yes, dear boy. How nice to see you again!"

"Me too, doc. I mean, I'm overjoyed to see *you*, I couldn't very well be overjoyed to see *me*, unless I had a mirror, and I don't! What happened? I was zapped by a ray gun, I guess."

"Yes, that's exactly what happened. Tits."

Stringent frowned and winced as sharp pains shot through his skull as a result. "I beg your pardon, doc? Did you just utter a dirty word? I must be mishearing things, mustn't I?"

"No, your fucking ears are fine, my boy."

"You did it again, doc! You said a bad word! What gives? You always told me that filthy language was indicative of a dirty soul. Have you had a change of heart about that, doc?"

The professor shrugged. "Piss."

"And again! What's going on here, doc?"

"Sod all, dear boy. Bums."

Stringent climbed off the pallet bed and stood up. "Do you have some weird tropical disease? Is that it?"

The professor shook his head. "Beaver."

"Then what gives, doc?"

Crinkle tapped his ultraglass brain jar with a tentacle. "It was the fault of Moonwash. He stabbed me twice in a gladiatorial duel and on the first

177

occasion his shitting trident destroyed my Anti-Swearing Cluster. There isn't a single cell left alive in that particular part of my brain! So now I'm compelled to blurt obscenities and there's nothing I can do about it. In my youth I uttered the occasional expletive and I even let slip a couple in this very book, but now I have no control: the faucet of buggering verbal filth in my subconscious is stuck open."

"That's just too bad, doc!"

"Yes, it frigging is, dear boy. Ah well!" Then the professor seemed to have an important afterthought. He leaned close to the apeman's ear and said with his metal lips: "Cock."

Stringent decided to overlook the professor's unsettling affliction and concentrate entirely on the plot.

"I'm not sure what happened, doc. After arriving on the shores of this lake I was blasted with a weapon identical to the one used on me by the Protogruppenführer all those chapters ago, and yet the man who pressed the trigger was someone else."

The professor laughed. "No, dear boy, it was the Protogruppenführer you encountered. He has established a colony on the shores of Lake Chad with his followers, the Pre-Emptive Nazis, except that now they're called the fucking Meta-Emptive Nazis."

"Ja!" came a strident voice, "and I also have changed my name. I am no longer the Protogruppenführer but the *Post*gruppenführer, because the time is the future, not the past."

Into the hut walked the figure that had assaulted Stringent. It turned its nonhuman head and winked at the professor, who winked back. Stringent was shocked by this behavior.

"But he's our deadly enemy, doc, and you . . ."

The professor held up a tentacle for silence. "Hold your shitty horses there, dear boy. I need to explain the situation to you. Remember the old dictum 'my enemy's enemy is my friend?' Well, Stringy, we are sodding compelled to form an alliance with the Postgruppenführer for the mutual benefit of the human race. Tits."

Stringent clenched his jaw and his buttock cheeks but said nothing to antagonize the metal-headed rascal who toyed with the ray gun slung at his naked hip like some pervert.

"OK, doc, I'm ready to hear the story."

The professor said, "Not every member of the Nazi Party was happy with the way things went after Hitler's death. Some believed the gradual fucking move towards peace and love was a betrayal of the original evil principles. So these members formed a splinter group. They were led by Postgruppenführer Kaspar Stumpf."

"That's me!" said the man with the metal head.

The professor waved aside this unnecessary comment and continued with a sigh, "Well, they decided to form their own colony somewhere in a place free from harassment, a remote location where the true viciousness of the Nazi ethos wouldn't be subjected to temptations of gentleness. The southern shore of Lake Chad in the Cameroons was chosen as a site. Yes, I know it's crapping weird that Lake Chad isn't wholly in Chad, but that's not my fault. Anyway, one night, they stole the Tarotplane, the invention that helped Germany win the war."

"I get it, doc," said Stringent encouragingly.

"The Tarotplane towed a glider behind it and this glider was full of the few Nazis who professed allegiance to the old values. Most of them were from the bloody ranks of the Pre-Emptive Nazis. The Tarotplane enabled them to avoid clear air turbulence all the way here; it would also serve as a precaution to preserve their independence. Any nation that had designs on the colony would be sure to think twice when they realized that such a formidable weapon was available to the colonists, for the Tarotplane is capable of flying utterly unscathed through any amount of antiaircraft fire to drop bombs on enemy heads!"

"Softer heads than mine," said the Postgruppenführer.

"Tee hee! Pisser," said Crinkle.

Stringent digested all this. "It was your plan all along to come here and borrow the Tarotplane off these guys?"

"Yes, my boy. We fucking need it to get the gun that can kill anything. There's no other aircraft capable of reaching the place where that gun is said to be located. Asswipe. Balls."

"And where," asked Stringent uneasily, "is that place?"

"Bronson Frigging Charlie!"

Stringent swallowed hard. "Outer space, doc?"

"Yes, my boy, but what's the issue? You've already been kidnapped by aliens and taken outside our atmosphere. Scrotum. So this will merely be a simple stroll in the park for you."

"Yeah, but it's a biplane, doc!"

The professor scratched his bell jar. "True. And?"

"It has an open cockpit. The fuselage isn't pressurized or sealed against leaks. There's no radiation shielding!"

"Well, I'm not crapping shielded either, Stringy."

"But you're clockwork, doc."

The professor and the Postgruppenführer roared with laughter; and the cruel Nazi leader even had the audacity to wipe tears of quicksilver from his dead cheeks. He cried, "Oh, Herr Hairy tells a most funny joke! He is being the clown again! Ha ha!"

"What's so amusing?" growled Stringent.

Crinkle finally recovered his composure enough to gasp, "I might well be powered by fucking clockwork, but what's the clockwork powered by? You don't believe my so-called 'mainspring' is actually a metal spring, do you? No, dear boy, it's composed of hydrogen and helium atoms crushed into a reactive spiral. My clockwork is powered by nuclear fission! What a cute notion: to believe I was some sort of relative of the chronometer! I regard that as absolutely hilarious."

"But you're unshielded, doc? So I have probably received a fatal dose of radiation? And the HIPZIS too?"

"Of course! You didn't think this novel could possibly have any sort of happy ending, did you? Bollocks!"

Stringent considered this objectively. "Fair enough."

"Look on the bright side," continued Crinkle, "your descendants might mutate into centaurs or spolcycs."

"I doubt it; the Pectorals insisted I used contraception, so the chances of me having any offspring are minimal. But what's a spolcycs, doc? Are you sure you didn't make it up?"

"Quite fucking sure, dear boy. A cyclops is a creature with one eye; so a spolcyc must be a creature *made* of eyes! Stands to reason, doesn't it? In my view, it's perfectly obvious."

"Gee, thanks, doc! Yes, I suppose it is."

The cyborg folded six arms.

"The crapping plan is this, Stringy: we use the Tarotplane to fly across the rogue gas clouds that are floating up there. The three Bronson worlds and Earth all lost some of their respective atmospheres because of the odd gravitational matrices set up by the complex orbits, so space isn't the total vacuum it once was. The Tarotplane will be able to guide us from one gas cloud to another, so we won't suffocate provided we trust it. Then we can land on Bronson Charlie alive!"

Stringent licked his lips. "I've got an alternative idea, doc."

"Does it involve whores, my boy?"

"Not *that* idea, doc; this idea. Listen! The engine of the airplane that crashed near Goodvibe is probably still intact. If we can fix it and reverse the polarity we'll be able to send the entire world back in time to the year 1932 and all this horrible nonsense about the Rushans will no longer be a problem. So what do you think?"

"No good, my boy. When I was still psychic I had a clairvoyant dream and it showed me that a tribe of More Lucks had entered the forest where you crashed and found the remains of Northrop's Stratospheric Cruiser; I am sorry to report that they dismantled it and dragged the engine away to their lair, wherever that might be."

"The More Lucks, doc? Where are they from?"

The professor shrugged. "I think they have escaped from another book by the same author.* I'm not sure."

Tantra entered the hut. "Hello, Mr. Strange!"

Crinkle said, "Here's the *aviatrix* that flew the Balbo seaplane here all the way from Leptis Magna. She's a wonderful girl and has forced me to reassess my casual 1930s prejudices. Isn't that right, my dear? Now fetch the men some coffee, will ya?"

"Glad to see you lost your chauvinism, doc!"

"Too pissing right, Stringy!"

The Postgruppenführer tapped the apeman on his shoulder. "Don't you have any curiosity about why I possess the body of a naked youth but the head of an empty suit of armor?"

Stringent pouted. "I suppose so. Tell me."

The Postgruppenführer said, "I'm a product of the same laboratory that turned Tobias Crinkle into the thing you see before you; but in my case a different experiment was performed. We are both cyborgs, but the Führer had his brain extracted and grafted onto the hull of a robot; whereas I had a robot head fixed to my body, a body pumped full of preserving fluids to stop it rotting. That's my answer."

Stringent sighed. "Yeah, thanks."

---

* *Engelbrecht Again!* Published by Dead Letter Press in 2008.

The professor said, "Do you feel ready to fly a Tarotplane to Bronson Charlie, dear boy? Please say yes."

"Why not, doc? Show me where she is."

They left the mud hut and Crinkle guided the apeman down a path that wound through tall reeds for about half a mile. Suddenly they broke into a clearing; it was a runway and the Tarotplane stood on the compressed dirt like a lunatic's dream of a Handley Page H.P.42 (the one with 4 x 555-hp Bristol-Jupiter XFBM 9-cylinder radial engines). It was big for a biplane and had a rather cumbersome appearance that betrayed a haughty disdain for streamlining, and yet it possessed soul. Stringent whistled through his teeth in unadulterated admiration.

"So this is what won the war for Hitler, doc?"

"Yes, my boy. Note the wings!"

The four wings were giant Tarot cards. At the moment they displayed the same symbol, the Seven of Coins, representing a readiness for a new adventure and preparation for a new strategy; but Stringent guessed they would change to other patterns the moment the plane took off. He turned to the professor with a sheepish grin.

"May I get inside her, doc?"

"Climb up, dear turd. I'm coming with you and so are Tantra, Nutloaf and the Postgruppenführer. The sooner we leave, the better. Any moment now the Rushans might invade!"

"What about Moonwash and Quorn Joy, doc?"

"It's more efficient if they stay here," answered Nutloaf. She followed the apeman into the cockpit; and Tantra, Crinkle and Kaspar Stumpf also climbed up and seated themselves.

Stringent pressed the ignition button.

The plane responded beautifully to his touch. He rolled her down the runway and lifted her easily up.

"Remember, my boy, there's no autopilot. You have to manually check the symbols on the wings and take their advice. Tits. If you fail to heed an omen or hint, we will still crash. The Tarotplane isn't a magical device, so don't let your attention wander!"

"No worries, doc, I'm the best in the business."

"But do you know the meanings of the Tarot symbols?" asked Nutloaf as she stared at the changing wings.

Stringent replied in a small voice, "No."

The professor smiled. "I'm an expert and I'll call out the interpretations as they occur. The lower left wing is now the Page of Sticks, which is an indication of a willingness to go in a new direction, so bank her steeply to the fucking left and take her higher."

The apeman did as he was told. They soon found themselves spiraling upwards through a rent in the dense clouds of aerial junk. Now they were above the cogs and levers and comedy weights. The Bronson worlds were vast in a sky that was a darker blue.

"The upper right wing has changed to the Wheel of Fortune. Bank her to the right and increase the angle of bastard ascent by ten degrees. Now bank her to the left, my boy. Piss."

They were on the very edge of space. In an earlier century or in a more sensible book they would have frozen and suffocated by now, but pockets of oxygen bobbed about randomly and the biplane remained within them. As these pockets moved, collided and absorbed each other, Stringent was able to navigate the Tarotplane beyond the Earth and nearer to the planet known as Bronson Charlie. Without the advice of the wings, however, the attempt would have been suicidal.

"Upper left wing has changed to the Eight of Swords. Lower right has changed to the High Priestess. Shift up a shitting gear and dip her nose by five degrees. That's it, boy. Tits."

Bronson Alpha fell away behind them; Bronson Bravo also. At last the enigmatic bulk of Bronson Charlie, most arcane of the rogue worlds, was expanding to meet them. The occupants of the Tarotplane gasped with an ineffable sense of wonder. They were fully caught in its gravity now and they entered its atmosphere at precisely the correct angle. Spiraling to the surface, Stringent grinned broadly.

"I did it, doc! I piloted her across space!"

"Congratulations. Beaver."

The Postgruppenführer craned his helmet at the continents beneath the plane. He sighed and said, "I can't see any evidence of civilization, just a few ruined cities on a plateau. Do you think this might be a dead world? If so, our time has been wasted!"

Crinkle tapped Stringent on the shoulder with a tentacle. "Head for the plateau. May as well investigate."

The apeman put the Tarotplane into a steep dive. When all four wings changed into the Ace of Coins, signifying practical accomplishment and tangible results, he pulled back on the stick. They were less than 50 feet above a collection of toppled pillars, broken arches and shattered towers. He found a clear place to land.

"That's it, doc. Down safe and sound."

But the professor seemed distraught and he clutched his brain jar in an impenetrable knot of tentacles.

THE GUN THAT CAN KILL ANYTHING

Stringent Strange ran to the side of his stepfather. "What's wrong, doc? Are you unwell or psychotic?" He tried to pull away the tentacles but it was impossible. Too many bears.

"I can hardly believe it, Stringy. A loose frigging end I had forgotten about has just now been tied up!"

"Will you explain to me what it is, doc?"

But before the cyborg could answer him, Tantra shouted, "Look over there! It's a living inhabitant. He's wearing a massive hat and watching us. Seems to be waiting for someone."

"So he cocking does, dear girl. Let's go over."

They walked towards a structure that was still largely intact. It looked like the platform of a railway station but there were no tracks or trains. A leaking pipe dripped water on the alien's hat. It was a wide-brimmed hat and it was almost full. The alien looked like a human male but he couldn't be, because this chapter insists he isn't. He was a typical Harmonican and an indigenous insect buzzed around his face, landing on his cheeks, brow and chin. His eyes followed it.

"I doubt he speaks English—I mean German," said Stringent. "So how can we communicate with him?"

"Try Esperanto, my boy," suggested the professor.

"What's that, doc? Isn't it something to do with chocolate? I don't think that feeding the alien will help!"

"No, Stringy, it's a language that was invented to render interplanetary conversation feasible. I'm not fucking fluent but I can try to make myself understood with the little I know."

185

"Go on then, doc!" encouraged Stringent.

The professor trundled over to the alien with the hat and said, "Ĉu vi miskomprenis min? Li ĉiam miskomprenas spritaĵojn. Ŝi misprononcas ĉiujn vortojn. Tits. Ĉu la esploristo suferis pro malvarmumo? Kio estas ventumilo? Ĉi vi cebumis pri la krucvort-enigmo? Scrotum. La mezuro estas nur proksimuma. Beaver."

He stood back and waited for a response. The alien looked up and his hat spilled water down his back.

"Don't rightly comprehend," he drawled.

"Hey, he speaks our lingo!" rejoiced Stringent. "I bet that spares the author an intricate digression!"

"What have you come for?" asked the alien.

"We're looking for the gun that can kill anything," said the professor with tentacles akimbo. A cold wind blew across the landscape and for a moment Crinkle shivered, but then he remembered that he didn't have a nervous system, so he stopped.

"It's not here," said the alien quietly.

"What?" roared Stringent.

The Postgruppenführer was equally dismayed. "This is a disaster! We shall have to return to Earth empty handed; and the Rushans will be free to impose their Canadian will!"

The professor addressed the alien. "Where is it?"

The alien lightly brushed away the persistent insect that had settled on his left sideburn. "It got left behind."

"Left behind where? Tell us!"

"The first time our planet passed yours."

"I didn't ask *when*, I asked where!" The professor extended a few arms to shake the alien, but then he realized that this would result in corrosive water being splashed over him.

"We tried to establish a colony on Earth," said the alien, "and the gun went with the colonists. Then Harmonica drifted out of your solar system. We maintained radio contact with the colony for a few centuries but they stopped transmitting one day and we heard nothing more from them. This time we weren't able to travel to your planet to retrieve it: we are a dying race and thus Bradburyesque."

That was clearly an indigenous word.

Crinkle gritted his alloyed teeth. "Yes, but where!"

The alien blinked. "I don't know. The knowledge has been forgotten. I simply can't tell you. I'm sorry."

"We're in trouble now, doc!" said Stringent.

To his astonishment, the professor grinned and shook his head. "That's not the fucking case at all, my sodding boy. I know the precise location of the original Harmonican colony! Quick, we need to get back in the shitty Tarotplane and return to Earth."

Stringent asked no more questions.

They ran back to the waiting craft and he took it back into the sky. As they departed, the alien didn't look up or wave. He remained immobile on his rocking chair, collecting water.

As Stringent worked the joystick and the wings changed their symbols he asked the professor from the corner of his mouth, "What gives, doc? I don't get how you know where the gun is located. Have you seen a proof copy of this book before printing?"

"No, my boy, that would be a form of cheating. Let me explain. I was overcome with memories when I glimpsed the architecture of the ruined cities on the surface of this world. The style of the buildings was identical to those of the ruins in the Congo jungle near the River Lomami where I found the infant version of you."

"Holy plot twist, doc! That's incredible!"

"Yes, Stringy, but it's true anyway. If you take us there now, we stand a good chance of getting the gun."

The apeman opened up the throttle and they accelerated into space and passed carefully from one rogue oxygen bubble to another until they were back in the more homely skies of Earth. The professor gave directions to the place where the ruins were hidden under a canopy of trees. There was now the problem of where to land.

"I don't perceive any clearings at all, doc!"

"Can you land on top, my boy?"

This was an eccentric request but the apeman took the biplane into the forest canopy. Branches pierced the wings and scraped the fuselage and the occupants of the craft were hurled around violently inside. Stringent broke his nose a second time on the console. Tantra ended up with a foot wedged inside the open visor of Kaspar Stumpf's empty helmet. That one might not have happened accidentally, as the Postgruppenführer seemed in no haste to extract it. He merely mumbled the word, "Toes!" again and again to himself. Tantra eventually managed to pull it out. The airplane had lurched to a vertiginous halt.

"Now what do we do, doc?"

"Isn't it buggering obvious, my boy? We climb down the trees right to the jungle floor. The ruins are almost directly beneath us. When we reach them we can split up five ways and search different buildings. Eventually one of us will discover the gun."

Stringent nodded and eased himself out of the cockpit. It was easy for him to climb down the tree and his gorilla arms rejoiced in the sensation of rough bark against his fur. Tantra and Nutloaf also found it simple, for they were nature lovers and skilled at such arboreal pursuits. For Kaspar Stumpf it was a little more tricky.

Nonetheless he eventually managed the task. As for the professor, his descent was the most effortless of all. He hung on by a single tentacle to a sturdy branch and extended his arm, lowering himself parallel to the thick trunk until his castors were on the ground. Then he relaxed his grip on the branch and retracted the tentacle.

The ruins gleamed before them. Crinkle danced.

"Come on, there isn't much time. I'll go this way; each of you can pick your own fifth of the complex to search. I fear the Rushans are already on their way. We might be too late!"

Stringent moved through a low archway into an empty chamber. There was a hole in the roof and sunlight streamed in. He blinked. No, the room wasn't entirely empty. An object stood propped against the far wall. It had a stock, a barrel and a trigger guard.

What could it be? The apeman approached it.

He picked it up. It was the gun.

The gun that could kill anything. Their only defense against Rush. He smiled to himself, aimed the gun through the hole in the roof and pressed the trigger. A bolt of orange energy spat out at ludicrous velocity and was gone in a tiny fraction of an instant.

He stepped outside the chamber and shouted, "I have it! I've found it! I have the weapon that will save us!"

The professor emerged from a doorway and trundled up to him, taking the weapon in his tentacles and examining it. "Well done, my boy! You're a frigging hero indeed! Now remember: the myth states that it can only be fired once, so we must be cautious."

"Um, doc," said Stringent.

"Yes, dear boy? Tits."

"Nothing. What shall we do now?"

"Good question. We ought to return to the Nazi colony on the shore of Lake Chad, but we don't have transport and it's too far to trek. This wasn't something I had planned for . . ."

A thunderous boom cracked open the sky!

Something enormous and white broke through the junk clouds.

They all looked up at the same time.

To confront a flying house!

A large stone house was descending to the ground.

It flattened the trees it landed on.

And came to a rest nearby.

Then the front door opened and three figures emerged.

They stood on the spacious porch.

They blinked at Stringent.

Laughed at the professor and the HIPZIS.

Ignored the Postgruppenführer.

Then they shouted, "Our names are Geddie, Lifesun and Pert. We have come direct from Canada to take over the world and this novel. The great hyperspatial being named Rush has been liberated into your universe and he is on his way here. You cannot resist Rush, for he is a potent avatar of the ultimate monster Tyrrrrinx."

"That last part is news to me!" cried the professor.

"Hey, doc, what's an avatar?"

The three prophets who might also be demigods overheard him. "We'll tell you what an avatar is! It's an aspect or sample. An aspect or sample of a bigger thing. We are the priests of the Sample of Tyrrrrinx and our great computers fill our hallowed halls."

"Hey, doc, what's a computer?"

"An electronic calculating machine, Stringy." The professor turned to face the prophets. "Exactly what kinds of great computers do you have in those hallowed halls of yours?"

Geddie seemed nonplussed by the question.

"Er, we have a couple of MIT Altair 8800s, a Rockwell AIM-65, four or five Intel SDK-85s, a COSMAC ELF, half a dozen IMSAI 8080s, one Apple 1, a Cromemco Z-1, six Motorola MEK6800D2s, a Tesla PMI-80, and several PSI Comp80s, I think."

The professor frowned. "Do any of them work?"

"Why should they?" blared Pert.

"What's the name of your house?" asked Stringent.

"La Villa Strangiato," said Geddie.

"It's very nice. Elegant."

"Thanks. It flies very well too."

"Is it hard to control?"

"No, not really. It is activated by antigravity engines so there's almost no risk of stalling. Doesn't do aerobatics easily, though, and that's a pity. The last time I tried an inverse loop, the bathroom ended up in a dreadful mess, and as for the kitchen . . ."

"Enough!" cried Lifesun, shaking his blond hair.

Pert cupped his ear with his hand. "Rush himself is coming! He has a peculiar form, so don't laugh or you'll be sorry! You'll be sorry anyway! Actually he's not that odd. He resembles a naked man grasping a giant red star that is bounded by a circle."

"Too many naked men in this story!" fretted Stringent. Then he asked Geddie, "How does Rush move?"

"By rolling. He's very fast! Don't try to escape his clutches, for even if you Fly By Night he'll still get you in his Caress of Steel. Behold! He has arrived! He's always rushing around. That's why he's called Rush. One of the reasons anyway. Watch out!"

The apparition that rolled into view was vast.

It was bigger than a Ferris wheel.

Trees collapsed as it ploughed through the forest.

It rolled to a stop behind La Villa Strangiato but more than half of it was still visible above the house.

Slowly it spoke. "Buenos Nochas, Mein Froinds!"

"Use the gun on him, Stringy!"

"I forgot to tell you, doc. It has been fired already."

"What? Who the hell did that?"

The apeman shrugged. "Dunno. Maybe the Belgians."

Crinkle considered this. "Yes, that's the sort of thing they would do. It means we're doomed, of course."

"Utterly, doc? Or just partly?"

"The entire human race is done for, Stringy!"

"Wait a moment, doc! What about my abnormalities? You still haven't told me what the other two are!"

"That's fucking true, my boy. I haven't."

"Maybe they can help us out of this tight spot now? Tell me what they are! Don't put it off any longer!"

The professor scratched his jar and inhaled deeply. "Very well. But I pray they won't make you arrogant. The first abnormality is that you have six fingers on both your hands."

"I already know that, doc, but to be honest it has never really helped me much, especially bearing in mind that in our world it's normal for both men and gorillas to have *seven* fingers on each hand. Maybe in a different version of this reality—a parallel cosmos imagined by a writer such as the brilliant Philip José Farmer or the vastly underrated John Sladek—having six fingers would be an advantage, because everybody else would possess only five. But that's pure theory."

"No, it's not a theory, Stringy, because there's no way of testing it, nor is it even a hypothesis. It's just a speculation. Anyway, the second of your abnormalities is the fact that . . ."

The apeman strained forward. "Yes, doc?"

"You can whistle and hum two different tunes at the same time!"

There was an awkward pause.

"Is that it, doc? Is that all?"

"Don't knock it until you've tried it, my boy!"

Stringent screwed up his face and whistled "Dixie" while humming "My Eyes Have Seen the Glory." The three prophets of Rush just watched him sullenly. Rush also watched him.

The tunes ended. Nothing had happened.

"Well, that was useless, doc! What about my third abnormality? That's the last hope for all mankind!"

"Yes, my boy. Ahem . . . Your third abnormality is that you are flexible enough to perform auto-fellatio."

"Is that a martial art, doc?"

"Ahem . . . Not really, dear boy. It means performing oral sex on your own prod. I must confess that I was always most worried about revealing this ability to you. I thought that if you knew about it, you'd never leave the house. It doesn't matter now."

Stringent looked at his groin area.

Then he shook his head.

And Rush laughed. "Bye bye, buster! Time to die!"

191

An orange bolt of energy fell out of the sky and pierced his skull. He didn't even have time to scream.

"What the heck?" bellowed the professor.

Stringent tugged his chin. "Do you think there's any possibility that the universe is spherical and that a bolt of special energy, call it *tachyonic* if you like, could go right round and arrive back at its departure point? It's a purely academic question, of course."

Crinkle waved his tentacles. "I suppose so."

Stringent smiled. He blinked.

Rush was tottering and teetering. His three priests rushed out and tried to comfort him, but it was clear there was nothing they could do. Then the wheel rolled over Geddie, crushing him. Lifesun tried to pull it back, but he was swept up by the upturn. He hung on for dear life but lost his grip at the highest point and plunged to the ground. As for Pert, he jumped out of the way, but suddenly Rush fell.

He fell like a coin at the end of its spin.

He fell directly on Pert.

So the prophets were all dead. And the god they worshipped was dead too. And I might as well admit, in case you aren't already aware, that they were inspired by a Canadian rock band that was one of my favorites in my youth. Check them out.

Impeccable drumming and bass playing.

Soaring guitar work . . .

Great lyrics and superb concepts.

And this is the only genuine advert in the entire book!

Anyhow . . . The menace to the world was over. Stringent turned to the professor and said, "Maybe we can requisition their flying house, doc? It should get us back to Lake Chad."

"Beaver. Hairy ass. Nutsack. Let's do it!"

They ran inside, tripping over a few computers in the hallway. It was in the sitting room that they found the controls. Stringent sat on the main sofa and pulled back on the stick.

La Villa Strangiato lifted gently upwards.

"North, Stringy! North!"

The apeman banked the house and opened the throttle. As he flew, the two girls went out onto the porch to enjoy the view. The forests appeared to be endless, the bright emerald canopy cut only by rivers yellowed with silt. Parrots flew up to meet the house, circling the chimneys, landing on the eaves or entering through the open front door and stealing the fruit in the glass fruit bowl in the lounge.

Many hours passed and finally they spotted Lake Chad in the distance. Stringent put the house into a shallow dive, but Tantra called out urgently and the professor went to see what the matter was. He returned with bad news. The colony was being attacked by dinosaurs! The tyrannosaurs and tricera-topses of Libya must have followed them from Tripoli. Gritting his teeth, the apeman spiraled down.

The battle below was messy but fierce. The Meta-Emptive Nazis were holding the beasts at bay with their stubby ray guns, and had even rigged up a defensive projector to show pornographic films featuring seductive pterodac-tyls, but the cohorts of Yyyshk weren't so easy to distract. Teeth snapped, horns jabbed, and it was only by a miracle of sentence structure that Moon-wash and Quorn Joy weren't cut to pieces. They looked up and beckoned to La Villa Strangiato.

Suddenly there was a new arrival on the scene. A limousine of absurd length hurtled through the reeds into the clearing; halfway along its vast chassis was an obvious scar where some welder had joined two separate pieces together. The car screeched to a halt and the professor cried, "The thugs of the Cosa Nostra Damus!"

"They must have followed the dinosaurs, doc!"

"That's surely right, Stringy!"

One of the many car doors opened, but what stepped out onto the dirt wasn't a man. It was a robot. A steam-powered robot. Muscle Leany! He held submachine guns in both hands. The professor was about to call out to him in joy, but something curious happened. Doors in the thighs of the leader of the Beatnikshirts creaked open, displaying alcoves, and two men in Armani suits jumped out of each.

"Fredo and Caldo!" gasped Professor Crinkle.

"What's going on, doc?"

"Well, dear boy, either Big Italy and Little Italy have recently become allies, which is something I seriously doubt, or else the whole thing was a set-up from the very beginning."

"The Beatnikshirt regime was just a front?"

"Yes, for organized crime. Let this be a lesson to us, Stringy. Now the gangsters and the dinosaurs seem to be fighting each other! Bugger. It's a chaotic stew of bullets and teeth."

"It has turned into a three-way fight, doc!"

At this point I'd like to write that the professor extended a tentacle and touched his Stepson on his Stetson, but Stringent wasn't actually wearing a hat, so I can't. Instead he said, "Land the house right on top of them all! Squash the blighters totally flat!"

"It'll be my pleasure, doc!"

And that's what he did. In the notes I prepared before writing this story there is one that states: be sure to describe the squashing of the dinosaurs and gangsters in lots of gory detail. But now I don't think I can. You see, it was just a little too horrible . . .

The surviving Meta-Emptive Nazis were ecstatic to see the five heroes emerge in single file from La Villa Strangiato. Tantra and Nutloaf were eager to relate their exploits to Moonwash and Quorn Joy. After they had finished, Moonwash smiled and said, "That sounds really far out! But we haven't been idle either, dudes!"

"Really? What have you been up to?" asked Stringent.

"Why, we converted the Meta-Emptive Nazis to peace and love, man! They are HIPZIS now, and this colony is henceforth to be known as New Goodvibe. Even though the Debonair Werewolves destroyed our former utopia in Germany, we can begin again and rebuild it here! Like, flowers and mushrooms all round, man!"

This news was welcomed by everyone.

Except for Kaspar Stumpf.

He shook his fist and roared, "Bah! Now I'm the only one left in the world who believes in the old values of war and oppression! I must leave this place and find my own destiny elsewhere! Perhaps I will embark on a personal crusade against the Zombie Scholars! Yes, I think I'll do that. So now I will bid you all goodbye!"

And off he marched, the naked man with the empty helmet, and never again was he seen or heard of, and that's only because I can't be bothered to write about him any longer.

"Doc! We can use La Villa Strangiato to live in," said Stringent with a frown, "but I think we ought to change its name. Bearing in mind we sat in the west wing when it landed on our enemies, I think it's safe to define it as a kind of *flying wing*. So there's only one option for a name. Tell me if you agree? Northrop House!"

"That's an excellent suggestion, Stringy!"

The apeman looked thoughtful.

"What's up, dear boy?" asked the professor.

"I'm just wondering if I should give my third abnormality a try, that's all, doc. But I'm a bit nervous."

"Ahem . . . Yes, well, maybe you can wait until after the novel is over? For the sake of all our privacy."

Stringent nodded. Tantra wandered over.

She stared at him. "There's something shining on your chest under the fur. I never noticed it before."

"Oh yes? What is it?"

She reached and touched him. "It's a zipper!"

He fumbled for it. "What the . . ."

With a jerking motion he undid it. His gorilla suit fell away. At long last his true body was revealed.

It was the body of a human male. A man.

"Doc! It's unbelievable!"

He paced back and forth, flexing his abdominal muscles in front of the girls, enjoying the feel of the air on his skin. All his life he had accepted the fact he was half gorilla. But now . . .

"Why, doc? Why did someone put me in a suit?"

The professor scratched his jar. "I don't know, my boy. But I guess we can work out the reason. Your mother was an English actress; your father was a gorilla. You were born as a hybrid and clearly your parents wanted to protect you from the truth."

"You've got it all wrong, doc! If that was the case, they would have let me walk around like this, with a human head and a human body! I think somebody has played a joke!"

The professor pointed at Stringent's neck.

"There's a join," he said.

Stringent touched it with his human hands, worked his fingers under it, pulled with all his might. And his head came off. And beneath his head he had another. A gorilla's head.

"Your human head was just a mask, my boy!"

"So I'm a hybrid after all!"

"Yes, but the other way around."

"That was unexpected!"

"But it explains a lot, Stringy," said the professor.

"Oh really, doc? What?"

"Ever since I found you, I assumed you'd have the physical strength of a gorilla and the intelligence of a man; in fact, you have the strength of a man and the mind of a gorilla."

"That's the worst of both," explained Nutloaf.

"So I'm utterly useless!"

"I wouldn't go that far, Stringy. Ineffectual, yes; moronic, indeed; but never useless. That's too strong."

Tantra frowned. "It's likely that when you were born your parents were deeply shocked by the fact you had a gorilla's head on a man's body; they couldn't alter your hybrid nature, but they could swap the positions of the two parts to give a more acceptable mix, or at least *appear* to swap those parts with the aid of a special suit and mask, both designed to grow older at the same rate as their wearer."

Stringent scratched his buttocks, but it wasn't as entirely satisfying as before. Picking his nose was a different matter: hugely enjoyable. With a wink he turned to the professor.

"Hey, doc, you haven't uttered a dirty word for quite a while! Is there a possibility your brain has healed?"

"Fucking hell! You're sodding right, Stringy!"

They looked at each other.

Stringent said, "Now I'm more ineffectual and moronic than I was, the chance of starring in any sequels is reduced to zero, I suppose? Grappling new threats is a forlorn hope . . ."

The professor produced a rolled up piece of paper from a compartment inside his trapezoid hull. "Funnily enough, dear boy, you're wrong about that. The author of this novel was good (or vain) enough to give me a list of the novels he's planning to write that feature you. Most of them feature me too! Care to take a peek?"

Stringent snatched at the scroll impatiently. He unrolled it and his eyes devoured the following text:

WATCH OUT FOR THE NEXT STARTLING ADVENTURES OF STRINGENT STRANGE!

COMING SOON! INCLUDING:

THE ABNORMALITIES OF STRINGENT STRANGE

On Her Majesty's Secret Phallus
Stringent Strange and the Acceptable Perversion
The Eardrums of Tapajos
Mustard Knob Oil
Stringent Strange and the Zeppelin Fuckers
Rune Caster of Aspersions
The Unmitigated Bullcrap of Fassbinder Hopsnoggle
I Wish I Were a Wereclown
The Teapot Menace
Gamma-Ray Russell and the Tartarus Device
The Hilton as Big as the Ritz
Bring Back Atavism
Backgammon Among the Owls
The Stinkypoos of Uranus
Stringent Strange Versus Captain Kettle
The Minimal Colossus
I Capture the Man in the High Castle
The Eidetic Amnesiacs
Bolo Sax and the Frenzied Nut Kickers
The Pink Baron Goes Straight
Say One Thing, Dr Freud, but Mean a Mother
Liar! Liar! Your Monkey's on Fire
The Tendrils of Eliot
Stringent Strange and the Restraining Order
The Bum Drummers
Zicky Picky and his Doodah
Stringent Strange and the Overplayed Joke
Bash No More Monkeys
Oddity O'Clock
The Neverending Nuptials of the Nubile Nubian Necrophiles
Captain Kettle Meets the Teapot
Ornithopter Capers
Fibber! Fibber! Your Gibbon Can't Gibber
Go Fetch Auntie Apocalypse
Sigh in the Ointment
The Fecund Anticipators of Grokk
What the Yeti Apprehends

The Meddlesome Dabblers of Atlantis
Quicksand Slurpings
Stringent Strange and the Bland Baboons
Shylock Goes Metric
Zumboo's Banana Canoe
Belated Invasion of the Naked Norman Slave Girls
Tobias Crinkle's Negative Equity
Blubber Kissy Lips
Beware the Cracker Tour
Stringent Strange and the Wonderful Wizard of Australia
The Hall of the Cows of Russia
Beyond Paraparapara
The Nostalgia Merchants of Yore
Taking the Plutonian Piss
Stringent Strange has Difficulties Getting Published
Half Past Oddity O'Clock
The Catastrophic Costermongers of the Callous Comet
Goosing der Führer
The Jangling Quays of Jeremiah Quiche
King Stringent of Redonda
Who Gives a Monkey's Ass?
Sailing the Limitless Seas of Liechtenstein
Triumph of the Willy
If it Ain't Tempus Don't Fugit

THE END

Stringent tugged his chin and said, "Will all those adventures be issued by the publisher of this book, doc?"

"It depends on the reader, my dear boy."

"What do you mean by that?"

"If the reader enjoyed the tale so much he feels obliged to demand the sequels, there's a decent chance."

They both approached the front of the page they were standing on and stared directly out at you sitting there; and for the space of this paragraph they continued watching you, trying to discern your deepest feelings from your expression and movements.

Finally they had the information they wanted . . .

"No. Not by this publisher."

"Ah well, doc! You win some . . ."

"Winsome? You were never that, Stringy! Come on, let's go elsewhere before all our prose runs out."

The apeman and the cyborg laughed softly as they walked side by side towards the final word. Which is this one. No, actually it's over here. My mistake, it's right there. Now.

F I N I S

THE READERS WHO PRE-ORDERED THIS BOOK

A s has already been stated, the few Human Spectators in the amphitheatre were given special permission to attend the gladiatorial fights by Yyyshk, the Chief Plenipotentiary of Zyra. That was very thoughtful of him, don't you agree? What a considerate telepathic winking dinosaur! Anyway, the spectators in question were those who pre-ordered the book before it was published; and they witnessed plenty of bouts that later readers will never get to see. They were divided into four rough sections and the extra fights they were treated to ran as follows:

Section One

1. A three-way battle between Michael Bishop, Christopher Priest and Alexander Pope, with Oliver Goldsmith watching from the sidelines and thus taking part *vicariously*.

2. John Barth using a flaming barrel of tar against Marcel Proust, who was armed with a massive madeleine, not a cake but a fifty-foot high girl by that name. Barth-tub versus giantess.

3. Michael Moorcock, Milorad Pavić and Jack Vance against Lord Dunsany, David I. Masson and J.G. Ballard . . . Tormented albinos, magic mirrors and convoluted spells versus unicorns, time dilation and crashed cars. The outcome is still unknown.

And the spectators who got to watch them were: Robert Craig, Nathan Blumenfeld, Neal Chuang, Jason Aiken, Daniel Ferranti, Norris H. Hart, Juan Carlos Castresana, Steve A. Heinrich, Arthur Sippo, Richard Moore, Peter Nuro, Lisa Eckert, Ralph Carlson, Bill Drummonds, Karl Schodrok, and Zacharias Nuninga.

Section Two

1.Flann O'Brien mounted on a bicycle charging John Buchan, who was balanced on a portable staircase with thirty-nine steps. I don't know how much he charged him, probably more than was affordable.

2. Yevgeny Zamyatin and Ursula Le Guin using hollow glass rapiers filled with acid against John Kennedy Toole, who was armed with a lute that played music capable of destroying minds, and Leonora Carrington, who amplified this music with an enormous hearing trumpet.

3. William Gass versus William Gaddis.

And the spectators who got to watch them were: Goran Zadravec, Georgina Eloise Spiteri, Madeleine Lucy Spiteri, John Purdie, Bryan Curtis, Denise Pike, David Brzeski, Paul Niedernhofer, Enrico Barisione, William Thom, George R. Ibarra, Peggy Hailey, David Chamberlain, Des Lewis, Douglas Smith, and Gino Dros.

Section Three

1. Friedrich Dürrenmatt versus Boiledpoor Riddlerug. Dürrenmatt is a genuine writer, the brilliant author of the novel *The Judge and His Hangman*, among others; but Riddlerug is a person I made up just now. Riddlerug's most famous work is probably *Fudging the Issue*, which is about sticky situations and is set on a grounded flying carpet in Devon. Not really a carpet, more of a mat. A "Devon-Mat." Perhaps some sort of allusion to the name "Dürrenmatt." Who knows?

2. L. Sprague de Camp against Fletcher Pratt. They worked together very successfully and entertainingly for years. But now they are forced to kill each other with the aid of a roaring trumpet and a wall of serpents inside a miniature castle of iron. The roaring trumpet is possibly Leonora Carrington's hearing device from her own fight.

3. Washington Irving and a pumpkin catapult versus James Branch Cabell mounted on a silver stallion and armed with a tree branch, the very same one that his middle name was named after . . .

And the spectators who got to watch them were: Chase Mattsson, Sage Mattsson, Gerraint Oakley, Bob Lock, Andrea Rolfe Dittmer, Jim Dittmer, Martien Verbruggen, Andrew Hatchell, Jonathan Barlow, Margaret Hindle, Lisa Summers, Aaron French, Huw Rees, Gary Fry, Garth Hill, and Hannah Lawson.

Section Four

1. Alasdair Gray and Amin Maalouf versus Joanna Russ and Hannes Bok. This bout was notable for one of the gladiators killing her comrade and taking on the two opponents alone. "I don't need the aid of men. Men are silly and outdated," she announced.

2. Apuleius and his Golden Ass against Aristophanes with his wasps, frogs and clouds.

3. Dylan Thomas, armed with two hundred and fifty bottles of beer, versus Alphonse Daudet, who trundled around the arena in a motorized windmill and tried to decapitate his antagonist with spinning sails. Dylan drank the beer and hurled the bottles at the windmill, missing each time. As he grew drunker, his aim worsened, and he began hitting dinosaurs in the audience. Eventually one jumped into the arena and ripped the Welsh poet apart, then took on the windmill, whose occupant, Daudet, thought he was being attacked by a giant version of the author Cervantes. Plainly this situation was ironic, though what kind of irony is hard to determine. Pieces of Dylan were available to take home as souvenirs later and I have one of his burps on my own mantelpiece.

And the spectators who got to watch them were: Mihai Adascalitei, Edward Ashby, Stevan Apter, Olga Zolle, Niall Gordon, Christopher Paul Carey, Jeff Nelson, Stephen Redwood, Alan Barnes, Paulo Brito, Ron Bachman, James Smith, Jerome-Luc Paulin, Michael Croteau, Paul Saarma, David Cruces, and Dr. Jimmy.

Congratulations! YOU are the reader who spotted the most inconsistencies and you have therefore won the competition! Your prize has just been sent to you on the LZ 129 *Hindenburg* airship and should arrive on Thursday 6th May 1937. Please be there on time! We hope you enjoy it!